THE PIRATE
&
THE THREE CUTTERS

THE PIRATE
&
THE THREE CUTTERS

Captain Marryat

NONSUCH

First published 1836
Copyright © in this edition 2006
Nonsuch Publishing Ltd

Nonsuch Publishing Limited
The Mill, Brimscombe Port, Stroud, Gloucestershire, GL5 2QG
www.nonsuch-publishing.com

For comments or suggestions, please email the editor of this series at:
classics@tempus-publishing.com

Nonsuch Publishing Ltd is an imprint of Tempus Publishing Group

British Library Cataloguing in Publication Data.
A catalogue record for this book is available from the British Library.

ISBN 1-84588-205-9
ISBN-13 (from January 2007) 978-1-84588-205-1

Typesetting and origination by Nonsuch Publishing Limited
Printed in Great Britain by Oaklands Book Services Limited

CONTENTS

INTRODUCTION TO THE MODERN EDITION

Frederick Marryat was born in 1792, the son of a Member of Parliament for Sandwich and chairman of Lloyd's of London. He was educated privately, although he tried to run away to sea several times, until his father got him entered as a midshipman aboard the frigate HMS *Impérieuse*, commanded by Thomas, Lord Cochrane. Cochrane was one of the most daring captains of the Napoleonic Wars, nick-named '*le loup des mers*,' ('the sea-wolf,') by the French; under his command, the young Marryat took part in the defence of the castle of Trinidad in 1808, and the attack on the French fleet in Aix roads and the Walcheren expedition in 1809, as well as innumerable attacks on privateers, shore batteries and telegraph stations. In 1810 he joined HMS *Centaur*, the flagship of Rear Admiral Sir Samuel Hood in the Mediterranean, before serving aboard HMS *Æolus* and HMS *Spartan* in the Caribbean and off the coast of North America.

From 1813 to 1815 he was a lieutenant aboard the *Espiègle* and the *Newcastle* on the same stations, before being invalided home and promoted to commander. He spent the next five years ashore, marrying Catherine Shairp in 1819, with whom he had four sons and seven daughters; one of his daughters, Florence, also became a writer. 1820 saw his return to active duty, in command of the sloop *Beaver*, guarding the South Atlantic island of St Helena during the final exile of Napoleon Bonaparte. Upon Napoleon's death in 1821 Marryat was transferred to the *Rosario* and sent home with the despatches, following which he was on patrol in the English Channel to prevent smuggling, until the *Rosario* was paid off in 1822. In 1823 he took command of the brand-new ship *Larne* and was promptly sent to the East Indies, where he arrived just in time to participate in the First Burmese War.

The Kingdom of Burma had been expanding its territory to the east, towards British India, since the end of the eighteenth century, but, in early 1824 they invaded Cachar, which was under British protection because it controlled strategic territory that would be important for any potential attack on Bengal; Britain consequently declared war on Burma. After a series of Anglo-Burmese wars, Burma would eventually become a province of British India. For a short period during 1824 Frederick Marryat was the senior British naval officer in Rangoon, and was officially thanked for 'his able, gallant, and zealous co-operation'. In 1825 he was in charge of an expedition up the Pathein river, occupying Pathein itself, where a fort and garrison were later established. He was appointed to the command of HMS *Tees* later the same year, achieving the rank of post captain and, in 1826, he was made a Companion of the Order of the Bath, following his return to Britain.

In 1828 Marryat was appointed captain of HMS *Ariadne* but, two years later, he resigned his commission in order to concentrate on writing. He had risen steadily, although not spectacularly, in his profession; he had been awarded the gold medal of the Royal Humane Society in 1818 for saving more than a dozen lives; he had invented a new type of lifeboat; and he had adapted a signalling code for use by ships at sea, in recognition of which he was elected a Fellow of the Royal Society in 1819 and awarded the Légion d'honneur by

King Louis-Philippe of France in 1833. However, in 1829, while captain of the *Ariadne*, he had published *The Naval Officer, or Scenes and Adventures in the Life of Frank Mildmay*, which was an immediate critical and commercial success. Over the next twenty years he wrote prolifically, producing fifteen books for adults, of which the most famous is *Mr Midshipman Easy* (1836), and six books for children, the best known being *The Children of the New Forest* (1847). He drew on the experiences of his own life as a naval officer for material, and *Frank Mildmay* was avowedly autobiographical. He also edited the *Metropolitan Magazine* from 1832 to 1835.

Marryat's health was never particularly strong, and the strain of so much writing told upon it. He believed that a change of occupation might be beneficial and therefore applied to the Admiralty for a return to active duty in 1847. Their refusal of this application angered him so much that he burst a blood vessel and was seriously ill for six months. The shock of learning of the death of his eldest son later that year may well have been too much for his shattered system to cope with. Frederick Marryat died in 1848.

THE PIRATE

I
THE BAY OF BISCAY

IT WAS IN THE LATTER part of the month of June, of the year seventeen hundred and ninety something, that the angry waves of the Bay of Biscay were gradually subsiding, after a gale of wind as violent as it was unusual during that period of the year. Still they rolled heavily; and, at times, the wind blew up in fitful, angry gusts, as if it would fain renew the elemental combat; but each effort was more feeble, and the dark clouds which had been summoned to the storm, now fled in every quarter before the powerful rays of the sun, who burst their masses asunder with a glorious flood of light and heat; and, as he poured down his resplendent beams, piercing deep into the waters of that portion of the Atlantic to which we now refer, with the exception of one object, hardly visible, as at creation, there was a vast circumference of water, bounded by the fancied canopy of heaven. We have said, with the exception of one object; for in the centre of this picture, so simple, yet so sublime, composed of the three great elements, there was a remnant of the fourth. We say a remnant, for it was but the hull of a vessel, dismasted, water-logged, its upper works only floating occasionally above the waves, when a transient repose from their still violent undulation permitted it to reassume its buoyancy. But this was seldom; one moment it was deluged by the seas, which broke as they poured over its gunwale; and the next, it rose from its submersion, as the water escaped from the portholes at its sides.

How many thousands of vessels—how many millions of property—have been abandoned, and eventually consigned to the all-receiving depths of the ocean, through ignorance or through fear! What a mine of wealth must lie buried in its sands! what riches lie entangled amongst its rocks, or remain suspended in its unfathomable gulf, where the compressed fluid is equal in gravity to that which it encircles, there to remain secured in its embedment from corruption and decay, until the destruction of the universe and the return of chaos!—Yet, immense as the accumulated loss may be, the major part of it has been occasioned from an ignorance of one of the first laws of nature, that of specific gravity. The vessel to which we have referred was, to all appearance, in a situation of as extreme hazard as that of a drowning man clinging to a single rope-yarn; yet, in reality, she was more secure from descending to the abyss below than many gallantly careering on the waters, their occupants dismissing all fear, and only calculating upon a quick arrival into port.

The *Circassian* had sailed from New Orleans, a gallant and well-appointed ship, with a cargo, the major part of which consisted of cotton. The captain was, in the usual acceptation of the term, a good sailor; the crew were hardy and able seamen. As they crossed the Atlantic, they had encountered the gale to which we have referred, were driven down into the Bay of Biscay, where, as we shall hereafter explain, the vessel was dismasted, and sprang a leak, which baffled all their exertions to keep under. It was now five days since the frightened crew had quitted the vessel in two of her boats, one of which had swamped, and every soul that occupied it had perished; the fate of the other was uncertain.

We said that the crew had deserted the vessel, but we did not assert that every existing being had been removed out of her. Had such been the case, we should not have taken up the reader's time in describing inanimate matter. It is life that we portray, and life there still was in the shattered hull thus abandoned to the mockery of the ocean. In the *caboose* of the *Circassian*, that is, in the cooking-house secured on deck, and which fortunately had been so well fixed as to resist the force of the breaking waves, remained three beings—a man, a woman, and a child. The two first mentioned were of that inferior race which have, for so long a period, been procured from the sultry Afric coast, to toil, but reap not for themselves; the child which lay at the breast of the female was of European blood, now, indeed, deadly pale, as it attempted in vain to draw sustenance from its exhausted nurse, down whose sable cheeks the tears coursed, as she occasionally pressed the infant to her breast, and turned it round to leeward to screen it from the spray which dashed over them at each returning swell. Indifferent to all else, save her little charge, she spoke not, although she shuddered with the cold as the water washed her knees each time that the hull was careened into the wave. Cold and terror had produced a change in her complexion, which now wore a yellow, or sort of copper hue.

The male, who was her companion, sat opposite to her upon the iron range which once had been the receptacle of light and heat, but was now but a weary seat to a drenched and worn-out wretch. He, too, had not spoken for many hours; with the muscles of his face relaxed, his thick lips pouting far in advance of his collapsed cheeks, his high cheekbones prominent as budding horns, his eyes displaying little but their whites, he appeared to be an object of greater misery than the female, whose thoughts were directed to the infant and not unto herself. Yet his feelings were still acute, although his faculties appeared to be deadened by excess of suffering.

"Eh, me!" cried the negro woman faintly, after a long silence, her head falling back with extreme exhaustion. Her companion made no reply, but, roused at the sound of her voice, bent forward, slided open the door a little, and looked out to windward. The heavy spray dashed into his glassy eyes, and obscured his vision; he groaned, and fell back into his former position. "What you tink, Coco?" inquired the negress, covering up more carefully the child, as she bent her head down upon it. A look of despair, and a shudder from cold and hunger, were the only reply.

It was then about eight o'clock in the morning, and the swell of the ocean was fast subsiding. At noon the warmth of the sun was communicated to them through the planks of the caboose, while its rays poured a small stream of vivid light through the chinks of the closed panels. The negro appeared gradually to revive; at last he rose, and with some difficulty contrived again to slide open the door. The sea had gradually decreased its violence, and but occasionally broke over the vessel; carefully holding on by the door-jambs, Coco gained the outside, that he might survey the horizon.

"What you see, Coco?" said the female, observing from the *caboose* that his eyes were fixed upon a certain quarter.

"So help me God, me tink me see something; but ab so much salt water in um eye, me no see clear," replied Coco, rubbing away the salt which had crystallised on his face during the morning.

"What you tink um like, Coco?"

"Only one bit cloud," replied he, entering the caboose, and resuming his seat upon the grate with a heavy sigh.

"Eh, me!" cried the negress, who had uncovered the child to look at it, and whose powers were sinking fast. "Poor lilly Massa Eddard, him look very bad indeed—him die very soon, me fear. Look, Coco, no ab breath."

The child's head fell back upon the breast of its nurse, and life appeared to be extinct.

"Judy, you no ab milk for piccaninny; suppose um ab no milk, how can live? Eh! stop, Judy, me put lilly fingers in um mouth; suppose Massa Eddard no dead, him pull."

Coco inserted his finger into the child's mouth, and felt a slight drawing pressure. "Judy," cried Coco, "Massa Eddard no dead yet. Try now, suppose you ab lilly drop oder side."

Poor Judy shook her head mournfully, and a tear rolled down her cheek; she was aware that nature was exhausted. "Coco," said she, wiping her cheek with the back of her hand, "me give me heart blood for Massa Eddard; but no ab milk—all gone."

This forcible expression of love for the child, which was used by Judy, gave an idea to Coco. He drew his knife out of his pocket, and very coolly sawed to the bone of his fore finger. The blood flowed and trickled down to the extremity, which he applied to the mouth of the infant.

"See, Judy, Massa Eddard suck—him not dead," cried Coco, chuckling at the fortunate result of the experiment, and forgetting at the moment their almost hopeless situation.

The child, revived by the strange sustenance, gradually recovered its powers, and in a few minutes it pulled at the finger with a certain degree of vigour.

"Look Judy, how Massa Eddard take it," continued Coco. "Pull away, Massa Eddard, pull away. Coco ab ten finger, and take long while suck em all dry." But the child was soon satisfied, and fell asleep in the arms of Judy.

"Coco, suppose you go see again," observed Judy. The negro again crawled out, and again he scanned the horizon.

"So help me God, dis time me tink, Judy—yes, so help me God, me see a ship!" cried Coco, joyfully.

"Eh!" screamed Judy, faintly, with delight: "den Massa Eddard no die."

"Yes, so help me God—he come dis way!" and Coco, who appeared to have recovered a portion of his former strength and activity, clambered on the top of the *caboose*, where he sat, cross-legged, waving his yellow handkerchief, with the hope of attracting the attention of those on board; for he knew that it was very possible that an object floating little more than level with the water's surface might escape notice.

As it fortunately happened, the frigate, for such she was, continued her course precisely for the wreck, although it had not been perceived by the look-out men at the mast-heads, whose eyes had been directed to the line of the horizon. In less than an hour our little party were threatened with a new danger, that of being run over by the frigate, which was now within a cable's length of them, driving the seas before her in one widely extended foam, as she pursued her rapid and impetuous course. Coco shouted to his utmost, and fortunately attracted the notice of the men who were on the bowsprit, stowing away the foretopmast-staysail, which had been hoisted up to dry after the gale.

"Starboard, hard!" was roared out.

"Starboard it is," was the reply from the quarterdeck, and the helm was shifted without inquiry, as it always is on board of a man-of-war, although, at the same time, it behoves people to be rather careful how they pass such an order, without being prepared with a subsequent and most satisfactory explanation.

The topmast studding-sail flapped and fluttered, the foresail shivered, and the jib filled as the frigate rounded to, narrowly missing the wreck, which was now under the bows, rocking so violently in the white foam of the agitated waters, that it was with difficulty that Coco could, by clinging to the stump of the mainmast, retain his elevated position. The frigate shortened sail, hove to, and lowered down a quarter-boat, and in less than five minutes Coco, Judy, and the infant, were rescued from their awful situation. Poor Judy, who had borne up against all for the sake of the child, placed it in the arms of the officer who relieved them, and then fell back in a state of insensibility, in which condition she was carried on board. Coco, as he took his place in the stern-sheets of the boat, gazed wildly round him, and then broke out into peals of extravagant laughter, which continued without intermission, and were the only replies which he could give to the interrogatories of the quarter-deck, until he fell down in a swoon, and was entrusted to the care of the surgeon.

II
THE BACHELOR

O N THE EVENING OF THE same day on which the child and the two negroes had been saved from the wreck by the fortunate appearance of the frigate, Mr Witherington, of Finsbury Square, was sitting alone in his dining-room wondering what could have become of the Circassian, and why he had not received intelligence of her arrival. Mr Witherington, as we said before, was alone; he had his port and his sherry before him; and although the weather was rather warm, there was a small fire in the grate, because, as Mr Witherington asserted, it looked comfortable. Mr Witherington having watched the ceiling of the room for some time, although there was certainly nothing new to be discovered, filled another glass of wine, and then proceeded to make himself more comfortable by unbuttoning three more buttons of his waistcoat, pushing his wig further off his head, and casting loose all the buttons at the knees of his breeches; he completed his arrangements by dragging towards him two chairs within his reach, putting his legs on one, while he rested his arm on the other. And why was not Mr Witherington to make himself comfortable? He had good health, a good conscience, and eight thousand a-year.

Satisfied with all his little arrangements, Mr Witherington sipped his port wine, and putting down his glass again, fell back in his chair, placed his hands on his breast, interwove his fingers; and in this most comfortable position recommenced his speculations as to the non-arrival of the Circassian.

We will leave him to his cogitations while we introduce him more particularly to our readers.

The father of Mr Witherington was a younger son of one of the oldest and proudest families in the West Riding of Yorkshire: he had his choice of the four professions allotted to younger sons whose veins are filled with patrician blood—the army, the navy, the law, and the church. The army did not suit him, he said, as marching and counter-marching were not comfortable; the navy did not suit him, as there was little comfort in gales of wind and mouldy biscuit: the law did not suit him, as he was not sure that he would be at ease with his conscience, which would not be comfortable; the church was also rejected, as it was, with him, connected with the idea of a small stipend, hard duty, a wife and eleven children, which were anything but comfortable. Much to the horror of his family he eschewed all the liberal professions, and embraced the offer of an old backslider of an uncle, who proposed to him a situation in his banking-house, and a partnership as soon as he deserved it; the consequence was, that his relations bade him an indignant farewell, and then made no further inquiries about him: he was as decidedly cut as one of the female branches of the family would have been had she committed a *faux pas*.

Nevertheless, Mr Witherington senior stuck diligently to his business, in a few years was partner, and, at the death of the old gentleman, his uncle, found himself in possession of a good property, and every year coining money at his bank.

Mr Witherington senior then purchased a house in Finsbury Square, and thought it advisable to look out for a wife.

Having still much of the family pride in his composition, he resolved not to muddle the blood of the Witheringtons by any cross from Cateaton Street or Mincing Lane; and, after a proper degree of research, he selected the daughter of a Scotch earl, who went to London with a bevy of nine in a Leith smack to barter blood for wealth. Mr Witherington being so unfortunate as to be the first comer, had the pick of the nine ladies by courtesy; his choice was light-haired, blue-eyed, a little freckled, and very tall, by no means bad-looking, and standing on the list in the family Bible No. IV. From this union Mr Witherington had issue; first, a daughter, christened Moggy, whom we shall soon have to introduce to our readers as a spinster of forty-seven, and second, Antony Alexander Witherington Esquire, whom we just now have left in a very comfortable position, and in a very brown study.

Mr Witherington senior persuaded his son to enter the banking-house, and, as a dutiful son, he entered it every day; but he did nothing more, having made the fortunate discovery that "his father was born before him;" or, in other words, that his father had plenty of money, and would be necessitated to leave it behind him.

As Mr Witherington senior had always studied comfort, his son had early imbibed the same idea, and carried his feelings, in that respect, to a much greater excess; he divided things into comfortable and uncomfortable. One fine day, Lady Mary Witherington, after paying all the household bills, paid the debt of Nature; that is, she died: her husband paid the undertaker's bill, so it is to be presumed that she was buried.

Mr Witherington senior shortly afterwards had a stroke of apoplexy, which knocked him down. Death, who has no feelings of honour, struck him when down. And Mr Witherington, after having laid a few days in bed, was by a second stroke laid in the same vault as Lady Mary Witherington: and Mr Witherington junior (our Mr Witherington) after deducting £40,000 for his sister's fortune, found himself in possession of a clear £8,000 per annum, and an excellent house in Finsbury Square. Mr Witherington considered this a comfortable income, and he therefore retired altogether from business.

During the lifetime of his parents he had been witness to one or two matrimonial scenes, which had induced him to put down matrimony as one of the things not comfortable: therefore he remained a bachelor.

His sister Moggy also remained unmarried; but whether it was from a very unprepossessing squint which deterred suitors, or from the same dislike to matrimony as her brother had imbibed, it is not in our power to say. Mr Witherington was three years younger than his sister; and although he had for some time worn a wig, it was only because he considered it more comfortable. Mr Witherington's whole character might be summed up in two words—eccentricity and benevolence: eccentric he certainly was, as most bachelors usually are. Man is but a rough pebble without the attrition received from contact with the gentler sex: it is wonderful how the ladies pumice a man down to a smoothness which occasions him to roll over and over with the rest of his species, jostling but not wounding his neighbours, as the waves of circumstances bring him into collision with them.

Mr Witherington roused himself from his deep reverie, and felt for the string connected with the bell-pull, which it was the butler's duty invariably to attach to the arm of his master's chair previous to his last exit from the dining-room; for, as Mr Witherington very truly observed, it was very uncomfortable to be obliged to get up and ring the bell: indeed, more than once Mr Witherington had calculated the advantages and disadvantages of having a daughter about eight years old who could ring bells, air the newspapers, and cut the leaves of a new novel.

When, however, he called to mind that she could not always remain at that precise age, he decided that the balance of comfort was against it.

Mr Witherington, having pulled the bell again, fell into a brown study.

Mr Jonathan, the butler, made his appearance; but observing that his master was occupied, he immediately stopped at the door, erect, motionless, and with a face as melancholy as if he was performing mute at the porch of some departed peer of the realm; for it is an understood thing, that the greater the rank of the defunct the longer must be the face, and, of course, the better must be the pay.

Now, as Mr Witherington is still in profound thought, and Mr Jonathan will stand as long as a hackney-coach horse, we will just leave them as they are, while we introduce the brief history of the latter to our readers. Jonathan Trapp has served as footboy, which term, we believe, is derived from those who are in that humble capacity receiving a *quantum suff.* of the application of the feet of those above them to increase the energy of their service; then as foot*man*; which implies that they have been promoted to the more agreeable right of administering instead of receiving the above dishonourable applications; and lastly, for promotion could go no higher in the family, he had been raised to the dignity of butler in the service of Mr Witherington senior. Jonathan then fell in love, for butlers are guilty of indiscretions as well as their masters: neither he nor his fair flame, who was a lady's maid in another family, notwithstanding that they had witnessed the consequences of this error in others, would take warning; they gave warning, and they married.

Like most butlers and ladies' maids who pair off, they set up a public-house; and it is but justice to the lady's maid to say, that she would have preferred an eating-house, but was overruled by Jonathan, who argued, that although people would drink when they were not dry, they never would eat unless they were hungry.

Now, although there was truth in the observation, this is certain, that business did not prosper: it has been surmised that Jonathan's tall, lank, lean figure injured his custom, as people are but too much inclined to judge of the goodness of the ale by the rubicund face and rotundity of the landlord; and therefore inferred that there could be no good beer where mine host was the picture of famine. There certainly is much in appearances in this world; and it appears that, in consequence of Jonathan's cadaverous appearance, he very soon

appeared in the *Gazette*; but what ruined Jonathan in one profession
procured him immediate employment in another. An appraiser,
upholsterer, and undertaker, who was called in to value the fixtures,
fixed his eye upon Jonathan, and knowing the value of his peculiarly
lugubrious appearance, and having a half-brother of equal height,
offered him immediate employment as a mute. Jonathan soon forgot
to mourn his own loss of a few hundreds in his new occupation
of mourning the loss of thousands; and his erect, stiff, statue-like
carriage, and long melancholy face, as he stood at the portals of those
who had entered the portals of the next world, were but too often a
sarcasm upon the grief of the inheritors. Even grief is worth nothing
in this trafficking world unless it be paid for. Jonathan buried many,
and at last buried his wife. So far all was well; but at last he buried his
master, the undertaker, which was not quite so desirable. Although
Jonathan wept not, yet did he express mute sorrow as he marshalled
him to his long home, and drank to his memory in a pot of porter as
he returned from the funeral, perched, with many others, like carrion
crows on the top of the hearse.

And now Jonathan was thrown out of employment from
a reason which most people would have thought the highest
recommendation. Every undertaker refused to take him, because
they could not match him. In this unfortunate dilemma, Jonathan
thought of Mr Witherington junior; he had served and he had buried
Mr Witherington his father, and Lady Mary his mother; he felt that
he had strong claims for such variety of services, and he applied to
the bachelor. Fortunately for Jonathan, Mr Witherington's butler-
incumbent was just about to commit the same folly as Jonathan had
done before, and Jonathan was again installed, resolving in his own
mind to lead his former life, and have nothing more to do with ladies'
maids. But from habit Jonathan still carried himself as a mute on all
ordinary occasions—never indulging in an approximation to mirth,
except when he perceived that his master was in high spirits, and then
rather from a sense of duty than from any real hilarity of heart.

Jonathan was no mean scholar for his station in life, and during his service with the undertaker, he had acquired the English of all the Latin mottoes which are placed upon the hatchments; and these mottoes, when he considered them as apt, he was very apt to quote. We left Jonathan standing at the door; he had closed it, and the handle still remained in his hand. "Jonathan," said Mr Witherington, after a long pause—"I wish to look at the last letter from New York, you will find it on my dressing-table."

Jonathan quitted the room without reply, and made his reappearance with the letter.

"It is a long time that I have been expecting this vessel, Jonathan," observed Mr Witherington, unfolding the letter.

"Yes, sir, a long while; *tempus fugit*," replied the butler in a low tone, half shutting his eyes.

"I hope to God no accident has happened," continued Mr Witherington: "my poor little cousin and her twins e'en now that I speak, they may be all at the bottom of the sea."

"Yes, sir," replied the butler; "the sea defrauds many an honest undertaker of his profits."

"By the blood of the Witheringtons! I may be left without an heir, and shall be obliged to marry, which would be very uncomfortable."

"Very little comfort," echoed Jonathan—"my wife is dead. *In caelo quies.*"

"Well, we must hope for the best; but this suspense is anything but comfortable," observed Mr Witherington, after looking over the contents of the letter for at least the twentieth time.

"That will do, Jonathan; I'll ring for coffee presently;" and Mr Witherington was again alone and with his eyes fixed upon the ceiling.

A cousin of Mr Witherington, and a very great favourite (for Mr Witherington, having a large fortune, and not having anything to do with business, was courted by his relations), had, to a certain degree, committed herself; that is to say, that, notwithstanding the injunctions of her parents, she had fallen in love with a young lieutenant in a marching regiment, whose pedigree was but respectable, and whose fortune was anything but respectable, consisting merely of a subaltern's pay. Poor men, unfortunately, always make love better than those who are rich, because, having less to care about, and not being puffed up with their own consequence, they are not so selfish and think much more of the lady than of themselves. Young ladies, also, who fall in love, never consider whether there is sufficient "to make the pot boil"—probably because young ladies in love lose their appetites, and, not feeling inclined to eat at that time, they imagine that love will always supply the want of food. Now, we will appeal to the married ladies whether we are not right in asserting that, although the collation spread for them and their friends on the day of the marriage is looked upon with almost loathing, they do not find their appetites return with interest soon afterwards. This was precisely the case with Cecilia, or rather, Cecilia Templemore, for she had changed her name the day before. It was also the case with her husband, who always had a good appetite, even during his days of courtship; and the consequence was, that the messman's account, for they lived in barracks, was, in a few weeks, rather alarming. Cecilia applied to her family, who very kindly sent her word that she might starve; but, the advice neither suiting her nor her husband, she then wrote to her cousin Antony, who sent her word that he would be most happy to receive them at his table, and that they should take up their abode in Finsbury Square. This was exactly what they wished; but still there was a certain difficulty; Lieutenant Templemore's regiment was quartered in a town in Yorkshire, which was some trifling distance from Finsbury Square; and to be at Mr Witherington's dinner-table at six P.M., with the necessity of appearing at parade every morning at nine A.M., was a dilemma not to be got out of. Several letters were interchanged upon this knotty subject: and at last it was agreed that Mr Templemore should sell out, and come up to Mr Witherington with his pretty wife: he did so, and found that it was much more comfortable to turn out at nine o'clock in the morning to a good breakfast than to a martial parade. But Mr Templemore had an honest pride and independence of character which would not permit him to eat the bread of idleness, and after a sojourn of two months in most comfortable quarters, without a messman's bill, he frankly stated his feelings to Mr Witherington, and requested his assistance to procure for himself an honourable livelihood. Mr Witherington, who had become attached to them both, would have remonstrated, observing that Cecilia was his own cousin, and that he was a confirmed bachelor; but, in this instance, Mr Templemore was firm, and Mr Witherington very unwillingly consented. A mercantile house of the highest respectability required a partner who could superintend their consignments to America. Mr Witherington advanced the sum required; and, in a few weeks, Mr and Mrs Templemore sailed for New York.

Mr Templemore was active and intelligent; their affairs prospered; and, in a few years, they anticipated a return to their native soil with a competence. But the autumn of the second year after their arrival proved very sickly; the yellow fever raged; and among the thousands who were carried off, Mr Templemore was a victim, about three weeks after his wife had been brought to bed of twins. Mrs Templemore rose from her couch a widow and the mother of two fine boys. The loss of Mr Templemore was replaced by the establishment with which he was connected, and Mr Witherington offered to his cousin that asylum which, in her mournful and unexpected bereavement, she so much required. In three months her affairs were arranged; and with her little boys hanging at the breasts of two negro nurses,—for no others could be procured who would undertake the voyage,—Mrs Templemore, with Coco as male servant, embarked on board of the good ship *Circassian*, A1, bound to Liverpool.

III
THE GALE

THOSE WHO, STANDING ON THE pier, had witnessed the proud bearing of the *Circassian* as she gave her canvas to the winds, little contemplated her fate: still less did those on board; for confidence is the characteristic of seamen, and they have the happy talent of imparting their confidence to whomsoever may be in their company. We shall pass over the voyage, confining ourselves to a description of the catastrophe.

It was during a gale from the north-west, which had continued for three days, and by which the *Circassian* had been driven into the Bay of Biscay, that at about twelve o'clock at night, a slight lull was perceptible. The captain, who had remained on deck, sent down for the chief mate. "Oswald," said Captain Ingram, "the gale is breaking, and I think before morning we shall have had the worst of it. I shall lie down for an hour or two; call me if there be any change."

Oswald Bareth, a tall, sinewy-built, and handsome specimen of transatlantic growth, examined the whole circumference of the horizon before he replied. At last his eyes were steadily fixed to leeward: "I've a notion not, sir," said he; "I see no signs of clearing off to leeward: only a lull for relief, and a fresh hand at the bellows, depend upon it."

"We have now had it three days," replied Captain Ingram, "and that's the life of a summer gale."

"Yes," rejoined the mate; "but always provided that it don't blow back again. I don't like the look of it, sir; and have it back we shall, as sure as there's snakes in Virginny."

"Well, so be if so be," was the safe reply of the captain. "You must keep a sharp look out, Bareth, and don't leave the deck to call me; send a hand down."

The captain descended to his cabin. Oswald looked at the compass in the binnacle—spoke a few words to the man at the helm—gave one or two terrible kicks in the ribs to some of the men who were *caulking*—sounded the pump-well—put a fresh quid of tobacco into his cheek, and then proceeded to examine the heavens above. A cloud, much darker and more descending than the others, which obscured the firmament, spread over the zenith, and based itself upon the horizon to leeward. Oswald's eye had been fixed upon it but a few seconds, when he beheld a small lambent gleam of lightning pierce through the most opaque part; then another, and more vivid. Of a sudden the wind lulled, and the *Circassian* righted from her careen. Again the wind howled, and again the vessel was pressed down to her bearings by its force: again another flash of lightning, which was followed by a distant peal of thunder.

"Had the worst of it, did you say, captain? I've a notion that the worst is yet to come," muttered Oswald, still watching the heavens.

"How does she carry her helm, Matthew?" inquired Oswald, walking aft.

"Spoke a-weather."

"I'll have the trysail off her, at any rate," continued the mate. "Aft, there my lads! and lower down the trysail. Keep the sheet fast till it's down, or the flogging will frighten the lady-passenger out of her wits. Well, if ever I own a craft, I'll have no women on board. Dollars shan't tempt me."

The lightning now played in rapid forks; and the loud thunder, which instantaneously followed each flash, proved its near approach. A deluge of slanting rain descended—the wind lulled—roared again—then lulled—shifted a point or two, and the drenched and heavy sails flapped.

"Up with the helm, Mat!" cried Oswald, as a near flash of lightning for a moment blinded, and the accompanying peal of thunder deafened, those on deck. Again the wind blew strong—it ceased, and it was a dead calm. The sails hung down from the yards, and the rain descended in perpendicular torrents, while the ship rocked to and fro in the trough of the sea, and the darkness became suddenly intense.

"Down there, one of you! and call the captain," said Oswald. "By the Lord! we shall have it. Main braces there, men, and square the yards. Be smart! That topsail should have been in," muttered the mate; "but I'm not captain. Square away the yards, my lads!" continued he; "quick, quick!—there's no child's play here!"

Owing to the difficulty of finding and passing the ropes to each other, from the intensity of the darkness, and the deluge of rain which blinded them, the men were not able to execute the order of the mate so soon as it was necessary; and before they could accomplish their task, or Captain Ingram could gain the deck, the wind suddenly burst upon the devoted vessel from the quarter directly opposite to that from which the gale had blown, taking her all a-back, and throwing her on her beam-ends. The man at the helm was hurled over the wheel; while the rest, who were with Oswald at the main-bits, with the coils of ropes, and every other article on deck not secured, were rolled into the scuppers, struggling to extricate themselves from the mass of confusion and the water in which they floundered. The sudden revulsion awoke all the men below, who imagined that the ship was foundering; and, from the only hatchway not secured, they poured up in their shirts with their other garments in their hands, to put them on—if fate permitted.

Oswald Bareth was the first who clambered up from to leeward. He gained the helm, which he put hard up. Captain Ingram and some of the seamen also gained the helm. It is the rendezvous of all good seamen in emergencies of this description: but the howling of the gale—the blinding of the rain and salt spray—the seas checked in their running by the shift of wind, and breaking over the ship in vast masses of water—the tremendous peals of thunder—and the intense darkness which accompanied these horrors, added to the inclined position of the vessel, which obliged them to climb from one part of the deck to another, for some time checked all profitable communication. Their only friend, in this conflict of the elements, was the lightning (unhappy, indeed, the situation in which lightning can be welcomed as a friend); but its vivid and forked flames, darting down upon every quarter of the horizon, enabled them to perceive their situation; and, awful as it was, when momentarily presented to their sight, it was not so awful as darkness and uncertainty. To those who have been accustomed to the difficulties and dangers of a sea-faring life, there are no lines which speak more forcibly to the imagination, or prove the beauty and power of the Greek poet, than those in the noble prayer of Ajax:—

> "Lord of earth and air,
> O king! O father! hear my humble prayer.
> Dispel this cloud, that light of heaven restore;
> Give me to see—and Ajax asks no more,
> If Greece must perish—we Thy will obey;
> But *let us perish in the face of day*!"

Oswald gave the helm to two of the seamen, and with his knife cut adrift the axes, which were lashed round the mizen-mast in painted canvas covers. One he retained for himself,—the others he put into the hands of the boatswain and the second mate. To speak so as to be heard was almost impossible, from the tremendous roaring of the

wind; but the lamp still burned in the binnacle, and by its feeble light
Captain Ingram could distinguish the signs made by the mate, and
could give his consent. It was necessary that the ship should be put
before the wind; and the helm had no power over her. In a short time
the lanyards of the mizen rigging were severed, and the mizen-mast
went over the side, almost unperceived by the crew on the other parts
of the deck, or even those near, had it not been from blows received
by those who were too close to it, from the falling of the topsail-
sheets and the rigging about the mast.

Oswald, with his companions, regained the binnacle, and for a little
while watched the compass. The ship did not pay off, and appeared to
settle down more into the water. Again Oswald made his signs, and
again the captain gave his assent. Forward sprang the undaunted mate,
clinging to the bulwark and belaying-pins, and followed by his hardy
companions, until they had all three gained the main channels. Here,
their exposure to the force of the breaking waves, and the stoutness
of the ropes yielding but slowly to the blows of the axes, which
were used almost under water, rendered the service one of extreme
difficulty and danger. The boatswain was washed over the bulwark
and dashed to leeward, where the lee-rigging only saved him from a
watery grave. Unsubdued, he again climbed up to windward, rejoined
and assisted his companions. The last blow was given by Oswald—the
lanyards flew through the dead-eyes—and the tall mast disappeared
in the foaming seas. Oswald and his companions hastened from their
dangerous position, and rejoined the captain, who, with many of the
crew, still remained near the wheel. The ship now slowly paid off
and righted. In a few minutes she was flying before the gale, rolling
heavily, and occasionally striking upon the wrecks of the masts, which
she towed with her by the lee-rigging.

Although the wind blew with as much violence as before, still it
was not with the same noise, now that the ship was before the wind
with her after-masts gone. The next service was to clear the ship of
the wrecks of the masts; but, although all now assisted, but little could

be effected until the day had dawned, and even then it was a service of danger, as the ship rolled gunwale under. Those who performed the duty were slung in ropes, that they might not be washed away; and hardly was it completed, when a heavy roll, assisted by a jerking heave from a sea which struck her on the chess-tree, sent the foremast over the starboard cathead. Thus was the *Circassian* dismasted in the gale.

IV
THE LEAK

THE WRECK OF THE FOREMAST was cleared from the ship; the gale continued, but the sun shone brightly and warmly. The *Circassian* was again brought to the wind. All danger was now considered to be over, and the seamen joked and laughed as they were busied in preparing jury-masts to enable them to reach their destined port.

"I wouldn't have cared so much about this spree," said the boatswain, "if it warn't for the mainmast; it was such a beauty. There's not another stick to be found equal to it in the whole length of the Mississippi."

"Bah! man," replied Oswald; "there's as good fish in the sea as ever came out of it, and as good sticks growing as ever were felled; but I guess we'll pay pretty dear for our spars when we get to Liverpool,— but that concerns the owners."

The wind, which, at the time of its sudden change to the southward and eastward, had blown with the force of a hurricane, now settled into a regular strong gale, such as sailors are prepared to meet and laugh at. The sky was also bright and clear, and they had not the danger of a lee shore. It was a delightful change after a night of darkness, danger, and confusion and the men worked that they might get sufficient sail on the ship to steady her, and enable them to shape a course.

"I suppose now that we have the trysail on her forward, the captain will be for running for it," observed one who was busy turning in a dead-eye.

"Yes," replied the boatswain; "and with this wind on our quarter we shan't want much sail, I've a notion."

"Well, then, one advantage in losing your mast—you haven't much trouble about the rigging."

"Trouble enough, though, Bill, when we get in," replied another, gruffly; "new lower rigging to parcel and sarve, and every block to turn in afresh."

"Never mind, longer in port—I'll get spliced."

"Why, how often do you mean to get spliced, Bill? You've a wife in every State, to my sartin knowledge."

"I ain't got one at Liverpool, Jack."

"Well, you may take one there, Bill; for you've been sweet upon that nigger girl for these last three weeks."

"Any port in a storm, but she won't do for harbour duty. But the fact is, you're all wrong there, Jack, its the babbies I likes—I likes to see them both together, hanging at the niggers' breasts, I always think of two spider-monkeys nursing two kittens."

"I knows the women, but I never knows the children. It's just six of one and half-a-dozen of the other; ain't it, Bill?"

"Yes; like two bright bullets out of the same mould. I say, Bill, did any of your wives ever have twins?"

"No; nor I don't intend, until the owners give us double pay."

"By-the-bye," interrupted Oswald, who had been standing under the weather bulk-head, listening to the conversation, and watching the work in progress, "we may just as well see if she has made any water with all this straining and buffeting. By the Lord I never thought of that. Carpenter, lay down your adze and sound the well."

The carpenter, who, notwithstanding the uneasiness of the dismasted vessel, was performing his important share of the work, immediately complied with the order. He drew up the rope-yarn, to which an iron rule had been suspended, and lowered down into the pump-well, and perceived that the water was dripping from it. Imagining that it must have been wet from the quantity of water shipped over all, the carpenter disengaged the rope-yarn from the rule, drew another from the junk lying on the deck, which the seamen were working up, and then carefully proceeded to plumb the well. He hauled it up, and, looking at it for some moments aghast, exclaimed, "*Seven feet* of water in the hold, by G—d."

If the crew of the *Circassian*, the whole of which were on deck, had been struck with an electric shock, the sudden change of their countenances could not have been greater than was produced by this appalling intelligence.

Heap upon sailors every disaster, every danger which can be accumulated from the waves, the wind, the elements, or the enemy, and they will bear up against them with a courage amounting to heroism. All that they demand is, that the one plank "between them and death" is sound, and they will trust to their own energies, and will be confident in their own skill: but *spring a leak* and they are half paralysed; and if it gain upon them they are subdued; for when they find that their exertions are futile, they are little better than children.

Oswald sprang to the pumps when he heard the carpenter's report. "Try again, Abel—it cannot be: cut away that line; hand us here a dry rope-yarn."

Once more the well was sounded by Oswald, and the result was the same. "We must rig the pumps, my lads," said the mate, endeavouring to conceal his own fears; "half this water must have found its way in when she was on her beam-ends."

This idea, so judiciously thrown out, was caught at by the seamen, who hastened to obey the order, while Oswald went down to acquaint the captain, who, worn out with watching and fatigue, had, now that danger was considered to be over, thrown himself into his cot to obtain a few hours' repose.

"Do you think, Bareth, that we have sprung a leak?" said the captain, earnestly, "She never could have taken in that quantity of water."

"Never, sir," replied the mate; "but she has been so strained, that she may have opened her top-sides. I trust it is no worse."

"What is your opinion, then?"

"I am afraid that the wrecks of the masts have injured her: you may recollect how often we struck against them before we could clear ourselves of them; once, particularly, the mainmast appeared to be right under her bottom, I recollect, and she struck very heavy on it."

"Well, it is God's will: let us get on deck as fast as we can."

When they arrived on deck, the carpenter walked up to the captain, and quietly said to him, "Seven feet three, sir." The pumps were then in full action; the men had divided, by the direction of the boatswain, and, stripped naked to the waist, relieved each other every two minutes. For half an hour they laboured incessantly.

This was the half-hour of suspense: the great point to be ascertained was, whether she leaked through the top-sides, and had taken in the water during the second gale; if so, there was every hope of keeping it under. Captain Ingram and the mate remained in silence near the capstan, the former with his watch in his hand, during the time that the sailors exerted themselves to the utmost. It was ten minutes past seven when the half hour had expired; the well was sounded and the line carefully measured—*Seven feet six inches*! So that the water had gained upon them, notwithstanding that they had plied the pumps to the utmost of their strength.

A mute look of despair was exchanged among the crew, but it was followed up by curses and execrations. Captain Ingram remained silent, with his lips compressed.

"It's all over with us!" exclaimed one of the men.

"Not yet, my lads; we have one more chance," said Oswald. "I've a notion that the ship's sides have been opened by the infernal straining of last night, and that she is now taking it in at the top-sides generally: if so, we have only to put her before the wind again, and have another good spell at the pumps. When no longer strained, as she is now with her broadside to the sea, she will close all up again."

"I shouldn't wonder if Mr Bareth is not right," replied the carpenter; "however, that's my notion, too."

"And mine," added Captain Ingram. "Come, my men! never say die while there's a shot in the locker. Let's try her again." And, to encourage the men, Captain Ingram threw off his coat and assisted at the first spell, while Oswald went to the helm and put the ship before the wind.

As the *Circassian* rolled before the gale, the lazy manner in which she righted proved how much water there was in the hold. The seamen exerted themselves for a whole hour without intermission, and the well was again sounded—*eight feet*!

The men did not assert that they would pump no longer; but they too plainly showed their intentions by each resuming in silence his shirt and jacket, which had been taken off at the commencement of his exertions.

"What's to be done, Oswald?" said Captain Ingram, as they walked aft. "You see the men will pump no longer: nor, indeed, would it be of any use. We are doomed."

"The *Circassian* is, sir, I am afraid," replied the mate: "pumping is of no avail; they could not keep her afloat till day-break. We must therefore, trust to our boats, which I believe to be all sound, and quit her before night."

"Crowded boats in such a sea as this!" replied Captain Ingram, shaking his head mournfully.

"Are bad enough, I grant; but better than the sea itself. All we can do now is to try and keep the men sober, and if we can do so it will be better than to fatigue them uselessly; they'll want all their strength before they put foot again upon dry land—if ever they are so fortunate. Shall I speak to them?"

"Do, Oswald," replied the captain; "for myself I care little, God knows; but my wife—my children!"

"My lads," said Oswald, going forward to the men, who had waited in moody silence the result of the conference—"as for pumping any longer it would be only wearing out your strength for no good. We must now look to our boats; and a good boat is better than a bad ship. Still this gale and cross-running sea are rather too much for boats at present; we had therefore better stick to the ship as long as we can. Let us set to with a will and get the boats ready, with provisions, water, and what may be needful, and then we must trust to God's mercy and our own endeavours."

"No boat can stand this sea," observed one of the men. "I'm of opinion, as it's to be a short life, it may as well be a merry one. What d'ye say, my lads?" continued he, appealing to the men.

Several of the crew were of the same opinion: but Oswald, stepping forward, seized one of the axes which lay at the main-bits, and going up to the seaman who had spoken, looked him steadfastly in the face:—

"Williams," said the mate, "a short life it may be to all of us, but not a merry one; the meaning of which I understand very well. Sorry I shall be to have your blood, or that of others, on my hands; but as sure as there's a heaven, I'll cleave to the shoulder the first man who attempts to break into the spirit-room. You know I never joke. Shame upon you! Do you call yourselves men, when, for the sake of a little liquor now, you would lose your only chance of getting drunk every day as soon as we get on shore again? There's a time for all things; and I've a notion this is a time to be sober."

As most of the crew sided with Oswald, the weaker party were obliged to submit, and the preparations were commenced. The two boats on the booms were found to be in good condition. One party was employed cutting away the bulwarks, that the boats might be launched over the side, as there were no means of hoisting them out. The well was again sounded. Nine feet of water in the hold, and the ship evidently settling fast. Two hours had now passed, and the gale was not so violent; the sea, also, which at the change of wind had been cross, appeared to have recovered its regular run. All was ready; the sailors, once at work again, had, in some measure, recovered their spirits, and were buoyed up with fresh hopes at the slight change in their favour from the decrease of the wind. The two boats were quite large enough to contain the whole of the crew and passengers; but, as the sailors said among themselves (proving the kindness of their hearts), "What was to become of those two poor babbies, in an open boat for days and nights, perhaps?" Captain Ingram had gone down to Mrs Templemore, to impart to her their melancholy prospects; and the mother's heart, as well as the mother's voice, echoed the words of the seamen, "What will become of my poor babes?"

It was not till nearly six o'clock in the evening that all was ready: the ship was slowly brought to the wind again, and the boats launched over the side. By this time the gale was much abated; but the vessel was full of water, and was expected soon to go down.

There is no time in which coolness and determination are more required than in a situation like the one which we have attempted to describe. It is impossible to know the precise moment at which a water-logged vessel, in a heavy sea, may go down: and its occupants are in a state of mental fever, with the idea of their remaining in her so late that she will suddenly submerge, and leave them to struggle in the waves. This feeling actuated many of the crew of the *Circassian*, and they had already retreated to the boats. All was arranged; Oswald had charge of one boat, and it was agreed that the larger should receive Mrs Templemore and her children, under the protection of Captain Ingram. The number appointed to Oswald's boat being completed, he shoved off, to make room for the other, and laid-to to leeward, waiting to keep company. Mrs Templemore came up with Captain Ingram, and was assisted by him into the boat. The nurse, with one child, was at last placed by her side; Coco was leading Judy, the other nurse, with the remaining infant in her arms, and Captain Ingram, who had been obliged to go into the boat with the first child, was about to return to assist Judy with the other, when the ship gave a heavy pitch, and her forecastle was buried in the wave: at the same time the gunwale of the boat was stove by coming in contact with the side of the vessel. "She's down, by G—d!" exclaimed the alarmed seamen in the boat; shoving off to escape from the vortex.

Captain Ingram, who was standing on the boat's thwarts to assist Judy, was thrown back into the bottom of the boat; and, before he could extricate himself, the boat was separated from the ship, and had drifted to leeward.

"My child!" screamed the mother: "my child!"

"Pull to again, my lads!" cried Captain Ingram, seizing the tiller.

The men, who had been alarmed at the idea that the ship was going down, now that they saw that she was still afloat, got out the oars and attempted to regain her, but in vain—they could not make head against the sea and wind. Further and further did they drift to leeward, notwithstanding their exertions; while the frantic mother extended her arms, imploring and entreating. Captain Ingram, who had stimulated the sailors to the utmost, perceived that further attempts were useless.

"My child! my child!" screamed Mrs Templemore, standing up, and holding out her arms towards the vessel. At a sign from the captain, the head of the boat was veered round. The bereaved mother knew that all hope was gone, and she fell down in a state of insensibility.

V
The Old Maid

O NE MORNING, SHORTLY AFTER THE disasters which we have described, Mr Witherington descended to his breakfast-room somewhat earlier than usual, and found his green morocco easy-chair already tenanted by no less a personage than William the footman, who, with his feet on the fender, was so attentively reading the newspaper that he did not hear his master's entrance. "By my ancestor, who fought on his stumps! but I hope you are quite comfortable, Mr William; nay, I beg I may not disturb you, sir."

William, although as impudent as most of his fraternity, was a little taken aback. "I beg your pardon, sir, but Mr Jonathan had not time to look over the paper."

"Nor is it required that he should, that I know of, sir."

"Mr Jonathan says, sir, that it is always right to look over the *deaths*, that news of that kind may not shock you."

"Very considerate, indeed."

"And there is a story there, sir, about a shipwreck."

"A shipwreck! where, William? God bless me! where is it?"

"I am afraid it is the same ship you are so anxious about, sir,— the—I forget the name, sir."

Mr Witherington took the newspaper, and his eye soon caught the paragraph in which the rescue of the two negroes and child from the wreck of the *Circassian* was fully detailed.

"It is indeed!" exclaimed Mr Witherington. "My poor Cecilia in an open boat! one of the boats was seen to go down,—perhaps she's dead—merciful God! one boy saved. Mercy on me! where's Jonathan?"

"Here, sir," replied Jonathan, very solemnly, who had just brought in the eggs, and now stood erect as a mute behind his master's chair, for it was a case of danger, if not of death.

"I must go to Portsmouth immediately after breakfast—shan't eat though—appetite all gone."

"People seldom do, sir, on these melancholy occasions," replied Jonathan. "Will you take your own carriage, sir, or a mourning coach?"

"A mourning coach at fourteen miles an hour, with two pair of horses! Jonathan, you're crazy."

"Will you please to have black silk hatbands and gloves for the coachman and servants who attend you, sir?"

"Confound your shop! no; this is a resurrection, not a death; it appears that the negro thinks only one of the boats went down."

"*Mors omnia vincit*," quoth Jonathan, casting up his eyes.

"Never you mind that; mind your own business. That's the postman's knock—see if there are any letters."

There were several; and amongst the others there was one from Captain Maxwell, of the *Eurydice*, detailing the circumstances already known, and informing Mr Witherington that he had despatched the two negroes and the child to his address by that day's coach, and that one of the officers, who was going to town by the same conveyance, would see them safe to his house.

Captain Maxwell was an old acquaintance of Mr Witherington— had dined at his house in company with the Templemores, and therefore had extracted quite enough information from the negroes to know where to direct them.

"By the blood of my ancestors! they'll be here to night," cried Mr Witherington; "and I have saved my journey. What is to be done? better tell Mary to get rooms ready: d'ye hear, William? beds for one little boy and two niggers."

"Yes, sir," replied William; "but where are the black people to be put?"

"Put! I don't care; one may sleep with cook, the other with Mary."

"Very well, sir, I'll tell them," replied William, hastening away, delighted at the row which he anticipated in the kitchen.

"If you please, sir," observed Jonathan, "one of the negroes is, I believe, a man."

"Well, what then?"

"Only, sir, the maids may object to sleep with him."

"By all the plagues of the Witheringtons! this is true; well, you may take him, Jonathan—you like that colour."

"Not in the dark, sir," replied Jonathan with a bow.

"Well, then, let them sleep together: so that affair is settled."

"Are they man and wife, sir?" said the butler.

"The devil take them both! how should I know? Let me have my breakfast, and we'll talk over the matter by-and-by."

Mr Witherington applied to his eggs, and muffin, eating his breakfast as fast as he could, without knowing why; but the reason was that he was puzzled and perplexed with the anticipated arrival, and longed to think quietly over the dilemma, for it was a dilemma to an old bachelor. As soon as he had swallowed his second cup of tea he put himself into his easy-chair, in an easy attitude, and was very soon soliloquising as follows:—

"By the blood of the Witheringtons! what am I, an old bachelor, to do with a baby, and a wet-nurse as black as the ace of spades, and another black fellow in the bargain. Send him back again? yes, that's best: but the child—woke every morning at five o'clock with its squalling—obliged to kiss it three times a-day—pleasant!—and then that nigger of a nurse—thick lips—kissing child all day, and then holding it out to me—ignorant as a cow—if child has the stomach-ache she'll cram a pepper-pod down its throat—West India fashion—children never without the stomach-ache!—my poor, poor cousin!—what has become of her and the other child, too?—wish they may pick her up, poor dear! and then she will come and take care of her own children—don't know what to do—great mind to send for sister Moggy—but she's so *fussy*—won't be in a hurry. Think again."

Here Mr Witherington was interrupted by two taps at the door.

"Come in," said he; and the cook, with her face as red as if she had been dressing a dinner for eighteen, made her appearance without the usual clean apron.

"If you please, sir," said she, curtseying, "I will thank you to suit yourself with another cook."

"Oh, very well," replied Mr Witherington, angry at the interruption.

"And if you please, sir, I should like to go this very day—indeed, sir, I shall not stay."

"Go to the devil! if you please," replied Mr Witherington, angrily; "but first go out and shut the door after you."

The cook retired, and Mr Witherington was again alone.

"Confound the old woman—what a huff she is in! won't cook for black people, I suppose—yes, that's it."

Here Mr Witherington was again interrupted by a second double tap at the door.

"Oh! thought better of it, I suppose. Come in."

It was not the cook, but Mary, the housemaid, that entered.

"If you please, sir," said she, whimpering, "I should wish to leave my situation."

"A conspiracy, by heavens! Well, you may go."

"To-night, sir, if you please," answered the woman.

"This moment, for all I care!" exclaimed Mr Witherington in his wrath.

The housemaid retired; and Mr Witherington took some time to compose himself.

"Servants all going to the devil in this country," said he at last; "proud fools—won't clean rooms after black people, I suppose—yes, that's it, confound them all, black and white! here's my whole establishment upset by the arrival of a baby. Well, it is very uncomfortable—what shall I do?—send for sister Moggy?—no, I'll send for Jonathan."

Mr Witherington rang the bell, and Jonathan made his appearance.

"What is all this, Jonathan?" said he; "cook angry—Mary crying— both going away—what's it all about?"

"Why, sir, they were told by William that it was your positive order that the two black people were to sleep with them; and I believe he told Mary that the man was to sleep with her."

"Confound that fellow! he's always at mischief; you know, Jonathan, I never meant that."

"I thought not, sir, as it is quite contrary to custom," replied Jonathan.

"Well, then, tell them so, and let's hear no more about it."

Mr Witherington then entered into a consultation with his butler, and acceded to the arrangements proposed by him. The parties arrived in due time, and were properly accommodated. Master Edward was not troubled with the stomach-ache, neither did he wake Mr Witherington at five o'clock in the morning; and, after all, it was not very uncomfortable. But, although things were not quite so uncomfortable as Mr Witherington had anticipated, still they were not comfortable; and Mr Witherington was so annoyed by continual skirmishes with his servants, complaints from Judy, in bad English, of the cook, who, it must be owned, had taken a prejudice against her and Coco, occasional illness of the child, *et cætera*, that he found his house no longer quiet and peaceable. Three months had now nearly passed, and no tidings of the boats had been received; and Captain Maxwell, who came up to see Mr Witherington, gave it as his decided opinion that they must have foundered in the gale. As, therefore, there appeared to be no chance of Mrs Templemore coming to take care of her child, Mr Witherington at last resolved to write to Bath, where his sister resided, and acquaint her with the whole story, requesting her to come and superintend his domestic concerns. A few days afterwards he received the following reply:—

"BATH, August.

"MY DEAR BROTHER ANTONY,—"Your letter arrived safe to hand on Wednesday last, and I must say that I was not a little surprised at its contents; indeed, I thought so much about it that I revoked at Lady Betty Blabkin's whist-party, and lost four shillings and sixpence. You say that you have a child at your house belonging to your cousin, who married in so indecorous a manner. I hope what you say is true; but, at the same time, I know what bachelors are guilty of; although, as Lady Betty says, it is better never to talk or even to hint about these improper things. I cannot imagine why men should consider themselves, in an unmarried state, as absolved from that purity which maidens are so careful to preserve; and so says Lady Betty, with whom I had a little conversation on the subject. As, however, the thing is done, she agrees with me that it is better to hush it up as well as we can.

"I presume that you do not intend to make the child your heir, which I should consider as highly improper; and, indeed, Lady Betty tells me that the legacy-duty is ten per cent., and that it cannot be avoided. However, I make it a rule never to talk about these sort of things. As for your request that I will come up and superintend your establishment, I have advised with Lady Betty on the subject, and she agrees with me that, for the honour of the family, it is better that I should come, as it will save appearances. You are in a peck of troubles, as most men are who are free-livers and are led astray by artful and alluring females. However, as Lady Betty says, 'the least said, the soonest mended.'

"I will, therefore, make the necessary arrangements for letting my house, and hope to join you in about ten days; sooner, I cannot, as I find that my engagements extend to that period. Many questions have already been put to me on this unpleasant subject; but I always give but one answer, which is, that bachelors will be bachelors; and that, at all events, it is not so bad as if you were a married man: for I make it a rule never to talk about, or even to hint about, these sort of things, for, as Lady Betty says, 'Men will get into scrapes, and the sooner things are hushed up the better.' So no more at present from your affectionate sister,

"MARGARET WITHERINGTON.

"*P.S.*—Lady Betty and I both agree that you are very right in hiring two black people to bring the child into your house, as it makes the thing look foreign to the neighbours, and we can keep our own secrets.

"M. W."

"Now, by all the sins of the Witheringtons, if this is not enough to drive a man out of his senses!—Confound the suspicious old maid! I'll not let her come into this house. Confound Lady Betty, and all scandal-loving old tabbies like her! Bless me!" continued Mr Witherington, throwing the letter on the table with a deep sigh, "this is anything but comfortable."

But if Mr Witherington found it anything but comfortable at the commencement, he found it unbearable in the sequel.

His sister Moggy arrived, and installed herself in the house with all the pomp and protecting air of one who was the saviour of her brother's reputation and character. When the child was first brought down to her, instead of perceiving at once its likeness to Mr Templemore, which was very strong, she looked at it and at her brother's face with her only eye, and shaking her finger, exclaimed,—

"Oh, Antony! Antony! and did you expect to deceive me?—the nose—the mouth exact—Antony, for shame! fie, for shame!"

But we must hurry over the misery that Mr Witherington's kindness and benevolence brought upon him. Not a day passed—scarcely an hour, without his ears being galled with his sister's insinuations. Judy and Coco were sent back to America; the servants, who had remained so long in his service, gave warning one by one, and afterwards, were changed as often almost as there was a change in the moon. She ruled the house and her brother despotically; and all poor Mr Witherington's comfort was gone until the time arrived when Master Edward was to be sent to school. Mr Witherington then plucked up courage, and after a few stormy months drove his sister back to Bath, and once more found himself comfortable.

Edward came home during the holidays, and was a great favourite; but the idea had become current that he was the son of the old gentleman, and the remarks made were so unpleasant and grating to him, that he was not sorry, much as he was attached to the boy, when he declared his intention to choose the profession of a sailor.

Captain Maxwell introduced him into the service; and afterwards, when, in consequence of ill health and exhaustion, he was himself obliged to leave it for a time, he procured for his *protégé* other ships. We must, therefore, allow some years to pass away, during which time Edward Templemore pursues his career, Mr Witherington grows older and more particular, and his sister Moggy amuses herself with Lady Betty's remarks and her darling game of whist.

During all this period no tidings of the boats, or of Mrs Templemore and her infant, had been heard; it was therefore naturally conjectured that they had all perished, and they were remembered but as things that had been.

VI
THE MIDSHIPMAN

THE WEATHER SIDE OF THE quarter-deck of H.M. frigate *Unicorn* was occupied by two very great personages: Captain Plumbton, commanding the ship, who was very great in width if not in height, taking much more than his allowance of the deck, if it were not that he was the proprietor thereof, and entitled to the lion's share. Captain P. was not more than four feet ten inches in height; but then he was equal to that in girth: there was quite enough of him, if he had only been *rolled out*. He walked with his coat flying open, his thumbs stuck into the arm holes of his waistcoat, so as to throw his shoulders back and increase his horizontal dimensions. He also held his head well aft, which threw his chest and stomach well forward. He was the prototype of pomposity and good nature, and he strutted like an actor in a procession.

The other personage was the first lieutenant, whom Nature had pleased to fashion in another mould. He was as tall as the captain was short—as thin as his superior was corpulent. His long, lanky legs were nearly up to the captain's shoulders; and he bowed down over the head of his superior, as if he were the crane to hoist up, and the captain the bale of goods to be hoisted. He carried his hands behind his back, with two fingers twisted together; and his chief difficulty appeared to be to reduce his own stride to the parrot march of the captain. His features were sharp and lean as was his body, and wore every appearance of a cross-grained temper.

He had been making divers complaints of divers persons, and the captain had hitherto appeared imperturbable. Captain Plumbton was an even-tempered man, who was satisfied with a good dinner. Lieutenant Markitall was an odd-tempered man, who would quarrel with his bread and butter.

"Quite impossible, sir," continued the first-lieutenant, "to carry on the duty without support."

This oracular observation, which, from the relative forms of the two parties, descended as it were from above, was replied to by the captain with a "Very true."

"Then, sir, I presume you will not object to my putting that man in the report for punishment?"

"I'll think about it, Mr Markitall." This, with Captain Plumbton, was as much as to say, No.

"The young gentlemen, sir, I am sorry to say, are very troublesome."

"Boys always are," replied the captain.

"Yes sir: but the duty must be carried on, and I cannot do without them."

"Very true—midshipmen are very useful."

"But I am sorry to say, sir, that they are not. Now sir, there's Mr Templemore; I can do nothing with him—he does nothing but laugh."

"Laugh!—Mr Markitall, does he laugh at you?"

"Not exactly, sir; but he laughs at everything. If I send him to the mast-head, he goes up laughing; if I call him down, he comes down laughing; if I find fault with him, he laughs the next minute: in fact, sir, he does nothing but laugh. I should particularly wish, sir, that you would speak to him, and see if any interference on your part—"

"Would make him cry—eh? better to laugh than cry in this world. Does he never cry, Mr Markitall?"

"Yes, sir, and very unseasonably. The other day, you may recollect, when you punished Wilson the marine, whom I appointed to take care of his chest and hammock, he was crying the whole time; almost tantamount—at least an indirect species of mutiny on his part, as it implied—"

"That the boy was sorry that his servant was punished; I never flog a man but I'm sorry myself, Mr Markitall."

"Well, I do not press the question of his crying—that I might look over; but his laughing, sir, I must beg that you will take notice of that. Here he is, sir, coming up the hatchway. Mr Templemore, the captain wishes to speak to you."

Now the captain did not wish to speak to him, but, forced upon him as it was by the first-lieutenant, he could do no less. So Mr Templemore touched his hat, and stood before the captain, we regret to say, with such a good-humoured, sly, confiding smirk on his countenance, as at once established the proof of the accusation, and the enormity of the offence.

"So, sir," said Captain Plumbton, stopping in his perambulation, and squaring his shoulders still more, "I find that you laugh at the first-lieutenant."

"I, sir?" replied the boy, the smirk expanding into a broad grin.

"Yes; you, sir," said the first-lieutenant, now drawing up to his full height; "why you're laughing now, sir."

"I can't help it, sir—it's not my fault; and I'm sure it's not yours, sir," added the boy, demurely.

"Are you aware, Edward—Mr Templemore, I mean—of the impropriety of disrespect to your superior officer?"

"I never laughed at Mr Markitall but once, sir, that I can recollect, and that was when he tumbled over the messenger."

"And why did you laugh at him then, sir?"

"I always do laugh when any one tumbles down," replied the lad; "I can't help it, sir."

"Then, sir, I suppose you would laugh if you saw me rolling in the lee-scuppers?" said the captain.

"Oh!" replied the boy, no longer able to contain himself, "I'm sure I should burst myself with laughing—I think I see you now, sir."

"Do you, indeed! I'm very glad that you do not; though I'm afraid, young gentleman, you stand convicted by your own confession."

"Yes, sir, for laughing, if that is any crime; but it's not in the Articles of War."

"No, sir; but disrespect is. You laugh when you go to the mast-head."

"But I obey the order, sir, immediately—Do I not, Mr Markitall?"

"Yes, sir, you obey the order; but, at the same time, your laughing proves that you do not mind the punishment."

"No more I do, sir. I spend half my time at the mast-head, and I'm used to it now."

"But, Mr Templemore, ought you not to feel the disgrace of the punishment?" inquired the captain, severely.

"Yes, sir, if I felt I deserved it I should. I should not laugh, sir, if *you* sent me to the mast-head," replied the boy, assuming a serious countenance.

"You see, Mr Markitall, that he can be grave," observed the captain.

"I've tried all I can to make him so, sir," replied the first-lieutenant; "but I wish to ask Mr Templemore what he means to imply by saying, 'when he deserves it.' Does he mean to say that I have ever punished him unjustly?"

"Yes, sir," replied the boy, boldly; "five times out of six, I am mast-headed for nothing—and that's the reason why I do not mind it."

"For nothing, sir! Do you call laughing nothing?"

"I pay every attention that I can to my duty, sir; I always obey your orders; I try all I can to make you pleased with me—but you are always punishing me."

"Yes, sir, for laughing, and, what is worse, making the ship's company laugh."

"They 'haul and hold' just the same, sir—I think they work all the better for being merry."

"And pray, sir, what business have you to think?" replied the first-lieutenant, now very angry. "Captain Plumbton, as this young gentleman thinks proper to interfere with me and the discipline of the ship, I beg you will see what effect your punishing may have upon him."

"Mr Templemore," said the captain, "you are, in the first place, too free in your speech, and, in the next place, too fond of laughing. There is, Mr Templemore, a time for all things—a time to be merry, and a time to be serious. The quarter-deck is not a fit place for mirth."

"I'm sure the gangway is not," shrewdly interrupted the boy.

"No—you are right, nor the gangway; but you may laugh on the forecastle, and when below with your messmates."

"No, sir, we may not; Mr Markitall always sends out if he hears us laughing."

"Because, Mr Templemore, you're always laughing."

"I believe I am, sir; and if it's wrong I'm sorry to displease you, but I mean no disrespect. I laugh in my sleep—I laugh when I awake—I laugh when the sun shines—I always feel so happy; but though you do mast-head me, Mr Markitall, I should not laugh, but be very sorry, if any misfortune happened to you."

"I believe you would, boy—I do indeed, Mr Markitall," said the captain.

"Well, sir," replied the first-lieutenant, "as Mr Templemore appears to be aware of his error, I do not wish to press my complaint—I have only to request that he will never laugh again."

"You hear, boy, what the first-lieutenant says; it's very reasonable, and I beg I may hear no more complaints. Mr Markitall, let me know when the foot of that foretopsail will be repaired—I should like to shift it to-night."

Mr Markitall went down under the half-deck to make the inquiry.

"And, Edward," said Captain Plumbton, as soon as the lieutenant was out of ear-shot, "I have a good deal more to say to you upon this subject, but I have no time now. So come and dine with me—at my table, you know, I allow laughing in moderation."

The boy touched his hat, and with a grateful, happy countenance, walked away.

We have introduced this little scene, that the reader may form some idea of the character of Edward Templemore. He was indeed the soul of mirth, good-humour, and kindly feelings towards others; he even felt kindly towards the first-lieutenant, who persecuted him for his risible propensities. We do not say that the boy was right in laughing at all times, or that the first-lieutenant was wrong in attempting to check it. As the captain said, there is a time for all things, and Edward's laugh was not always seasonable; but it was his nature, and he could not help it. He was joyous as the May morning; and thus he continued for years, laughing at everything—pleased with everybody—almost universally liked—and his bold, free, and happy spirit unchecked by vicissitude or hardship.

He served his time—was nearly turned back when he was passing his examination for laughing, and then went laughing to sea again— was in command of a boat at the cutting-out of a French corvette, and when on board was so much amused by the little French captain skipping about with his rapier, which proved fatal to many, that at last he received a pink from the little gentleman himself, which laid him on deck. For this affair, and in consideration of his wound, he obtained his promotion to the rank of lieutenant—was appointed to a line-of-battle ship in the West Indies—laughed at the yellow-fever—was appointed to the tender of that ship, a fine schooner, and was sent to cruise for prize-money for the admiral, and promotion for himself, if he could, by any fortunate encounter, be so lucky as to obtain it.

VII
SLEEPER'S BAY

ON THE WESTERN COAST OF Africa, there is a small bay, which has received more than one name from its occasional visitors. That by which it was designated by the adventurous Portuguese, who first dared to cleave the waves of the Southern Atlantic, has been forgotten with their lost maritime pre-eminence; the name allotted to it by the woolly-headed natives of the coast has never, perhaps, been ascertained; it is, however, marked down in some of the old English charts as Sleeper's Bay.

The mainland which, by its curvature, has formed this little dent on a coast possessing, and certainly at present requiring few harbours, displays, perhaps, the least inviting of all prospects; offering to the view nothing but a shelving beach of dazzling white sand, backed with a few small hummocks beat up by the occasional fury of the Atlantic gales—arid, bare, and without the slightest appearance of vegetable life. The inland prospect is shrouded over by a dense mirage, through which here and there are to be discovered the stems of a few distant palm-trees, so broken and disjoined by refraction that they present to the imagination anything but the idea of foliage or shade. The water in the bay is calm and smooth as the polished mirror; not the smallest ripple is to be heard on the beach, to break through the silence of nature; not a breath of air sweeps over its glassy surface, which is heated with the intense rays of a vertical noonday sun, pouring down a withering flood of light and heat: not a sea-bird is to be discovered wheeling on its flight, or balancing on its wings as it pierces the deep with its searching eye, ready to dart upon its prey. All is silence, solitude, and desolation, save that occasionally may be seen the fin of some huge shark, either sluggishly moving through the heated element, or stationary in the torpor of the mid-day heat. A site so sterile, so stagnant, so little adapted to human life, cannot well be conceived, unless, by flying to extremes, we were to portray the chilling blast, the transfixing cold, and "close-ribbed ice," at the frozen poles.

At the entrance of this bay, in about three fathoms water, heedless of the spring cable which hung down as a rope which had fallen overboard, there floated, motionless as death, a vessel whose proportions would have challenged the unanimous admiration of those who could appreciate the merits of her build, had she been anchored in the most frequented and busy harbour of the universe. So beautiful were her lines, that you might almost have imagined her a created being that the ocean had been ordered to receive, as if fashioned by the Divine Architect, to add to the beauty and variety of His works; for, from the huge leviathan to the smallest of the finny tribe—from the towering albatross to the boding petrel of the storm—where could be found, among the winged or finned frequenters of the ocean, a form more appropriate, more fitting, than this specimen of human skill, whose beautiful model and elegant tapering spars were now all that could be discovered to break the meeting lines of the firmament and horizon of the offing.

Alas! she was fashioned, at the will of avarice, for the aid of cruelty and injustice, and now was even more nefariously employed. She had been a slaver—she was now the far-famed, still more dreaded, pirate-schooner, the *Avenger*.

Not a man-of-war which scoured the deep but had her
instructions relative to this vessel, which had been so successful in
her career of crime—not a trader in any portion of the navigable
globe but whose crew shuddered at the mention of her name, and
the remembrance of the atrocities which had been practised by
her reckless crew. She had been everywhere—in the east, the west,
the north, and the south, leaving a track behind her of rapine and
of murder. There she lay in motionless beauty; her low sides were
painted black, with one small, narrow riband of red—her raking
masts were clean scraped—her topmasts, her cross-trees, caps, and
even running-blocks, were painted in pure white. Awnings were
spread fore and aft to protect the crew from the powerful rays of
the sun; her ropes were hauled taut; and in every point she wore
the appearance of being under the control of seamanship and
strict discipline. Through the clear smooth water her copper shone
brightly; and as you looked over her taffrail down into the calm
blue sea, you could plainly discover the sandy bottom beneath her
and the anchor which then lay under her counter. A small boat
floated astern, the weight of the rope which attached her appearing,
in the perfect calm, to draw her towards the schooner.

We must now go on board, and our first cause of surprise will be
the deception relative to the tonnage of the schooner, when viewed
from a distance. Instead of a small vessel of about ninety tons, we
discover that she is upwards of two hundred; that her breadth of
beam is enormous; and that those spars, which appeared so light and
elegant, are of unexpected dimensions. Her decks are of narrow fir
planks, without the least spring or rise; her ropes are of Manilla hemp,
neatly secured to copper belaying-pins, and coiled down on the deck,
whose whiteness is well contrasted with the bright green paint of her
bulwarks; her capstern and binnacles are cased in fluted mahogany,
and ornamented with brass; metal stanchions protect the skylights,
and the bright muskets are arranged in front of the mainmast, while
the boarding-pikes are lashed round the mainboom.

In the centre of the vessel, between the fore and main masts, there is a long brass 32-pounder fixed upon a carriage revolving in a circle, and so arranged that in bad weather it can be lowered down and *housed*; while on each side of her decks are mounted eight brass guns of smaller calibre and of exquisite workmanship. Her build proves the skill of the architect; her fitting-out, a judgment in which nought has been sacrificed to, although everything has been directed by, taste; and her neatness and arrangement, that, in the person of her commander, to the strictest discipline there is united the practical knowledge of a thorough seaman. How, indeed, otherwise could she have so long continued her lawless yet successful career? How could it have been possible to unite a crew of miscreants, who feared not God nor man, most of whom had perpetrated foul murders, or had been guilty of even blacker iniquities? It was because he who commanded the vessel was so superior as to find in her no rivalry. Superior in talent, in knowledge of his profession, in courage, and, moreover, in physical strength—which in him was almost Herculean—unfortunately he was also superior to all in villainy, in cruelty, and contempt of all injunctions, moral and Divine.

What had been the early life of this person was but imperfectly known. It was undoubted that he had received an excellent education, and it was said that he was of an ancient border family on the banks of the Tweed: by what chances he had become a pirate—by what errors he had fallen from his station in society, until he became an outcast, had never been revealed; it was only known that he had been some years employed in the slave-trade previous to his seizing this vessel and commencing his reckless career. The name by which he was known to the crew of the pirate-vessel was "Cain," and well had he chosen this appellation; for, had not his hand for more than three years been against every man's, and every man's hand against his? In person he was about six feet high, with a breadth of shoulders and of chest denoting the utmost of physical force which, perhaps, has ever been allotted to man. His features would have been handsome had they not been scarred with wounds; and, strange to say, his eye was mild and of a soft blue. His mouth was well formed, and his teeth of a pearly white: the hair of his head was crisped and wavy, and his beard, which he wore, as did every person composing the crew of the pirate, covered the lower part of his face in strong, waving, and continued curls. The proportions of his body were perfect; but from their vastness they became almost terrific. His costume was elegant, and well adapted to his form: linen trousers, and untanned yellow leather boots, such as are made at the Western Isles; a broad-striped cotton shirt; a red Cashmere shawl round his waist as a sash; a vest embroidered in gold tissue, with a jacket of dark velvet, and pendant gold buttons, hanging over his left shoulder, after the fashion of the Mediterranean seamen; a round Turkish skull-cap, handsomely embroidered; a pair of pistols, and a long knife in his sash, completed his attire.

The crew consisted in all of 165 men, of almost every nation; but it was to be remarked that all those in authority were either Englishmen or from the northern countries; the others were chiefly Spaniards and Maltese. Still there were Portuguese, Brazilians, negroes, and others, who made up the complement, which at the time we now speak of was increased by twenty-five additional hands. These were Kroumen, a race of blacks well known at present, who inhabit the coast near Cape Palmas, and are often employed by our men-of-war stationed on the coast to relieve the English seamen from duties which would be too severe to those who were not inured to the climate. They are powerful, athletic men, good sailors, of a happy, merry disposition, and, unlike other Africans, will work hard. Fond of the English, they generally speak the language sufficiently to be understood, and are very glad to receive a baptism when they come on board. The name first given them they usually adhere to as long as they live; and you will now on the coast meet with a Blucher, a Wellington, a Nelson, etc., who will wring swabs, or do any other of the meanest description of work, without feeling that it is discreditable to sponsorials so grand.

It is not to be supposed that these men had voluntarily come on board of the pirate; they had been employed in some British vessels trading on the coast, and had been taken out of them when the vessels were burnt, and the Europeans of the crews murdered. They had received a promise of reward, if they did their duty; but, not expecting it, they waited for the earliest opportunity to make their escape.

The captain of the schooner is abaft with his glass in his hand, occasionally sweeping the offing in expectation of a vessel heaving in sight: the officers and crew are lying down, or lounging listlessly, about the decks, panting with the extreme heat, and impatiently waiting for the sea-breeze to fan their parched foreheads. With their rough beards and exposed chests, and their weather-beaten fierce countenances, they form a group which is terrible even in repose.

We must now descend into the cabin of the schooner. The fittings-up of this apartment are simple: on each side is a standing bed-place; against the after bulkhead is a large buffet, originally intended for glass and china, but now loaded with silver and gold vessels of every size and description, collected by the pirate from the different ships which he had plundered; the lamps are also of silver, and evidently had been intended to ornament the shrine of some Catholic saint.

In this cabin there are two individuals, to whom we shall now direct the reader's attention. The one is a pleasant-countenanced, good-humoured Krouman, who had been christened "Pompey the Great;" most probably on account of his large proportions. He wears a pair of duck trousers; the rest of his body is naked, and presents a sleek, glossy skin, covering muscle, which an anatomist or a sculptor would have viewed with admiration. The other is a youth of eighteen, or thereabouts, with an intelligent, handsome countenance, evidently of European blood. There is, however, an habitually mournful cast upon his features: he is dressed much in the same way as we have described the captain, but the costume hangs more gracefully upon his slender, yet well-formed limbs. He is seated on a sofa, fixed in the fore part of the cabin, with a book in his hand, which occasionally he refers to, and then lifts his eyes from, to watch the motions of the Krouman, who is busy in the office of steward, arranging and cleaning the costly articles in the buffet.

"Massa Francisco, dis really fine ting," said Pompey, holding up a splendidly embossed tankard, which he had been rubbing.

"Yes," replied Francisco, gravely; "it is, indeed, Pompey."

"How Captain Cain came by dis?"

Francisco shook his head, and Pompey put his finger up to his mouth, his eyes, full of meaning, fixed upon Francisco.

At this moment the personage referred to was heard descending the companion-ladder. Pompey recommenced rubbing the silver, and Francisco dropped his eyes upon the book.

What was the tie which appeared to bind the captain to this lad was not known; but, as the latter had always accompanied, and lived together with him, it was generally supposed that he was the captain's son; and he was as often designated by the crew as young Cain as he was by his Christian name of Francisco. Still it was observed that latterly they had frequently been heard in altercation, and that the captain was very suspicious of Francisco's movements.

"I beg I may not interrupt your conversation," said Cain, on entering the cabin; "the information you may obtain from a Krouman must be very important."

Francisco made no reply, but appeared to be reading his book. Cain's eyes passed from one to the other, as if to read their thoughts.

"Pray what were you saying, Mr Pompey?"

"Me say, Massa Captain? me only tell young Massa dis very fine ting; ask where you get him—Massa Francisco no tell."

"And what might it be to you, you black scoundrel?" cried the captain, seizing the goblet, and striking the man with it a blow on the head which flattened the vessel, and at the same time felled the Krouman, powerful as he was, to the deck. The blood streamed, as the man slowly rose, stupefied and trembling from the violent concussion. Without saying a word, he staggered out of the cabin, and Cain threw himself on one of the lockers in front of the standing bed-place, saying, with a bitter smile, "So much for your intimates, Francisco!"

"Rather, so much for your cruelty and injustice towards an unoffending man," replied Francisco, laying his book on the table. "His question was an innocent one,—for he knew not the particulars connected with the obtaining of that flagon."

"And you, I presume, do not forget them? Well, be it so, young man; but I warn you again—as I have warned you often—nothing but the remembrance of your mother has prevented me, long before this, from throwing your body to the sharks."

"What influence my mother's memory may have over you, I know not; I only regret that, in any way, she had the misfortune to be connected with you."

"She had the influence," replied Cain, "which a woman must have over a man when they have for years swung in the same cot; but that is wearing off fast. I tell you so candidly; I will not (even) allow even her memory to check me, if I find you continue your late course. You have shown disaffection before the crew—you have disputed my orders—and I have every reason to believe that you are now plotting against me."

"Can I do otherwise than show my abhorrence," replied Francisco, "when I witness such acts of horror, of cruelty—cold-blooded cruelty, as lately have been perpetrated? Why do you bring me here? and why do you now detain me? All I ask is, that you will allow me to leave the vessel. You are not my father; you have told me so."

"No, I am not your father; but—you are your mother's son."

"That gives you no right to have power over me, even if you had been married to my mother; which—"

"I was not."

"I thank God; for marriage with you would have been even greater disgrace."

"What!" cried Cain, starting up, seizing the young man by the neck, and lifting him off his seat as if he had been a puppet; "but no— I cannot forget your mother." Cain released Francisco, and resumed his seat on the locker.

"As you please," said Francisco, as soon as he had recovered himself; "it matters little whether I am brained by your own hand, or launched overboard as a meal for the sharks; it will be but one more murder."

"Mad fool! why do you tempt me thus?" replied Cain, again starting up, and hastily quitting the cabin.

The altercation which we have just described was not unheard on deck, as the doors of the cabin were open, and the skylight removed to admit the air. The face of Cain was flushed as he ascended the ladder. He perceived his chief mate standing by the hatchway, and many of the men, who had been slumbering abaft, with their heads raised on their elbows, as if they had been listening to the conversation below.

"It will never do, sir," said Hawkhurst, the mate, shaking his head.

"No," replied the captain; "not if he were my own son. But what is to be done?—he knows no fear."

Hawkhurst pointed to the entering port.

"When I ask your advice, you may give it," said the captain, turning gloomily away.

In the meantime, Francisco paced the cabin in deep thought. Young as he was, he was indifferent to death; for he had no tie to render life precious. He remembered his mother, but not her demise; that had been concealed from him. At the age of seven he had sailed with Cain in a slaver, and had ever since continued with him. Until lately, he had been led to suppose that the captain was his father. During the years that he had been in the slave-trade, Cain had devoted much time to his education; it so happened that the only book which could be found on board of the vessel, when Cain first commenced teaching, was a Bible belonging to Francisco's mother. Out of this book he learned to read; and, as his education advanced, other books were procured. It may appear strange that the very traffic in which his reputed father was engaged did not corrupt the boy's mind, but, accustomed to it from his infancy, he had considered these negroes as another species,—an idea fully warranted by the cruelty of the Europeans towards them.

There are some dispositions so naturally kind and ingenuous that even example and evil contact cannot debase them: such was the disposition of Francisco. As he gained in years and knowledge, he thought more and more for himself, and had already become disgusted with the cruelties practised upon the unfortunate negroes, when the slave-vessel was seized upon by Cain and converted into a pirate. At first, the enormities committed had not been so great; vessels had been seized and plundered, but life had been spared. In the course of crime, however, the descent is rapid: and as, from information given by those who had been released, the schooner was more than once in danger of being captured, latterly no lives had been spared; and but too often the murders had been attended with deeds even more atrocious.

Francisco had witnessed scenes of horror until his young blood curdled: he had expostulated to save, but in vain. Disgusted with the captain and the crew, and their deeds of cruelty, he had latterly expressed his opinions fearlessly, and defied the captain; for, in the heat of an altercation, Cain had acknowledged that Francisco was not his son.

Had any of the crew or officers expressed but a tithe of what had fallen from the bold lips of Francisco, they would have long before paid the forfeit of their temerity; but there was a feeling towards Francisco which could not be stifled in the breast of Cain—it was the feeling of association and habit. The boy had been his companion for years: and from assuetude had become, as it were, a part of himself. There is a principle in our nature which, even when that nature is most debased, will never leave us—that of requiring something to love, something to protect and watch over: it is shown towards a dog, or any other animal, if it cannot be lavished upon one of our own species. Such was the feeling which so forcibly held Cain towards Francisco; such was the feeling which had hitherto saved his life.

After having paced up and down for some time, the youth took his seat on the locker which the captain had quitted: his eye soon caught the head of Pompey, who looked into the cabin and beckoned with his finger.

Francisco rose, and, taking up a flagon from the buffet which contained some spirits, walked to the door, and, without saying a word, handed it to the Krouman.

"Massa Francisco," whispered Pompey, "Pompey say—all Kroumen say—suppose they run away, you go too? Pompey say—all Kroumen say—suppose they try to kill you? Nebber kill you while one Krouman alive."

The negro then gently pushed Francisco back with his hand, as if not wishing to hear his answer, and hastened forward on the berth deck.

VIII
THE ATTACK

IN THE MEANTIME, THE SEA-BREEZE had risen in the offing, and was sweeping along the surface to where the schooner was at anchor. The captain ordered a man to the cross-trees, directing him to keep a good look-out, while he walked the deck in company with his first mate.

"She may not have sailed until a day or two later," said the captain, continuing the conversation; "I have made allowance for that, and, depend upon it, as she makes the eastern passage, we must soon fall in with her; if she does not heave in sight this evening, by daylight I shall stretch out in the offing; I know the Portuguese well. The sea-breeze has caught our craft: let them run up the inner jib, and see that she does not foul her anchor."

It was now late in the afternoon, and dinner had been sent into the cabin; the captain descended, and took his seat at the table with Francisco, who ate in silence. Once or twice the captain, whose wrath had subsided, and whose kindly feelings towards Francisco, checked for a time, had returned with greater force, tried, but in vain, to rally him to conversation, when "*Sail ho!*" was shouted from the mast-head.

"There she is, by G—d!" cried the captain, jumping from, and then, as if checking himself, immediately resuming, his seat.

Francisco put his hand to his forehead, covering his eyes as his elbow leant upon the table.

"A large ship, sir; we can see down to the second reef of her topsails," said Hawkhurst, looking down the skylight.

The captain hastily swallowed some wine from a flagon, cast a look of scorn and anger upon Francisco, and rushed on deck.

"Be smart, lads!" cried the captain, after a few seconds' survey of the vessel through his glass; "that's her: furl the awnings, and run the anchor up to the bows: there's more silver in that vessel, my lads, than your chests will hold: and the good saints of the churches at Goa will have to wait a little longer for their gold candlesticks."

The crew were immediately on the alert; the awnings were furled, and all the men, stretching aft the spring cable, walked the anchor up to the bows. In two minutes more the *Avenger* was standing out on the starboard tack, shaping her course so as to cut off the ill-fated vessel. The breeze freshened, and the schooner darted through the smooth water with the impetuosity of a dolphin after its prey. In an hour the hull of the ship was plainly to be distinguished; but the sun was near to the horizon, and before they could ascertain what their force might be, daylight had disappeared. Whether the schooner had been perceived or not, it was impossible to say; at all events, the course of the ship had not been altered, and if she had seen the schooner, she evidently treated her with contempt. On board the *Avenger*, they were not idle; the long gun in the centre had been cleared from the incumbrances which surrounded it, the other guns had been cast loose, shot handed up, and everything prepared for action, with all the energy and discipline of a man-of-war. The chase had not been lost sight of, the eyes of the pirate-captain were fixed upon her through a night-glass. In about an hour more the schooner was within a mile of the ship, and now altered her course so as to range up within a cable's length of her to leeward. Cain stood upon the gunwale and hailed. The answer was in Portuguese.

"Heave to, or I'll sink you!" replied he in the same language.

A general discharge from a broadside of carronades, and a heavy volley of muskets from the Portuguese, was the decided answer. The broadside, too much elevated to hit the low hull of the schooner, was still not without effect—the foretopmast fell, the jaws of the main-gaff were severed, and a large proportion of the standing as well as the running rigging came rattling down on her decks. The volley of musketry was more fatal: thirteen of the pirates were wounded, some of them severely.

"Well done! John Portuguese," cried Hawkhurst: "by the holy poker! I never gave you credit for so much pluck."

"Which they shall dearly pay for," was the cool reply of Cain, as he still remained in his exposed situation.

"Blood for blood! if I drink it," observed the second mate, as he looked at the crimson rivulet trickling down the fingers of his left hand from a wound in his arm—"just tie my handkerchief round this, Bill."

In the interim, Cain had desired his crew to elevate their guns, and the broadside was returned.

"That will do, my lads: starboard; ease off the boom-sheet; let her go right round, Hawkhurst,—we cannot afford to lose our men."

The schooner wore round, and ran astern of her opponent.

The Portuguese on board the ship, imagining that the schooner, finding she had met with unexpected resistance, had sheered off, gave a loud cheer.

"The last you will ever give, my fine fellows!" observed Cain, with a sneer.

In a few moments the schooner had run a mile astern of the ship.

"Now then, Hawkhurst, let her come too and about; man the long gun, and see that every shot is pitched into her, while the rest of them get up a new foretopmast, and knot and splice the rigging."

The schooner's head was again turned towards the ship; her position was right astern, about a mile distant or rather more; the long 82-pounder gun amidships was now regularly served, every shot passing through the cabin-windows, or some other part of the ship's stern, raking her fore and aft. In vain did the ship alter her course, and present her broadside to the schooner; the latter was immediately checked in her speed, so as to keep the prescribed distance at which the carronades of the ship were useless, and the execution from the long gun decisive. The ship was at the mercy of the pirate; and, as may be expected, no mercy was shown. For three hours did this murderous attack continue, when the gun, which, as before observed, was of brass, became so heated that the pirate-captain desired his men to discontinue. Whether the ship had surrendered or not it was impossible to say, as it was too dark to distinguish: while the long gun was served, the foretop-mast and main-gaff had been shifted, and all the standing and running rigging made good; the schooner keeping her distance, and following in the wake of the ship until daylight.

We must now repair on board of the ship; she was an Indiaman; one of the very few that occasionally are sent out by the Portuguese government to a country which once owned their undivided sway, but in which, at present, they hold but a few miles of territory. She was bound to Goa, and had on board a small detachment of troops, a new governor and his two sons, a bishop and his niece, with her attendant. The sailing of a vessel with such a freight was a circumstance of rare occurrence, and was, of course, generally bruited about long before her departure. Cain had, for some months, received all the necessary intelligence relative to her cargo and destination; but, as usual with the Portuguese of the present day, delay upon delay had followed, and it was not until about three weeks previous that he had been assured of her immediate departure. He then ran down the coast to the bay we have mentioned, that he might intercept her; and, as the event had proved, showed his usual judgment and decision. The fire of the schooner had been most destructive; many of the Indiaman's crew, as well as of the troops, had been mowed down one after another; until at last, finding that all their efforts to defend themselves were useless, most of those who were still unhurt had consulted their safety, and hastened down to the lowest recesses of the hold to avoid the raking and destructive shot. At the time that the schooner had discontinued her fire to allow the gun to cool, there was no one on deck but the Portuguese captain and one old weatherbeaten seaman who stood at the helm. Below, in the orlop-deck, the remainder of the crew and the passengers were huddled together in a small space: some were attending to the wounded, who were numerous; others were invoking the saints to their assistance, the bishop, a tall, dignified person, apparently nearly sixty years of age, was kneeling in the centre of the group, which was dimly lighted by two or three lanterns, at one time in fervent prayer, at another, interrupted, that he might give absolution to those wounded men whose spirits were departing, and who were brought down and laid before him by their comrades. On one side of him knelt his orphan niece, a young girl of about seventeen years of age, watching his countenance as he prayed, or bending down with a look of pity and tearful eyes on her expiring countrymen, whose last moments were gladdened by his holy offices. On the other side of the bishop, stood the governor, Don Philip de Ribiera, and his two sons, youths in their prime, and holding commissions in the king's service. There was melancholy on the brow of Don Ribiera; he was prepared for, and he anticipated, the worst. The eldest son had his eyes fixed upon the sweet countenance of Teresa de Silva—that very evening, as they walked together on the deck, had they exchanged their vows—that very evening they had luxuriated in the present, and had dwelt with delightful anticipation on the future. But we must leave them and return on deck.

The captain of the Portuguese ship had walked aft, and now went up to Antonio, the old seaman, who was standing at the wheel.

"I still see her with the glass, Antonio, and yet she has not fired for nearly two hours; do you think any accident has happened to her long gun? if so, we may have some chance."

Antonio shook his head. "We have but little chance, I am afraid, my captain; I knew by the ring of the gun, when she fired it, that it was brass; indeed, no schooner could carry a long iron gun of that calibre. Depend upon it, she only waits for the metal to cool and daylight to return: a long gun or two might have saved us; but now, as she has the advantage of us in heels, we are at her mercy."

"What can she be—a French privateer?"

"I trust it may be so; and I have promised a silver candlestick to St. Antonio that it may prove no worse: we then may have some chance of seeing our homes again; but I fear not."

"What, then, do you imagine her to be, Antonio?"

"The pirate which we have heard so much of."

"Jesu protect us! we must then sell our lives as dearly as we can."

"So I intend to do, my captain," replied Antonio, shifting the helm a spoke.

The day broke, and showed the schooner continuing her pursuit at the same distance astern, without any apparent movement on board. It was not until the sun was some degrees above the horizon that the smoke was again seen to envelop her bows, and the shot crashed through the timbers of the Portuguese ship. The reason for this delay was, that the pirate waited till the sun was up to ascertain if there were any other vessels to be seen, previous to his pouncing on his quarry. The Portuguese captain went aft and hoisted his ensign, but no flag was shown by the schooner. Again whistled the ball, and again did it tear up the decks of the unfortunate ship: many of those who had re-ascended to ascertain what was going on, now hastily sought their former retreat.

"Mind the helm, Antonio," said the Portuguese captain; "I must go down and consult with the governor."

"Never fear, my captain; as long as these limbs hold together, I will do my duty," replied the old man, exhausted as he was by long watching and fatigue.

The captain descended to the orlop-deck, where he found the major part of the crew and passengers assembled.

"My lords," said he, addressing the governor and the bishop, "the schooner has not shown any colours, although our own are hoisted. I am come down to know your pleasure. Defence we can make none; and I fear that we are at the mercy of a pirate."

"A pirate!" ejaculated several, beating their breasts, and calling upon their saints.

"Silence, my good people, silence," quietly observed the bishop; "as to what it may be best to do," continued he, turning to the captain, "I cannot advise; I am a man of peace, and unfit to hold a place in a council of war. Don Ribiera, I must refer the point to you and your sons. Tremble not, my dear Teresa; are we not under the protection of the Almighty?"

"Holy Virgin, pity us!"

"Come, my sons," said Don Ribiera, "we will go on deck and consult: let not any of the men follow us; it is useless risking lives which may yet be valuable."

Don Ribiera and his sons followed the captain to the quarter deck, and with him and Antonio they held a consultation.

"We have but one chance," observed the old man, after a time: "let us haul down our colours as if in submission; they will then range up alongside, and either board us from the schooner, or from their boats; at all events, we shall find out what she is, and, if a pirate, we must sell our lives as dearly as we can. If, when we haul down the colours, she ranges up alongside, as I expect she will, let all the men be prepared for a desperate struggle."

"You are right, Antonio," replied the governor; "go aft captain, and haul down the colours!—let us see what she does now. Down, my boys! and prepare the men to do their duty."

As Antonio had predicted, so soon as the colours were hauled down, the schooner ceased firing and made sail. She ranged up on the quarter of the ship, and up to her main peak soared the terrific black flag; her broadside was poured into the Indiaman, and before the smoke had cleared away there was a concussion from the meeting sides, and the bearded pirates poured upon her decks.

The crew of the Portuguese, with the detachment of troops, still formed a considerable body of men. The sight of the black flag had struck ice into every heart, but the feeling was resolved into one of desperation.

"Knives, men, knives!" roared Antonio, rushing on to the attack, followed by the most brave.

"Blood for blood!" cried the second mate, aiming a blow at the old man.

"You have it," replied Antonio, as his knife entered the pirate's heart, while, at the same moment, he fell and was himself a corpse.

The struggle was deadly, but the numbers and ferocity of the pirates prevailed. Cain rushed forward followed by Hawkhurst, bearing down all who opposed them. With one blow from the pirate-captain, the head of Don Ribiera was severed to the shoulder; a second struck down the eldest son, while the sword of Hawkhurst passed through the body of the other. The Portuguese captain had already fallen, and the men no longer stood their ground. A general massacre ensued, and the bodies were thrown overboard as fast as the men were slaughtered. In less than five minutes there was not a living Portuguese on the bloody decks of the ill-fated ship.

IX
THE CAPTURE

"Pass the word for not a man to go below, Hawkhurst," said the pirate-captain.

"I have, sir; and sentries are stationed at the hatchways. Shall we haul the schooner off?"

"No, let her remain; the breeze is faint already: we shall have a calm in half an hour. Have we lost many men?"

"Only seven, that I can reckon; but we have lost Wallace." (the second mate).

"A little promotion will do no harm," replied Cain; "take a dozen of our best men and search the ship, there are others alive yet. By-the-by, send a watch on board of the schooner; she is left to the mercy of the Kroumen, and—"

"One who is better out of her," replied Hawkhurst.

"And those we find below—" continued the mate.

"Alive!"

"True; we may else be puzzled where to find that portion of her cargo which suits us," said Hawkhurst, going down the hatchway to collect the men who were plundering on the main deck and in the captain's cabin.

"Here, you Maltese! up, there! and look well round if there is anything in sight," said the captain, walking aft.

Before Hawkhurst had collected the men and ordered them on board of the schooner, as usual in those latitudes, it had fallen a perfect calm.

Where was Francisco during this scene of blood? He had remained in the cabin of the schooner. Cain had more than once gone down to him, to persuade him to come on deck and assist at the boarding of the Portuguese, but in vain—his sole reply to the threats and solicitations of the pirate was,—

"Do with me as you please—I have made up my mind—you know I do not fear death—as long as I remain on board of this vessel, I will take no part in your atrocities. If you do respect my mother's memory, suffer her son to seek an honest and honourable livelihood."

The words of Francisco were ringing in the ears of Cain as he walked up and down on the quarter-deck of the Portuguese vessel, and, debased as he was, he could not help thinking that the youth was his equal in animal, and his superior in mental, courage—he was arguing in his own mind upon the course he should pursue with respect to Francisco, when Hawkhurst made his appearance on deck, followed by his men, who dragged up six individuals who had escaped the massacre. These were the bishop; his niece, a Portuguese girl; her attendant; the supercargo of the vessel; a sacristan; and a servant of the ecclesiastic; they were hauled along the deck and placed in a row before the captain, who cast his eye upon them in severe scrutiny. The bishop and his niece looked round, the one proudly meeting the eye of Cain, although he felt that his hour was come; the other carefully avoiding his gaze, and glancing round to ascertain whether there were any other prisoners, and if so, if her betrothed was amongst them; but her eye discovered not what she sought—it was met only by the bearded faces of the pirate-crew, and the blood which bespattered the deck.

She covered her face with her hands.

"Bring that man forward," said Cain, pointing to the servant. "Who are you."

"A servant of my lord the bishop."

"And you?" continued the captain.

"A poor sacristan attending upon my lord the bishop."

"And you?" cried he to a third.

"The supercargo of this vessel."

"Put him aside, Hawkhurst!"

"Do you want the others?" inquired Hawkhurst significantly.

"No."

Hawkhurst gave a signal to some of the pirates, who led away the sacristan and the servant. A stifled shriek and a heavy plunge in the water were heard a few seconds after. During this time the pirate had been questioning the supercargo as to the contents of the vessel, and her stowage, when he was suddenly interrupted by one of the pirates, who in a hurried voice, stated that the ship had received several shot between wind and water, and was sinking fast. Cain, who was standing on the side of the carronade with his sword in his hand, raised his arm and struck the pirate a blow on the head with the hilt, which, whether intended or not, fractured his skull, and the man fell upon the deck.

"Take that, babbler! for your intelligence; if these men are obstinate, we may have worked for nothing."

The crew, who felt the truth of their captain's remark, did not appear to object to the punishment inflicted, and the body of the man was dragged away.

"What mercy can we expect from those who show no mercy even to each other?" observed the bishop, lifting his eyes to heaven.

"Silence!" cried Cain, who now interrogated the supercargo as to the contents of the hold—the poor man answered as well as he could—"the plate! the money for the troops—where are they?"

"The money for the troops is in the spirit-room, but of the plate I know nothing; it is in some of the cases belonging to my lord the bishop."

"Hawkhurst! down at once into the spirit-room, and see to the money; in the mean time I will ask a few questions of this reverend father."

"And the supercargo—do you want him any more?"

"No; he may go."

The poor man fell down on his knees in thankfulness at what he considered his escape: he was dragged away by the pirates, and, it is scarcely necessary to add that in a minute his body was torn to pieces by the sharks, who, scenting their prey from a distance, were now playing in shoals around the two vessels.

The party on the quarter-deck were now (unperceived by the captain) joined by Francisco, who, hearing from the Krouman, Pompey, that there were prisoners still on board, and amongst them two females, had come over to plead the cause of mercy.

"Most reverend father," observed Cain, after a short pause, "you have many articles of value in this vessel?"

"None," replied the bishop, "except this poor girl; she is, indeed, beyond price, and will, I trust, soon be an angel in heaven."

"Yet is this world, if what you preach be true, a purgatory which must be passed through previous to arriving there, and that girl may think death a blessing compared to what she may expect if you refuse to tell me what I would know. You have good store of gold and silver ornaments for your churches—where are they?"

"They are among the packages intrusted to my care."

"How many may you have in all?"

"A hundred, if not more."

"Will you deign to inform me where I may find what I require?"

"The gold and silver are not mine, but are the property of that God to whom they have been dedicated," replied the bishop.

"Answer quickly; no more subterfuge, good sir. Where is it to be found?"

"I will not tell, thou blood-stained man; at least; in this instance, there shall be disappointment, and the sea shall swallow up those earthly treasures to obtain which thou hast so deeply imbrued thy hands. Pirate! I repeat it, I will not tell."

"Seize that girl, my lads!" cried Cain; "she is yours, do with her as you please."

"Save me! oh, save me!" shrieked Teresa, clinging to the bishop's robe.

The pirates advanced and laid hold of Teresa. Francisco bounded from where he stood behind the captain, and dashed away the foremost.

"Are you men?" cried he, as the pirates retreated. "Holy sir, I honour you. Alas! I cannot save you," continued Francisco, mournfully. "Yet will I try. On my knees—by the love you bore my mother—by the affection you once bore me—do not commit this horrid deed. My lads!" continued Francisco, appealing to the pirates, "join with me and entreat your captain; ye are too brave, too manly, to injure the helpless and the innocent—above all, to shed the blood of a holy man, and of this poor trembling maiden."

There was a pause—even the pirates appeared to side with Francisco, though none of them dared to speak. The muscles of the captain's face quivered with emotion, but from what source could not be ascertained.

At this moment the interest of the scene was heightened. The girl who attended upon Teresa, crouched on her knees with terror, had been casting her fearful eyes upon the men who composed the pirate-crew; suddenly she uttered a scream of delight as she discovered among them one that she well knew. He was a young man, about twenty-five years of age, with little or no beard. He had been her lover in his more innocent days; and she, for more than a year, had mourned him as dead, for the vessel in which he sailed had never been heard of. It had been taken by the pirate, and, to save his life, he had joined the crew.

"Filippo! Filippo!" screamed the girl, rushing into his arms. "Mistress! it is Filippo; and we are safe."

Filippo instantly recognised her: the sight of her brought back to his memory his days of happiness and of innocence; and the lovers were clasped in each other's arms.

"Save them! spare them!—by the spirit of my mother! I charge you," repeated Francisco, again appealing to the captain.

"May God bless thee, thou good young man!" said the bishop, advancing and placing his hand upon Francisco's head.

Cain answered not; but his broad expanded chest heaved with emotion—when Hawkhurst burst into the group.

"We are too late for the money, captain: the water is already six feet above it. We must now try for the treasure."

This intelligence appeared to check the current of the captain's feelings.

"Now, in one word, sir," said he to the bishop, "where is the treasure? Trifle not, or, by Heaven—!"

"Name not Heaven," replied the bishop; "you have had my answer."

The captain turned away, and gave some directions to Hawkhurst, who hastened below.

"Remove that boy," said Cain to the pirates, pointing to Francisco, "Separate those two fools," continued he, looking towards Filippo and the girl, who were sobbing in each other's arms.

"Never!" cried Filippo.

"Throw the girl to the sharks! Do you hear? Am I to be obeyed?" cried Cain, raising his cutlass.

Filippo started up, disengaged himself from the girl, and, drawing his knife, rushed towards the captain to plunge it in his bosom.

With the quickness of lightning the captain caught his uplifted hand, and, breaking his wrist, hurled him to the deck.

"Indeed!" cried he, with a sneer.

"You shall not separate us," said Filippo, attempting to rise.

"I do not intend it, my good lad," replied Cain. "Lash them both together and launch them overboard."

This order was obeyed: for the pirates not only quailed before the captain's cool courage, but were indignant that his life had been attempted. There was little occasion to tie the unhappy pair together; they were locked so fast in each other's arms that it would have been impossible almost to separate them. In this state they were carried to the entering-port, and cast into the sea.

"Monster!" cried the bishop, as he heard the splash, "thou wilt have a heavy reckoning for this."

"Now bring these forward," said Cain, with a savage voice.

The bishop and his niece were led to the gangway.

"What dost thou see, good bishop?" said Cain pointing to the discoloured water, and the rapid motion of the fins of the sharks, eager in the anticipation of a further supply.

"I see ravenous creatures after their kind," replied the bishop, "who will, in all probability, soon tear asunder those poor limbs; but I see no monster like thyself. Teresa, dearest, fear not; there is a God, an avenging God; as well as a rewarding one."

But Teresa's eyes were closed—she could not look upon the scene.

"You have your choice; first torture, and then your body to those sharks for your own portion: and as for the girl, this moment I hand her over to my crew."

"Never!" shrieked Teresa, springing from the deck and plunging into the wave.

There was a splash of contention, the lashing of tails, until the water was in a foam, and then the dark colour gradually cleared away, and nought was to be seen, but the pure blue wave and the still unsatisfied monsters of the deep.

"The screws—the screws! quick! we'll have the secret from him," cried the pirate-captain, turning to his crew, who, villains as they were, had been shocked at this last catastrophe. "Seize him!"

"Touch him not!" cried Francisco, standing on the hammock-netting; "touch him not! if you are men."

Boiling with rage, Cain let go the arm of the bishop, drew his pistol, and levelled it at Francisco. The bishop threw up the arm of Cain as he fired; saw that he had missed his aim, and clasping his hands, raised his eyes to heaven in thankfulness at Francisco's escape. In this position he was collared by Hawkhurst, whose anger overcame his discretion, and who hurled him through the entering-port into the sea.

"Officious fool!" muttered Cain, when he perceived what the mate had done. Then, recollecting himself, he cried,—"Seize that boy and bring him here."

One or two of the crew advanced to obey his orders; but Pompey and the Kroumen, who had been attentive to what was going on, had collected round Francisco, and a scuffle ensued. The pirates, not being very determined, nor very anxious to take Francisco, allowed him to be hurried away in the centre of the Kroumen, who bore him safely to the schooner.

In the meantime Hawkhurst, and the major part of the men on board of the ship, had been tearing up the hold to obtain the valuables, but without success. The water had now reached above the orlop-deck, and all further attempts were unavailing. The ship was settling fast, and it became necessary to quit her, and haul off the schooner; that she might not be endangered by the vortex of the sinking vessel. Cain and Hawkhurst, with their disappointed crew, returned on board the schooner, and before they had succeeded in detaching the two vessels a cable's length the ship went down with all the treasure so coveted. The indignation and rage which were expressed by the captain as he rapidly walked the deck in company with his first mate—his violent gesticulation—proved to the crew that there was mischief brewing. Francisco did not return to the cabin; he remained forward with the Kroumen, who, although but a small portion of the ship's company, were known to be resolute and not to be despised. It was also observed that all of them had supplied themselves with arms, and were collected forward, huddled together, watching every motion and manoeuvre, and talking rapidly in their own language. The schooner was now steered to the north-westward under all press of sail. The sun again disappeared, but Francisco returned not to the cabin—he went below, surrounded by the Kroumen, who appeared to have devoted themselves to his protection. Once during the night Hawkhurst summoned them on deck, but they obeyed not the order; and to the expostulation of the boatswain's mate, who came down, they made no reply. But there were many of the pirates in the schooner who appeared to coincide with the Kroumen in their regard for Francisco. There are shades of villainy in the most profligate of societies; and among the pirate's crew some were not yet wholly debased. The foul murder of a holy man—the cruel fate of the beautiful Teresa—and the barbarous conduct of the captain towards Filippo and his mistress, were deeds of an atrocity to which even the most hardened were unaccustomed. Francisco's pleadings in behalf of mercy were at least no crime; and yet they considered that Francisco was doomed. He was a general favourite; the worst-disposed of the pirates, with the exception of Hawkhurst, if they did not love him, could not forbear respecting him; although at the same time they felt that if Francisco remained on board the power even of Cain himself would soon be destroyed. For many months Hawkhurst, who detested the youth, had been most earnest that he should be sent out of the schooner. Now he pressed the captain for his removal in any way, as necessary for their mutual safety, pointing out to Cain the conduct of the Kroumen, and his fears that a large proportion of the ship's company were equally disaffected. Cain felt the truth of Hawkhurst's representation, and he went down to his cabin to consider upon what should be done.

It was past midnight, when Cain, worn out with the conflicting passions of the day, fell into an uneasy slumber. His dreams were of Francisco's mother—she appeared to him pleading for her son, and Cain "babbled in his sleep." At this time Francisco, with Pompey, had softly crawled aft, that they might obtain, if they found the captain asleep, the pistols of Francisco, with some ammunition. Pompey slipped in first, and started back when he heard the captain's voice. They remained at the cabin-door listening. "No, no," murmured Cain, "he must die—useless—plead not, woman!—I know I murdered thee—plead not, he dies!"

In one of the sockets of the silver lamp there was a lighted wick, the rays of which were sufficient to afford a dim view of the cabin. Francisco, overhearing the words of Cain, stepped in, and walked up to the side of the bed. "Boy! plead not," continued Cain, lying on his back and breathing heavily "plead not woman! to-morrow he dies." A pause ensued, as if the sleeping man was listening to a reply. "Yes, as I murdered thee, so will I murder him."

"Wretch!" said Francisco, in a low, solemn voice, "didst thou kill my mother?"

"I did—I did!" responded Cain, still sleeping.

"And why?" continued Francisco, who at this acknowledgment on the part of the sleeping captain was careless of discovery.

"In my mood she vexed me," answered Cain.

"Fiend; thou hast then confessed it!" cried Francisco in a loud voice, which awoke the captain, who started up; but before his senses were well recovered, or his eyes open so as to distinguish their forms, Pompey struck out the light, and all was darkness; he then put his hand to Francisco's mouth, and led him out of the cabin.

"Who's there?—who's there?" cried Cain.

The officer in charge of the deck hastened down. "Did you call, sir?"

"Call!" repeated the captain. "I thought there was some one in the cabin. I want a light—that's all," continued he, recovering himself, as he wiped the cold perspiration from his forehead.

In the meantime Francisco, with Pompey, had gained his former place of refuge with the Kroumen. The feelings of the young man changed from agony to revenge; his object in returning to the cabin to recover his weapons had been frustrated, but his determination now was to take the life of the captain if he possibly could. The following morning the Kroumen again refused to work or go on deck; and the state of affairs was reported by Hawkhurst to his chief. The mate now assumed another tone: for he had sounded not the majority but the most steady and influential men on board, who, like himself, were veterans in crime.

"It must be, sir; or you will no longer command this vessel. I am desired to say so."

"Indeed!" replied Cain, with a sneer. "Perhaps you have already chosen my successor?"

Hawkhurst perceived that he had lost ground, and he changed his manner. "I speak but for yourself: if you do not command this vessel I shall not remain in her: if you quit her, I quit also; and we must find another."

Cain was pacified, and the subject was not renewed.

"Turn the hands up," at last said the captain. The pirate-crew assembled aft.

"My lads, I am sorry that our laws oblige me to make an example; but mutiny and disaffection must be punished. I am equally bound as yourselves by the laws which we have laid down for our guidance while we sail together; and you may believe that in doing my duty in this instance I am guided by a sense of justice, and wish to prove to you that I am worthy to command. Francisco has been with me since he was a child; he has lived with me, and it is painful to part with him: but I am here to see that our laws are put in force. He has been guilty of repeated mutiny and contempt, and—he must die."

"Death! death!" cried several of the pirates in advance: "death and justice!"

"No more murder!" said several voices from behind.

"Who's that that speaks?"

"Too much murder yesterday—no more murder!" shouted several voices at once.

"Let the men come forward who speak," cried Cain with a withering look. No one obeyed this order. "Down, then, my men! and bring up Francisco."

The whole of the pirate-crew hastened below, but with different intentions. Some were determined to seize Francisco, and hand him over to death—others to protect him. A confused noise was heard—the shouts of "*Down and seize him!*" opposed to those of "*No murder! No murder!*"

Both parties had snatched up their arms; those who sided with Francisco joined the Kroumen, whilst the others also hastened below to bring him on deck. A slight scuffle ensued before they separated, and ascertained by the separation the strength of the contending parties. Francisco, perceiving that he was joined by a large body, desired his men to follow him, went up the fore-ladder, and took possession of the forecastle. The pirates on his side supplied him with arms, and Francisco stood forward in advance. Hawkhurst, and those of the crew who sided with him, had retreated to the quarter-deck, and rallied round the captain, who leaned against the capstern. They were then able to estimate their comparative strength. The number, on the whole, preponderated in favour of Francisco; but on the captain's side were the older and more athletic of the crew, and, we may add, the more determined. Still, the captain and Hawkhurst perceived the danger of their situation, and it was thought advisable to parley for the present, and wreak their vengeance hereafter. For a few minutes there was a low consultation between both parties; at last Cain advanced.

"My lads," said he, addressing those who had rallied round Francisco, "I little thought that a fire-brand would have been cast in this vessel to set us all at variance. It was my duty, as your captain, to propose that our laws should be enforced. Tell me now what is it that you wish. I am only here as your captain, and to take the sense of the whole crew. I have no animosity against that lad: I have loved him—I have cherished him; but like a viper, he has stung me in return. Instead of being in arms against each other, ought we not to be united? I have, therefore, one proposal to make to you, which is this: let the sentence go by vote, or ballot, if you please; and whatever the sentence may be, I shall be guided by it. Can I say more?"

"My lads," replied Francisco, when the captain had done speaking, "I think it better that you should accept this proposal rather than that blood should be shed. My life is of little consequence; say, then, will you agree to the vote, and submit to those laws, which, as the captain says, have been laid down to regulate the discipline of the vessel?"

The pirates on Francisco's side looked round among their party, and, perceiving that they were the most numerous, consented to the proposal; but Hawkhurst stepped forward and observed: "Of course the Kroumen can have no votes, as they do not belong to the vessel."

This objection was important, as they amounted to twenty-five, and, after that number was deducted, in all probability, Francisco's adherents would have been in the minority. The pirates, with Francisco, objected, and again assumed the attitude of defence.

"One moment," said Francisco, stepping in advance; "before this point is settled, I wish to take the sense of all of you as to another of your laws. I ask you, Hawkhurst, and all who are now opposed to me, whether you have not one law, which is *Blood for blood*?"

"Yes—yes," shouted all the pirates.

"Then let your captain stand forward, and answer to my charge, if he dares."

Cain curled his lip in derision, and walked within two yards of Francisco.

"Well, boy, I'm here; and what is your charge?"

"First—I ask you, Captain Cain, who are so anxious that the laws should be enforced, whether you acknowledge that 'Blood for blood' is a just law?"

"Most just: and, when shed, the party who revenges is not amenable."

"'Tis well: then villain that thou art, answer—Didst thou not murder my mother?"

Cain, at this accusation, started.

"Answer the truth, or lie like a recreant!" repeated Francisco. "Did you not murder my mother?"

The captain's lips and the muscles of his face quivered, but he did not reply.

"*Blood for blood*!" cried Francisco, as he fired his pistol at Cain, who staggered, and fell on the deck.

Hawkhurst and several of the pirates hastened to the captain, and raised him.

"She must have told him last night," said Cain, speaking with difficulty, as the blood flowed from the wound.

"He told me so himself," said Francisco, turning round to those who stood by him.

Cain was taken down into the cabin. On examination, his wound was not mortal, although his loss of blood had been rapid and very great. In a few minutes Hawkhurst joined the party on the quarter deck. He found that the tide had turned more in Francisco's favour than he had expected; the law of "Blood for blood" was held most sacred: indeed, it was but the knowledge that it was solemnly recognised, and that, if one pirate wounded another, the other was at liberty to take his life, without punishment, which prevented constant affrays between parties, whose knives would otherwise have been the answer to every affront. It was a more debased law of duelling, which kept such profligate associates on good terms. Finding, therefore, that this feeling predominated, even among those who were opposed to Francisco on the other question, Hawkhurst thought it advisable to parley.

"Hawkhurst," said Francisco, "I have but one request to make, which, if complied with, will put an end to this contention; it is, that you will put me on shore at the first land that we make. If you and your party engage to do this, I will desire those who support me to return to their obedience."

"I grant it," replied Hawkhurst; "and so will the others. Will you not, my men?"

"Agreed—agreed upon all sides," cried the pirates, throwing away their weapons, and mingling with each other, as if they had never been opposed.

There is an old saying, that there is honour amongst thieves; and so it often proves. Every man in the vessel knew that this agreement would be strictly adhered to; and Francisco now walked the deck with as much composure as if nothing had occurred.

Hawkhurst, who was aware that he must fulfil his promise, carefully examined the charts when he went down below, came up and altered the course of the schooner two points more to the northward. The next morning he was up at the mast-head nearly half an hour, when he descended, and again altered the course. By nine o'clock a low sandy island appeared on the lee bow; when within half a mile of it, he ordered the schooner to be hove to, and lowered down the small boat from the stern. He then turned the hands up. "My lads, we must keep our promise, to put Francisco on shore at the first land which we made. There it is!" And a malicious smile played on the miscreant's features as he pointed out to them the barren sand-bank, which promised nothing but starvation and a lingering death. Several of the crew murmured; but Hawkhurst was supported by his own party, and had, moreover, taken the precaution quietly to remove all the arms, with the exception of those with which his adherents were provided.

"An agreement is an agreement; it is what he requested himself, and we promised to perform. Send for Francisco."

"I am here, Hawkhurst; and I tell you candidly, that, desolate as is that barren spot, I prefer it to remaining in your company. I will bring my chest up immediately."

"No—no; that was not a part of the agreement," cried Hawkhurst.

"Every man here has a right to his own property: I appeal to the whole of the crew."

"True—true," replied the pirates; and Hawkhurst found himself again in the minority.

"Be it so."

The chest of Francisco was handed into the boat.

"Is that all?" cried Hawkhurst.

"My lads, am I to have no provisions or water?" inquired Francisco.

"No," replied Hawkhurst.

"Yes—yes," cried most of the pirates.

Hawkhurst did not dare put it to the vote, he turned sulkily away. The Kroumen brought up two breakers of water, and some pieces of pork.

"Here, massa," said Pompey, putting into Francisco's hand a fishing-line with hooks.

"Thank you, Pompey; but I had forgot—that book in the cabin—you know which I mean."

Pompey nodded his head, and went below; but it was some time before he returned, during which Hawkhurst became impatient. It was a very small boat which had been lowered down; it had a lug-sail and two pair of sculls in it, and was quite full when Francisco's chest and the other articles had been put in.

"Come! I have no time to wait," said Hawkhurst; "in the boat!"

Francisco shook hands with many of the crew, and wished all of them farewell. Indeed, now that they beheld the poor lad about to be cast on the desolate island, even those most opposed to him felt some emotions of pity. Although they acknowledged that his absence was necessary, yet they knew his determined courage; and with them that quality was always a strong appeal.

"Who will row this lad ashore, and bring the boat off?"

"Not I," replied one; "it would haunt me ever afterwards."

So they all appeared to think, for no one volunteered. Francisco jumped into the boat.

"There is no room for any one but me; and I will row myself on shore," cried he. "Farewell, my lads! farewell!"

"Stop? not so; he must not have the boat—he may escape from the island," cried Hawkhurst.

"And why shouldn't he, poor fellow?" replied the men. "Let him have the boat."

"Yes—yes, let him have the boat;" and Hawkhurst was again overruled.

"Here, Massa Francisco—here de book."

"What's that, sir?" cried Hawkhurst, snatching the book out of Pompey's hand.

"Him, massa, Bible." Francisco waited for the book.

"Shove off!" cried Hawkhurst.

"Give me my book, Mr Hawkhurst!"

"No!" replied the malignant rascal, tossing the Bible over the taffrail; "he shall not have that. I've heard say that *there is consolation in it for the afflicted.*"

Francisco shoved off his boat, and seizing his sculls, pushed astern, picked up the book, which still floated, and laid it to dry on the after-thwart of the boat. He then pulled in for the shore. In the meantime the schooner had let draw her fore-sheet, and had already left him a quarter of a mile astern. Before Francisco had gained the sand-bank she was hull-down to the northward.

X

THE SAND-BANK

THE FIRST HALF HOUR THAT Francisco was on this desolate spot he watched the receding schooner: his thoughts were unconnected and vague. Wandering through the various scenes which had passed on the decks of that vessel, and recalling to his memory the different characters of those on board of her, much as he had longed to quit her—disgusted as he had been with those with whom he had been forced to associate—still, as her sails grew fainter and fainter to his view, as she increased her distance, he more than once felt that even remaining on board of her would have been preferable to his present deserted lot. "No, no!" exclaimed he, after a little further reflection, "I had rather perish here, than continue to witness the scenes which I have been forced to behold."

He once more fixed his eyes upon her white sails, and then sat down on the loose sand, and remained in deep and melancholy reverie until the scorching heat reminded him of his situation; he afterwards rose and turned his thoughts upon his present situation, and to what would be the measures most advisable to take. He hauled his little boat still farther on the beach, and attached the painter to one of the oars, which he fixed deep in the sand; he then proceeded to survey the bank, and found that but a small portion was uncovered at high water; for trifling as was the rise of the tide, the bank was so low that the water flowed almost over it. The most elevated part was not more than fifteen feet above high-water mark, and that was a small knoll of about fifty feet in circumference.

To this part he resolved to remove his effects: he returned to the boat, and having lifted out his chest, the water, the provisions, with the other articles which he had obtained, he dragged them up, one by one, until they were all collected at the spot he had chosen. He then took out of the boat the oars and little sail, which, fortunately, had remained in her. His last object, to haul the little boat up to the same spot, was one which demanded all his exertion; but, after considerable fatigue, he contrived, by first lifting round her bow, and then her stern, to effect his object.

Tired and exhausted, he then repaired to one of the breakers of water and refreshed himself. The heat, as the day advanced, had become intolerable; but it stimulated him to fresh exertion. He turned over the boat, and contrived that the bow and stern should rest upon two little hillocks, so as to raise it above the level of the sand beneath it two or three feet; he spread out the sail from the keel above, with the thole-pins as pegs, so as to keep off the rays of the sun. Dragging the breakers of water and the provisions underneath the boat, he left his chest outside; and having thus formed for himself a sort of covering which would protect him from the heat of the day and the damp of the night, he crept in, to shelter himself until the evening.

Although Francisco had not been on deck, he knew pretty well whereabouts he then was. Taking out a chart from his chest, he examined the coast to ascertain the probable distance which he might be from any prospect of succour. He calculated that he was on one of a patch of sand-banks off the coast of Loango, and about seven hundred miles from the Isle of St. Thomas—the nearest place where he might expect to fall in with a European face. From the coast he felt certain that he could not be more than forty or fifty miles at the most; but could he trust himself among the savage natives who inhabited it? He knew how ill they had been treated by Europeans; for at that period, it was quite as common for the slave-trader to land and take away the inhabitants as slaves by force, as to purchase them in the more northern territories: still, he might be fortunate enough to fall in with some trader on the coast, as there were a few who still carried on a barter for gold-dust and ivory.

We do not know—we cannot conceive a situation much more deplorable than the one we have just described to have been that of Francisco. Alone—without a chance of assistance—with only a sufficiency of food for a few days, and cut off from the rest of his fellow-creatures, with only so much terra firma as would prevent his being swallowed up by the vast, unfathomable ocean, into which the horizon fell on every side around him! And his chance of escape how small! Hundreds of miles from any from whom he might expect assistance, and the only means of reaching them a small boat—a mere cockleshell, which the first rough gale would inevitably destroy.

Such, indeed, were the first thoughts of Francisco; but he soon recovered from his despondency. He was young, courageous, and buoyant with hope; and there is a feeling of pride—of trust in our own resources and exertions, which increases and stimulates us in proportion to our danger and difficulty; it is the daring of the soul, proving its celestial origin and eternal duration.

So intense was the heat that Francisco almost panted for sufficient air to support life, as he lay under the shade of the boat during the whole of that day; not a breath of wind disturbed the glassy wave—all nature appeared hushed into one horrible calm. It was not until the shades of night were covering the solitude that Francisco ventured forth from his retreat; but he found little relief; there was an unnatural closeness in the air—a suffocation unusual even in those climes. Francisco cast his eyes up to the vault of heaven, and was astonished to find that there were no stars visible—a grey mist covered the whole firmament. He directed his view downwards to the horizon, and that, too, was not to be defined; there was a dark bank all around it. He walked to the edge of the sand-bank; there was not even a ripple—the wide ocean appeared to be in a trance, in a state of lethargy or stupor.

He parted the hair from his feverish brow, and once more surveying the horrible, lifeless, stagnant waste, his soul sickened, and he cast himself upon the sand. There he lay for many hours in a state bordering upon wild despair. At last he recovered himself, and, rising to his knees, he prayed for strength and submission to the will of Heaven.

When he was once more upon his feet, and had again scanned the ocean, he perceived that there was a change rapidly approaching. The dark bank on the horizon had now risen higher up; the opaqueness was everywhere more dense; and low murmurs were heard, as if there was wind stirring aloft, although the sea was still glassy as a lake. Signs of some movement about to take place were evident, and the solitary youth watched and watched. And now the sounds increased, and here and there a wild thread of air—whence coming, who could tell? and as rapidly disappearing—would ruffle, for a second, a portion of the stagnant sea. Then came whizzing sounds and moans, and then the rumbling noise of distant thunder—loud and louder yet—still louder— a broad black line is seen sweeping along the expanse of water—fearful in its rapidity it comes!—and the hurricane burst, at once and with all its force, and all its terrific sounds, upon the isolated Francisco.

The first blast was so powerful and so unexpected that it threw him down, and prudence dictated to him to remain in that position, for the loose sand was swept off and whirled in such force as to blind and prevent his seeing a foot from him; he would have crawled to the boat for security, but he knew not in which direction to proceed. But this did not last; for now the water was borne up upon the strong wings of the hurricane, and the sand was rendered firm by its saturation with the element.

Francisco felt that he was drenched, and he raised his head. All he could discover was, that the firmament was mantled with darkness, horrible from its intensity, and that the sea was in one extended foam—boiling everywhere, and white as milk—but still smooth, as if the power of the wind had compelled it to be so; but the water had encroached, and one half the sand-bank was covered with it, while

over the other the foam whirled, each portion chasing the other with
wild rapidity.

And now the windows of heaven were opened, and the rain, mingled
with the spray caught up by the hurricane, was dashed and hurled
upon the forlorn youth, who still lay where he had been first thrown
down. But of a sudden, a wash of water told him that he could remain
there no longer: the sea was rising—rising fast; and before he could
gain a few paces on his hands and knees, another wave, as if it chased
him in its wrath, repeated the warning of his extreme danger, and he
was obliged to rise on his feet and hasten to the high part of the sand-
bank, where he had drawn up his boat and his provisions.

Blinded as he was by the rain and spray, he could distinguish
nothing. Of a sudden, he fell violently; he had stumbled over one
of the breakers of water, and his head struck against a sea-chest.
Where, then, was the boat? It was gone!—it must have been swept
away by the fury of the wind. Alas, then, all chance was over! and,
if not washed away by the angry waters, he had but to prolong his
existence but a few days, and then to die. The effect of the blow he
had received on his forehead, with the shock of mind occasioned by
the disappearance of the boat, overpowered him, and he remained for
some time in a state of insensibility.

When Francisco recovered, the scene was again changed: the wide
expanse was now in a state of wild and fearful commotion, and the
water roared as loud as did the hurricane. The whole sand-bank, with
the exception of that part on which he stood, was now covered with
tumultuous foam, and his place of refuge was occasionally invaded,
when some vast mass, o'erlording the other waves, expended all its
fury, even to his feet. Francisco prepared to die!

But gradually the darkness of the heavens disappeared, and there
was no longer a bank upon the horizon, and Francisco hoped—alas!
hoped what?—that he might be saved from the present impending
death to be reserved for one still more horrible; to be saved from
the fury of the waves, which would swallow him up, and in a few

seconds remove him from all pain and suffering, to perish for want of sustenance under a burning sun; to be withered—to be parched to death—calling in his agony for water; and as Francisco thought of this he covered his face with his hands, and prayed, "Oh, God, thy will be done! but in thy mercy, raise, still higher raise the waters!"

But the waters did not rise higher. The howling of the wind gradually decreased, and the foaming seas had obeyed the Divine injunction—they had gone so far, but no farther! And the day dawned, and the sky cleared: and the first red tints, announcing the return of light and heat, had appeared on the broken horizon, when the eyes of the despairing youth were directed to a black mass on the tumultuous waters. It was a vessel, with but one mast standing, rolling heavily, and running before the gale right on for the sand-bank where he stood; her hull, one moment borne aloft and the next disappearing from his view in the hollow of the agitated waters. "She will be dashed to pieces!" thought Francisco; "she will be lost!—they cannot see the bank!" And he would have made a signal to her, if he had been able, to warn her of her danger, forgetting at the time his own desolate situation.

As Francisco watched, the sun rose, bright and joyous over this scene of anxiety and pain. On came the vessel, flying before the gale, while the seas chased her as if they would fain overwhelm her. It was fearful to see her scud—agonising to know that she was rushing to destruction.

At last he could distinguish those on board. He waved his hand, but they perceived him not; he shouted, but his voice was borne away by the gale. On came the vessel, as if doomed. She was within two cables' length of the bank when those on board perceived their danger. It was too late!—they had rounded her to—another, and another wave hurled her towards the sand. She struck!—her only remaining mast fell over the side, and the roaring waves hastened to complete their work of destruction and of death!

XI
THE ESCAPE

Francisco's eyes were fixed upon the vessel, over which the sea now broke with terrific violence. There appeared to be about eight or nine men on her deck, who sheltered themselves under the weather bulwarks. Each wave, as it broke against her side and then dashed in foam over her, threw her, with a convulsive jerk, still further on the sand-bank. At last she was so high up that their fury was partly spent before they dashed against her frame. Had the vessel been strong and well built—had she been a collier coasting the English shores—there was a fair chance that she might have withstood the fury of the storm until it had subsided, and that by remaining on board, the crew might have survived: but she was of a very different mould, and, as Francisco justly surmised, an American brig, built for swift sailing, very sharp, and, moreover, very slightly put together.

Francisco's eyes, as may easily be supposed, were never removed from the only object which could now interest him—the unexpected appearance and imminent danger of his fellow-creatures at this desolate spot. He perceived that two of the men went to the hatches, and slid them over to leeward: they then descended, and although the seas broke over the vessel, and a large quantity of water must have poured into her, the hatches were not put on again by those who remained on deck. But in a few minutes this mystery was solved; one after another, at first, and then by dozens, poured forth, out of the hold, the kidnapped Africans who composed her cargo. In a short time the decks were covered with them: the poor creatures had been released by the humanity of two English sailors, that they might have the same chance with themselves of saving their lives. Still, no attempt was made to quit the vessel. Huddled together, like a flock of sheep, with the wild waves breaking over them, there they all remained, both European and African; and as the heavy blows of the seas upon the sides of the vessel careened and shook her, they were seen to cling, in every direction, with no distinction between the captured and their oppressors.

But this scene was soon changed; the frame of the vessel could no longer withstand the violence of the waves, and as Francisco watched, of a sudden it was seen to divide a-midships, and each portion to turn over. Then was the struggle for life; hundreds were floating on the raging element, and wrestling for existence, and the white foam of the ocean was dotted by the black heads of the negroes who attempted to gain the bank. It was an awful, terrible scene, to witness so many at one moment tossed and dashed about by the waves—so many fellow-beings threatened with eternity. At one moment they were close to the beach, forced on to it by some tremendous wave; at the next, the receding water and the undertow swept them all back; and of the many who had been swimming one half had disappeared to rise no more. Francisco watched with agony as he perceived that the number decreased, and that none had yet gained the shore. At last he snatched up the haulyards of his boat's sail which were near him, and hastened down to the spot to afford such succour as might be possible; nor were his efforts in vain. As the seas washed the apparently inanimate bodies on shore, and would then have again swept them away to return them in mockery, he caught hold of them and dragged them safe on the bank, and thus did he continue his exertions until fifteen of the bodies of the negroes were spread upon the beach. Although exhausted and senseless, they were not dead, and long before he had dragged up the last of the number, many of those previously saved had, without any other assistance than the heat of the sun, recovered from their insensibility.

Francisco would have continued his task of humanity, but the parted vessel had now been riven into fragments by the force of the waves, and the whole beach was strewed with her timbers and her stores, which were dashed on shore by the waters, and then swept back again by the return. In a short time the severe blows he received from these fragments disabled him from further exertion, and he sank exhausted on the sand; indeed, all further attempts were useless. All on board the vessel had been launched into the sea at the same moment, and those who were not now on shore were past all succour. Francisco walked up to those who had been saved: he found twelve of them were recovered and sitting on their hams; the rest were still in a state of insensibility. He then went up to the knoll, where his chest and provisions had been placed, and, throwing himself down by them, surveyed the scene.

The wind had lulled, the sun shone brightly, and the sea was much less violent. The waves had subsided, and, no longer hurried on by the force of the hurricane, broke majestically, and solemnly, but not with the wildness and force which, but a few hours before, they had displayed. The whole of the beach was strewed with the fragments of the vessel, with spars and water-casks; and at every moment was to be observed the corpse of a negro turning round and round in the froth of the wave, and then disappearing.

For an hour did he watch and reflect and then he walked again to where the men who had been rescued were sitting, not more than thirty yards from him; they were sickly, emaciated forms, but belonging to a tribe who inhabited the coast, and who having been accustomed from their infancy to be all the day in the water, had supported themselves better than the other slaves, who had been procured from the interior, or the European crew of the vessel, all of whom had perished.

The Africans appeared to recover fast by the heat of the sun, so oppressive to Francisco, and were now exchanging a few words with each other. The whole of them had revived, but those who were most in need of aid were neglected by the others. Francisco made signs to them, but they understood him not. He returned to the knoll, and pouring out water into a tin pan from the breaker, brought it down to them. He offered it to one, who seized it eagerly; water was a luxury seldom obtained in the hold of a slave-vessel. The man drank deeply, and would have drained the cup, but Francisco prevented him, and held it to the lips of another. He was obliged to refill it three times before they had all been supplied: he then brought them a handful of biscuit, and left them, for he reflected that, without some precautions, the whole sustenance would be seized by them and devoured. He buried half a foot deep, and covered over with sand, the breakers of water and the provisions, and by the time he had finished this task, unperceived by the negroes, who still squatted together, the sun had sunk below the horizon. Francisco had already matured his plans, which were, to form a raft out of the fragments of the vessel, and, with the assistance of the negroes, attempt to gain the mainland. He lay down, for the second night, on this eventful spot of desolation, and commending himself to the Almighty protection, was soon in a deep slumber.

It was not until the powerful rays of the sun blazed on the eyes of the youth that he awoke, so tired had he been with the anxiety and fatigue of the preceding day, and the sleepless harrowing night which had introduced it. He rose and seated himself upon his sea-chest: how different was the scene from that of yesterday! Again the ocean slept, the sky was serene, and not a cloud to be distinguished throughout the whole firmament; the horizontal line was clear, even, and well defined: a soft breeze just rippled over the dark blue sea, which now had retired to its former boundary, and left the sand-bank as extended as when first Francisco had been put on shore. But here the beauty of the landscape terminated: the foreground was horrible to look upon; the whole of the beach was covered with the timbers of the wreck, with water-casks, and other articles, in some parts heaped and thrown up one upon another; and among them lay, jammed and mangled, the bodies of the many who had perished. In other parts there were corpses thrown up high and dry, or still rolling and turning to the rippling wave: it was a scene of desolation and of death.

The negroes who had been saved were all huddled up together, apparently in deep sleep, and Francisco quitted his elevated position and walked down to the low beach, to survey the means which the disaster of others afforded him for his own escape. To his great joy he found not only plenty of casks, but many of them full of fresh water, provisions also in sufficiency, and, indeed, everything that could be required to form a raft, as well as the means of support for a considerable time for himself and the negroes who had survived. He then walked up to them and called to them, but they answered not, nor even moved. He pushed them, but in vain; and his heart beat quick, for he was fearful that they were dead from previous exhaustion. He applied his foot to one of them, and it was not until he had used force, which in any other case he would have dispensed with, that the negro awoke from his state of lethargy and looked vacantly about him. Francisco had some little knowledge of the language of the Kroumen, and he addressed the negro in that tongue. To his great joy, he was answered in a language which, if not the same, had so great an affinity to it that communication became easy. With the assistance of the negro, who used still less ceremony with his comrades, the remainder of them were awakened, and a palaver ensued.

Francisco soon made them understand that they were to make a raft and go back to their own country; explaining to them that if they remained there, the water and provisions would soon be exhausted, and they would all perish. The poor creatures hardly knew whether to consider him a supernatural being or not; they talked among

themselves; they remarked at his having brought them fresh water the day before; they knew that he did not belong to the vessel in which they had been wrecked, and they were puzzled.

Whatever might be their speculations, they had one good effect, which was, that they looked upon the youth as a superior and a friend, and most willingly obeyed him. He led them up to the knoll, and, desiring them to scrape away the sand, supplied them again with fresh water and biscuit. Perhaps the very supply, and the way in which it was given to them, excited their astonishment as much as anything. Francisco ate with them, and, selecting from his sea-chest the few tools in his possession, desired them to follow him. The casks were collected and rolled up; the empty ones arranged for the raft: the spars were hauled up and cleared of the rigging, which was carefully separated for lashings; the one or two sails which had been found rolled up on the spars were spread out to dry; and the provisions and articles of clothing, which might be useful, laid together on one side. The negroes worked willingly, and showed much intelligence: before the evening closed, everything which might be available was secured, and the waves now only tossed about lifeless forms, and the small fragments of timber which could not be serviceable.

It would occupy too much time were we to detail all the proceedings of Francisco and the negroes for the space of four days, during which they laboured hard. Necessity is truly the mother of invention, and many were the ingenious resources of the party before they could succeed in forming a raft large enough to carry them and their provisions, with a mast and sail well secured. At length it was accomplished; and on the fifth day, Francisco and his men embarked; and, having pushed clear of the bank with poles, they were at last able to hoist their sail to a fine breeze, and steer for the coast before the wind at the rate of about three miles an hour. But it was not until they had gained half a mile from the bank that they were no longer annoyed by the dreadful smell arising from the putrefaction of so many bodies, for to bury them all would have been a work of too great time. The last two days of their remaining on the island, the effluvia had become so powerful as to be a source of the greatest horror and disgust even to the negroes.

But before night when the raft was about eight leagues from the sand-bank, it fell calm, and continued so for the next day, when a breeze sprang up from the south-east, to which they trimmed their sail with their head to the northward.

This wind, and the course steered, sent them off from the land, but there was no help for it; and Francisco felt grateful that they had such an ample supply of provisions and water as to enable them to yield to a few days' contrary wind without danger of want. But the breeze continued steady and fresh, and they were now crossing the Bight of Benin; the weather was fine and the sea smooth; the flying-fish rose in shoals, and dropped down into the raft, which still forced its way through the water to the northward.

Thus did Francisco and his negro crew remain for a fortnight floating on the wide ocean, without any object meeting their view. Day after day it was the same dreary "sky and water," and by the reckoning of Francisco they could not be far from the land, when, on the fifteenth day, they perceived two sails to the northward.

Francisco's heart bounded with joy and gratitude to Heaven; he had no telescope to examine them, but he steered directly for them, and, about dark, he made them out to be a ship and a schooner, hove to.

As Francisco scanned them, surmising what they might be, the sun set behind the two vessels, and after it had sunk below the horizon their forms were, for a few minutes, delineated with remarkable precision and clearness. There could be no mistake. Francisco felt convinced that the schooner was the *Avenger*; and his first impulse was to run to the sweep with which they were steered, and put the head of the raft again to the northward. A moment's reflection determined him to act otherwise; he lowered down his sail that he might escape observation, and watched the motions of the vessels

during the few minutes of light which remained. That the ship had
been captured, and that her capture had been attended with the
usual scene of outrage and violence, he had no doubt. He was now
about four miles from them, and just as they were vanishing from
his straining eyes he perceived that the schooner had made all sail to
the westward. Francisco, feeling that he was then secure from being
picked up by her, again hoisted his sail with the hope of reaching
the ship, which, if not scuttled, he intended to remove on board of,
and then make sail for the first port on the coast. But hardly had
the raft regained her way when the horizon was lighted up, and he
perceived that the pirates had set fire to the vessel. Then it was useless
to proceed towards her; and Francisco again thought of putting
the head of the raft to the northward, when the idea struck him,
knowing the character and cruelty of the pirates, that there might
be some unfortunate people left on board to perish in the flames.
He therefore continued his course, watching the burning vessel; the
flames increased in violence, mounting up to the masts and catching
the sails one after another. The wind blew fresh, and the vessel was
kept before the wind—a circumstance that assured Francisco that
there were people on board. At first she appeared to leave the raft, but
as her sails, one after another, were consumed by the element, so did
she decrease her speed, and Francisco, in about an hour, was close to
her and under her counter.

The ship was now one mass of fire from her bows to her mainmast;
a volume of flame poured from her main hold, rising higher than her
lower masts, and ending in a huge mass of smoke carried by the wind
ahead of her; the quarter-deck was still free from fire, but the heat on
it was so intense that those on board were all collected at the taffrail;
and there they remained, some violent, others in mute despair; for
the *Avenger's* people, in their barbarity, had cut away and destroyed
all the boats, to prevent their escape. From the light thrown round
the vessel, those on board had perceived the approach of Francisco
to their rescue, and immediately that it was under the counter, and

the sail lowered, almost all of them had descended by ropes, or the stern ladder, and gained a place in her. In a few minutes, without scarcely an exchange of a word, they were all out of the brig, and Francisco pushed off just as the flames burst from the cabin-windows, darting out in a horizontal line like the tongues of fiery serpents. The raft, now encumbered with twelve more persons, was then steered to the northward; and as soon as those who had been saved had been supplied with some water, which they so much needed, Francisco obtained the intelligence which he desired. The ship was from Carthagena, South America; had sailed from thence to Lisbon with a Don Cumanos, who had large property up the Magdalen river. He had wished to visit a part of his family at Lisbon, and from thence had sailed to the Canary Isles, where he also had property. In their way from Lisbon to South America they had been beaten by stress of weather to the southward, and afterwards had been chased by the *Avenger*; being a very fast sailer she had run down several degrees before she had been captured. When the pirate took possession, and found that she had little or no cargo of value to them, for her hold was chiefly filled with furniture and other articles for the use of Don Cumanos, angry at their disappointment, they had first destroyed all their boats and then set fire to the vessel, taking care not to leave her until all chance of the fire being put out was hopeless. And thus had these miscreants left innocent and unfortunate people to perish.

Francisco heard the narrative of Don Cumanos, and then informed him in what manner he had left the schooner, and his subsequent adventures. Francisco was now very anxious to make the land, or obtain succour from some vessel. The many who were now on board, and the time that he had already been at sea, obliged him to reduce the allowance of water. Fortune favoured him after all his trials; on the third day a vessel hove in sight, and they were seen by her. She made sail for them, and took them all on board. It was a schooner trafficking on the coast for gold-dust and ivory; but the magnificent offers of Don Cumanos induced them to give up their voyage and run across the Atlantic to Carthagena. To Francisco it was of little moment where he went, and in Don Cumanos he had found a sincere friend.

"You have been my preserver," said the Spaniard, "allow me to return the obligation—come and live with me."

As Francisco was equally pleased with Don Cumanos, he accepted the offer; they all arrived safely at Carthagena, and from thence proceeded to his estate on the Magdalen river.

XII
THE LIEUTENANT

WHEN WE LAST MENTIONED EDWARD Templemore, we stated that he was a lieutenant of the admiral's ship on the West India station, commanding the tender. Now the name of the tender was the *Enterprise*: and it was singular that she was one of two schooners built at Baltimore, remarkable for their beauty and good qualities; yet how different were their employments! Both had originally been built for the slave-trade; now one hoisted the English pennant, and cruised as the *Enterprise*; the other threw out the black flag, and scoured the seas as the *Avenger*.

The *Enterprise* was fitted much in the same way as we have already described her sister vessel—that is, with one long brass gun amidships, and smaller ones for her broadside. But in the numbers of their crew there was a great disparity; the *Enterprise* not being manned with more than sixty-five English sailors, belonging to the admiral's ship. She was employed, as most admirals' tenders usually were, sometimes carrying a tender made for a supply of provisions, or a tender of services, if required, from the admiral; or, if not particularly wanted, with the important charge of a tender *billet-doux* to some fair friend. But this is a tender subject to touch upon. In the meantime it must be understood that she had the same commission to sink, burn, and destroy, as all other of his Majesty's vessels, if anything came in her way; but as she usually carried despatches, the real importance of which were, of course, unknown, she was not to go out of her way upon such service.

Edward Templemore did, however, occasionally go a little out of his way, and had lately captured a very fine privateer after a smart action, for which he anticipated his promotion; but the admiral thought him too young, and therefore gave the next vacancy to his own nephew, who, the admiral quite forgot, was much younger.

Edward laughed when he heard of it, upon his arrival at Port Royal; and the admiral, who expected that he would make his appearance pouting with disappointment, when he came up to the Penn to report himself, was so pleased with his good humour that he made a vow that Templemore should have the next vacancy; but this he also quite forgot, because Edward happened to be, at the time it occurred, on a long cruise,— and "out of sight out of mind" is a proverb so well established, that it may be urged as an excuse for a person who had so many other things to think of as the admiral entrusted with the command of the West India station.

Lieutenant Templemore had, in consequence, commanded the *Enterprise* for nearly two years, and without grumbling; for he was of a happy disposition, and passed a very happy sort of life. Mr Witherington was very indulgent to him, and allowed him to draw liberally; he had plenty of money for himself or for a friend who required it, and he had plenty of amusement. Amongst other diversions, he had fallen most desperately in love; for, in one of his trips to the Leeward Isles (so called from their being to windward) he had succoured a Spanish vessel, which had on board the new Governor of Porto Rico, with his family, and had taken upon himself to land them on that island in safety; for which service the English admiral received a handsome letter, concluding with the moderate wish that his Excellency might live a thousand years, and

Edward Templemore an invitation to go and see them whenever he might pass that way; which, like most general invitations, was as much a compliment as the wish which wound up the letter to the admiral. It did, however, so happen that the Spanish governor had a very beautiful and only daughter, carefully guarded by a duenna, and a monk who was the depository of all the sins of the governor's establishment; and it was with this daughter that Edward Templemore fell into the heresy of love.

She was, indeed, very beautiful; and, like all her countrywomen, was ardent in her affection. The few days that she was on board the schooner with her father, during the time that the *Enterprise* convoyed the Spanish vessel into port, were quite sufficient to ignite two such inflammable beings as Clara d'Alfarez and Edward Templemore. The monk had been left on board of the leaky vessel; there was no accommodation in the schooner for him or the duenna, and Don Felix de Maxos de Cobas de Manilla d'Alfarez was too busy with his cigar to pay attention to his daughter.

When they were landed, Edward Templemore was asked to their residence, which was not in the town, but at a lovely bay on the south side of the island. The town mansion was appropriated to business and the ceremony of the court: it was too hot for a permanent abode, and the governor only went there for a few hours each day.

Edward Templemore remained a short time at the island, and at his departure received the afore-mentioned letter from the father to the English admiral, and an assurance of unalterable fidelity from the daughter to the English lieutenant. On his return he presented the letter, and the admiral was satisfied with his conduct.

When ordered out to cruise, which he always was when there was nothing else to do, he submitted to the admiral whether, if he should happen to be near Porto Rico, he could not leave an answer to the Spanish governor's letter; and the admiral, who knew the value of keeping up a good understanding with foreign relations, took the hint, and gave him one to deliver, if *convenient*. The second meeting was, as may be supposed, more cordial than the first on the part of the young lady; not so, however, on the part of the duenna and holy friar, who soon found out that their charge was in danger from heretical opinions.

Caution became necessary; and as secrecy adds a charm to an amour, Clara received a long letter and a telescope from Edward. The letter informed her that, whenever he could, he would make his appearance in his schooner off the south of the island, and await a signal made by her at a certain window, acknowledging her recognition of his vessel. On the night of that signal he would land in his boat and meet her at an appointed spot. This was all very delightful; and it so happened that Edward had four or five times contrived, during the last year, to meet Clara without discovery, and again and again to exchange his vows. It was agreed between them that when he quitted the station, she would quit her father and her home, and trust her future happiness to an Englishman and a heretic.

It may be a matter of surprise to some of our readers that the admiral should not have discovered the frequent visits of the *Enterprise* to Porto Rico, as Edward was obliged to bring his log for examination every time that he returned; but the admiral was satisfied with Edward's conduct, and his anxiety to cruise when there was nothing else for him to do. His logs were brought on shore to the admiral's secretary, carefully rolled and sealed up. The admiral's secretary threw the packages on one side, and thought no more of the matter, and Edward had always a ready story to tell when he took his seat at the admiral's dinner-table; besides, he is a very unfit person to command a vessel who does not know how to write a log that will bear an investigation. A certain latitude is always allowed in every degree of latitude as well as longitude.

The *Enterprise* had been despatched to Antigua, and Edward thought this an excellent opportunity to pay a visit to Clara d'Alfarez: he therefore, upon his return, hove to off the usual headland, and soon perceived the white curtain thrown out of the window.

"There it is, sir," said one of the midshipmen who was near him—for he had been there so often that the whole crew of the *Enterprise* were aware of his attachment—"She has shown her flag of truce."

"A truce to your nonsense, Mr Warren," replied Edward, laughing; "how came you to know anything about it?"

"I only judge by cause and effect, sir; and I know that I shall have to go on shore and wait for you tonight."

"That's not unlikely; but let draw the foresheet; we must now get behind the headland."

The youngster was right: that evening, a little before dark, he attended his commander on shore, the *Enterprise* lying to with a lantern at her peak.

"Once more, dearest Clara!" said Edward, as he threw off her long veil and pressed her in his arms.

"Yes, Edward, once more—but I am afraid only once more; for my maid, Inez, has been dangerously ill, and has confessed to Friar Ricardo. I fear much that, in her fright (for she thought that she was dying), she has told all. She is better now."

"Why should you imagine so, Clara?"

"Oh, you know not what a frightened fool that Inez is when she is ill! Our religion is not like yours."

"No, dear, it is not; but I will teach you a better."

"Hush, Edward, you must not say that. Holy Virgin! if Friar Ricardo should hear you! I think that Inez must have told him, for he fixes his dark eyes upon me so earnestly. Yesterday he observed to me that I had not confessed."

"Tell him to mind his own business."

"That is his business, and I was obliged to confess to him last night. I told him a great many things, and then he asked if that was all. His eyes went through me. I trembled as I uttered an untruth, for I said it was."

"I confess my sins but to my Maker, Clara! and I confess my love but to you. Follow my plan, dearest!"

"I will half obey you, Edward. I will not tell my love."

"And sins you have none, Clara; so you will obey me in all."

"Hush, Edward, you must not say that. We all have sins; and, oh! what a grievous sin they say it is to love you, who are a heretic! Holy Virgin, pardon me! but I could not help it."

"If that is your only sin, dearest, I can safely give you absolution."

"Nay, Edward, don't joke, but hear me. If Inez has confessed, they will look for me here, and we must not meet again—at least not in this place. You know the little bay behind the rock, it is not much farther off, and there is a cave where I can wait: another time it must be there."

"It shall be there, dearest; but is it not too near the beach? will you not be afraid of the men in the boat, who must see you?"

"But we can leave the beach. It is Ricardo alone that I am in dread of, and the Donna Maria. Merciful Heaven! should my father know all, we should be lost—be separated for ever!" and Clara laid her forehead on Edward's shoulder, as her tears fell fast.

"There is nought to fear, Clara. Hush! I heard a rustling in those orange-trees. Listen!"

"Yes! yes!" whispered Clara, hastily; "there is some one. Away! dear Edward, away!"

Clara sprang from his side, and hastened up the grove. Edward made his retreat, and flying down the rocky and narrow path through the underwood, was soon on the beach and into his boat. The *Enterprise* arrived at headquarters, and Edward reported himself to the admiral.

"I have work for you, Mr Templemore," said the admiral; "you must be ready to proceed on service immediately. We've found your match."

"I hope I may find her, sir," replied the lieutenant.

"I hope so, too; for, if you give a good account of her, it will put another swab on your shoulder. The pirate schooner, which has so long infested the Atlantic, has been seen and chased off Barbadoes by the *Amelia*: but it appears that there is not a vessel in the squadron which can come near her unless it be the *Enterprise*. She has since captured two West Indiamen, and was seen steering with them towards the coast of Guiana. Now, I am going to give you thirty additional hands, and send you after her."

"Thank you, sir," replied Edward, his countenance beaming with delight.

"How soon will you be ready?" inquired the admiral.

"To-morrow morning, sir."

"Very good. Tell Mr Hadley to bring me the order for the men and your sailing orders, and I will sign them; but recollect, Mr Templemore, you will have an awkward customer. Be prudent—brave I know you to be."

Edward Templemore promised everything, as most people do in such cases; and before the next evening the *Enterprise* was well in the offing, under a heavy press of sail.

XIII
THE LANDING

THE PROPERTY OF DON CUMANOS, to which he had retired with his family, accompanied by Francisco, extended from the mouth of, to many miles up, the Magdalen river. It was a fine alluvial soil, forming one vast strip of rich meadow, covered with numerous herds of cattle. The house was not a hundreds yards from the bank of the magnificent stream, and a small but deep creek ran up to the adjacent buildings; for Don Cumanos had property even more valuable, being proprietor of a gold mine near the town of Jambrano, about eight miles farther up, and which mine had latterly become exceedingly productive. The ore was brought down the river in boats, and smelted in the outhouses near the creek to which we have just referred.

It will be necessary to observe that the establishment of the noble Spaniard was numerous, consisting of nearly one hundred persons, employed in the smelting-house or attached to the household.

For some time Francisco remained here happy and contented; he had become the confidential supervisor of Don Cumanos' household, proved himself worthy of a trust so important, and was considered as one of the family.

One morning, as Francisco was proceeding down to the smelting-house to open the hatches of the small deck boats which had arrived from Jambrano with ore, and which were invariably secured with a padlock by the superintendent above, to which Don Cumanos had a corresponding key, one of the chief men informed him that a vessel had anchored off the mouth of the river the day before, and weighed again early that morning, and that she was now standing off and on.

"From Carthagena, probably, beating up," replied Francisco.

"Valga me Dios, if I know that, sir," said Diego, "I should have thought nothing about it; but Giacomo and Pedro, who went out to fish last night, as usual, instead of coming back before midnight, have not been heard of since."

"Indeed! that is strange. Did they ever stay so long before?"

"Never, sir; and they have fished together now for seven years."

Francisco gave the key to the man, who opened the locks of the hatches, and returned it.

"There she is!" cried the man; the head-sails making their appearance as the vessel opened to their view from the projecting point distant about four miles. Francisco directed his eye towards her, and, without further remark, hastened to the house.

"Well, Francisco," said Don Cumanos, who was stirring a small cup of chocolate, "what's the news this morning?"

"The *Nostra Senora del Carmen* and the *Aguilla* have arrived, and I have just unlocked the hatches. There is a vessel off the point which requires examination, and I have come for the telescope."

"Requires examination! Why, Francisco?"

"Because Giacomo and Pedro, who went fishing last night, have not returned, and there are no tidings of them."

"That is strange! But how is this connected with the vessel?"

"That I will explain as soon as I have had an examination of her," replied Francisco, who had taken up the telescope, and was drawing out the tube. Francisco fixed the glass against the sill of the window, and examined the vessel some time in silence.

"Yes! by the living God, it is the *Avenger*, and no other," exclaimed he, as he removed the telescope from his eye.

"Eh?" cried Don Cumanos.

"It is the pirate vessel—the *Avenger*—I'll forfeit my life upon it! Don Cumanos, you must be prepared. I know that they have long talked of a visit to this quarter, and anticipate great booty, and they have those on board who know the coast well. The disappearance of your two men convinces me that they sent up their boats last night to reconnoitre, and have captured them. Torture will extract the information which the pirates require, and I have little doubt but that the attack will be made, when they learn how much bullion there is at present on your premises."

"You may be right," replied Don Cumanos, thoughtfully; "that is, provided you are sure that it is the pirate vessel."

"Sure, Don Cumanos! I know every timber and plank in her; there is not a rope nor a block but I can recognise. At the distance of four miles, with such a glass as this, I can discover every little variety in her rigging from other craft, I will swear to her," repeated Francisco, once more looking through the telescope.

"And if they attack, Francisco?"

"We must defend ourselves, and, I trust, beat them off. They will come in their boats, and at night. If they were to run in the schooner by daylight and anchor abreast of us, we should have but a poor chance. But they little think that I am here, and that they are recognised. They will attack this night, I rather think."

"And what do you then propose, Francisco?"

"That we should send all the females away to Don Teodoro's—it is but five miles—and call the men together as soon as possible. We are strong enough to beat them off if we barricade the house. They cannot land more than from ninety to one hundred men, as some must remain in charge of the schooner; and we can muster quite as many. It may be as well to promise our men a reward if they do their duty."

"That is all right enough; and the bullion we have here."

"Here we had better let it remain; it will take too much time to remove it, and, besides, will weaken our force by the men who must be in charge of it. The out-houses must be abandoned, and everything which is of consequence taken from them. Fire them they will, in all probability. At all events we have plenty of time before us, if we begin at once."

"Well, Francisco, I shall make you commandant, and leave the arrangements to you, while I go and speak to Donna Isidora. Send for the men and speak to them; promise them rewards, and act as if you were ordering upon your own responsibility."

"I trust I shall prove myself worthy of your confidence, sir," replied Francisco.

"Carambo!" exclaimed the old don, as he left the room; "but it is fortunate you are here. We might all have been murdered in our beds."

Francisco sent for the head men of the establishment, and told them what he was convinced they would have to expect; and he then explained to them his views. The rest were all summoned; and Francisco pointed out to them the little mercy they would receive if the pirates were not repulsed, and the rewards which were promised by Don Cumanos if they did their duty.

Spaniards are individually brave; and, encouraged by Francisco, they agreed that they would defend the property to the last.

The house of Don Cumanos was well suited to resist an attack of this description, in which musketry only was expected to be employed. It was a long parallelogram of stone walls, with a wooden veranda on the first floor,—for it was only one story high. The windows on the first story were more numerous, but at the basement there were but two, and no other opening but the door in the whole line of building. It was of a composite architecture, between the Morisco and the Spanish. If the lower part of the house, which was of stone, could be secured from entrance, the assailants would, of course, fight under a great disadvantage. The windows below were the first secured by piling a heavy mass of stones in the interior of the rooms against them, rising to the ceiling from a base like the segment of a pyramid, extending to the opposite side of the chamber; and every preparation was made for effectually barricading the door before night. Ladders were then fixed to ascend to the veranda, which was rendered musket-proof nearly as high as its railings, to protect the men. The Donna Isidora, and the women of the establishment, were, in the afternoon, despatched to Don Teodoro's; and, at the request of Francisco, joined to the entreaties of Donna Isidora, Don Cumanos was persuaded to accompany them. The don called his men, and telling them that he left Francisco in command, expected them to do their duty; and then shaking hands with him, the cavalcade was soon lost in the woods behind the narrow meadows which skirted the river.

There was no want of muskets and ammunition. Some were employed casting bullets, and others in examining the arms which had long been laid by. Before evening all was ready; every man had received his arms and ammunition; the flints had been inspected; and Francisco had time to pay more attention to the schooner, which had, during the day, increased her distance from the land, but was now again standing in for the shore. Half-an-hour before dusk, when within three miles, she wore round and put her head to the offing.

"They'll attack this night," said Francisco, "I feel almost positive: their yards and stay-tackles are up, all ready for hoisting out the long-boat."

"Let them come, senor; we will give them a warm reception," replied Diego, the second in authority.

It was soon too dark to perceive the vessel. Francisco and Diego ordered every man, but five, into the house; the door was firmly barricaded, and some large pieces of rock, which had been rolled into the passage, piled against it. Francisco then posted the five men down the banks of the river, at a hundred yards' distance from each other, to give notice of the approach of the boats. It was about ten o'clock at night, when Francisco and Diego descended the ladder and went to examine their outposts.

"Senor," said Diego, as he and Francisco stood on the bank of the river, "at what hour is it your idea that these villains will make their attempt?"

"That is difficult to say. If the same captain commands them who did when I was on board of her, it will not be until after the moon is down, which will not be till midnight; but should it be any other who is in authority, they may not be so prudent."

"Holy Virgin! senor, were you ever on board of that vessel?"

"Yes, Diego, I was, and for a long while, too; but not with my own good will. Had I not been on board I never should have recognised her."

"Very true, senor; then we may thank the saints that you have once been a pirate."

"I hope that I never was that, Diego," replied Francisco, smiling; "but I have been a witness to dreadful proceedings on board of that vessel, at the remembrance of which, even now, my blood curdles."

To pass away the time, Francisco then detailed many scenes of horror to Diego which he had witnessed when on board of the *Avenger*; and he was still in the middle of a narrative when a musket was discharged by the farthermost sentinel.

"Hark, Diego!"

Another, and another, nearer and nearer to them, gave the signal that the boats were close at hand. In a few minutes the men all came in, announcing that the pirates were pulling up the stream in three boats, and were less than a quarter of a mile from the landing-place.

"Diego, go to the house with these men, and see that all is ready," said Francisco. "I will wait here a little longer; but do not fire till I come to you."

Diego and the men departed, and Francisco was left on the beach alone.

In another minute, the sound of the oars was plainly distinguishable, and Francisco's ears were directed to catch, if possible, the voices. "Yes," thought he, "you come with the intentions of murder and robbery; but you will, through me, be disappointed." As the boats approached, he heard the voice of Hawkhurst. The signal muskets fired had told the pirates that they were discovered, and that, in all probability, they would meet with resistance; silence was, therefore, no longer of any advantage.

"Oars, my lads!—oars!" cried Hawkhurst.

One boat ceased rowing, and soon afterwards the two others. The whole of them were now plainly seen by Francisco, at the distance of about one cable's length from where he stood; and the clear still night carried the sound of their voices along the water.

"Here is a creek, sir," said Hawkhurst, "leading up to those buildings. Would it not be better to land there, as, if they are not occupied, they will prove a protection to us if we have a hard fight for it?"

"Very true, Hawkhurst," replied a voice, which Francisco immediately recognised to be that of Cain.

"He is alive, then," thought Francisco, "and his blood is not yet upon my hands."

"Give way, my lads!" cried Hawkhurst.

The boats dashed up the creek, and Francisco hastened back to the house.

"Now, my lads," said he, as he sprang up the ladder, "you must be resolute; we have to deal with desperate men. I have heard the voices of the captain and the chief mate; so there is no doubt as to its being the pirate. The boats are up the creek and will land behind the out-buildings. Haul up these ladders, and lay them fore and aft on the veranda; and do not fire without taking a good aim. Silence! my men—silence! Here they come."

The pirates were now seen advancing from the out-buildings in strong force. In the direction in which they came, it was only from the side of the veranda, at which not more than eight or ten men could be placed, that the enemy could be repulsed. Francisco therefore gave orders that as soon as some of the men had fired they should retreat and load their muskets, to make room for others.

When the pirates had advanced halfway to the house, on the clear space between it and the outbuildings, Francisco gave the word to fire. The volley was answered by another, and a shout from the pirates, who, with Hawkhurst and Cain at their head, now pressed on, but not until they had received a second discharge from the Spaniards, and the pirates had fired in return. As the Spaniards could not at first fire a volley of more than a dozen muskets at a time, their opponents imagined their force to be much less than it really was. They now made other arrangements. They spread themselves in a semicircle in front of the veranda, and kept up a continued galling fire. This was returned by the party under Francisco for nearly a quarter of an hour; and as all the muskets were now called into action, the pirates found out that they had a more formidable enemy to cope with than they had anticipated.

It was now quite dark, and not a figure was to be distinguished, except by the momentary flashing of the fire-arms. Cain and Hawkhurst, leaving their men to continue the attack, had gained the house, and a position under the veranda. Examining the windows and door, there appeared but little chance of forcing an entrance; but it immediately occurred to them that under the veranda their men would not be exposed, and that they might fire through the wooden floor of it upon those above. Hawkhurst hastened away, and returned with about half the men, leaving the others to continue their attack as before. The advantage of this manoeuvre was soon evident. The musket-balls of the pirates pierced the planks, and wounded many of the Spaniards severely; and Francisco was at last obliged to order his men to retreat into the house, and fire out of the windows.

But even this warfare did not continue; for the supporting-pillars of the veranda being of wood, and very dry, they were set fire to by the pirates. Gradually the flames wound round them, and their forked tongues licked the balustrade. At last, the whole of the veranda was in flames. This was a great advantage to the attacking party, who could now distinguish the Spaniards without their being so clearly seen themselves. Many were killed and wounded. The smoke and heat became so intense in the upper story that the men could no longer remain there; and, by the advice of Francisco, they retreated to the basement of the house.

"What shall we do now, senor?" said Diego, with a grave face.

"Do?" replied Francisco; "they have burnt the veranda, that is all. The house will not take fire; it is of solid stone: the roof indeed may; but still here we are. I do not see that they are more advanced than they were before. As soon as the veranda has burnt down, we must return above, and commence firing again from the windows."

"Hark, sir! they are trying the door."

"They may try a long while; they should have tried the door while the veranda protected them from our sight. As soon as it is burnt, we shall be able to drive them away from it. I will go up again and see how things are."

"No, senor; it is of no use. Why expose yourself now that the flames are so bright?"

"I must go and see if that is the case, Diego. Put all the wounded men in the north chamber, it will be the safest, and more out of the way."

Francisco ascended the stone staircase, and gained the upper story. The rooms were filled with smoke, and he could distinguish nothing. An occasional bullet whistled past him. He walked towards the windows, and sheltered himself behind the wall between them.

The flames were not so violent, and the heat more bearable. In a short time, a crash, and then another told him that the veranda had fallen in. He looked through the window. The mass of lighted embers had fallen down in front of the house, and had, for a time, driven away the assailants. Nothing was left of the veranda but the burning ends of the joists fixed in the wall above the windows, and the still glowing remains of the posts which once supported it.

But the smoke from below now cleared away, and the discharge of one or two muskets told Francisco that he was perceived by the enemy.

"The roof is safe," thought he, as he withdrew from the window; "and now I do not know whether the loss of the veranda may not prove a gain to us."

What were the intentions of the pirates it was difficult to ascertain. For a time they had left off firing, and Francisco returned to his comrades. The smoke had gradually cleared away, and they were able to resume their position above; but as the pirates did not fire, they, of course, could do nothing, as it was only by the flashing of the muskets that the enemy was to be distinguished. No further attempts were made at the door or windows below; and Francisco in vain puzzled himself as to the intended plans of the assailants.

Nearly half an hour of suspense passed away. Some of the Spaniards were of opinion that they had retreated to their boats and gone away, but Francisco knew them better. All he could do was to remain above, and occasionally look out to discover their motions. Diego, and one or two more, remained with him; the other men were kept below, that they might be out of danger.

"Holy Francis! but this has been a dreadful night, senor! How many hours until daylight?" said Diego.

"Two hours at least, I should think," replied Francisco; "but the affair will be decided before that."

"The saints protect us! See, senor, are they not coming?"

Francisco looked through the gloom, in the direction of the outbuildings, and perceived a group of men advancing. A few moments and he could clearly make them out.

"Yes, truly, Diego; and they have made ladders, which they are carrying. They intend to storm the windows. Call them up; and now we must fight hard indeed."

The Spaniards hastened up and filled the room above, which had three windows in the front, looking towards the river, and which had been sheltered by the veranda.

"Shall we fire now, senor?"

"No—no: do not fire till your muzzles are at their hearts. They cannot mount more than two at a time at each window. Recollect, my lads, that you must now fight hard, for your lives will not be spared; they will show no quarter and no mercy."

The ends of the rude ladders now made their appearance above the sill of each window. They had been hastily, yet firmly, constructed; and were nearly as wide as the windows. A loud cheer was followed by a simultaneous mounting of the ladders.

Francisco was at the centre window, when Hawkhurst made his appearance, sabre in hand. He struck aside the musket aimed at him, and the ball whizzed harmless over the broad water of the river. Another step, and he would have been in, when Francisco fired his pistol; the ball entered the left shoulder of Hawkhurst, and he dropped his hold. Before he could regain it, a Spaniard charged at him with a musket, and threw him back. He fell, bearing down with him one or two of his comrades, who had been following him up the ladder.

Francisco felt as if the attack at that window was of little consequence after the fall of Hawkhurst, whose voice he had recognised; and he hastened to the one on the left, as he had heard Cain encouraging his men in that direction. He was not wrong in his conjecture; Cain was at the window, attempting to force an entrance, but was opposed by Diego and other resolute men. But the belt of the pirate-captain was full of pistols, and he had already fired three with effect. Diego and the two best men were wounded, and the others who opposed him were alarmed at his giant proportions. Francisco rushed to attack him; but what was the force of so young a man against the Herculean power of Cain! Still Francisco's left hand was at the throat of the pirate, and the pistol was pointed in his right, when a flash of another pistol, fired by one who followed Cain, threw its momentary vivid light upon the features of Francisco, as he cried out, "Blood for blood!" It was enough; the pirate captain uttered a yell of terror at the supposed supernatural appearance; and he fell from the ladder in a fit among the still burning embers of the veranda.

The fall of their two chiefs, and the determined resistance of the Spaniards, checked the impetuosity of the assailants. They hesitated; and they at last retreated, bearing away with them their wounded The Spaniards cheered, and, led by Francisco, followed them down the ladders, and, in their turn, became the assailants. Still the pirates' retreat was orderly: they fired, and retired rank behind rank successively. They kept the Spaniards at bay, until they had arrived at the boats, when a charge was made, and a severe conflict ensued. But the pirates had lost too many men, and, without their commander, felt dispirited. Hawkhurst was still on his legs and giving his orders as coolly as ever. He espied Francisco, and rushing at him, while the two parties were opposed muzzle to muzzle, seized him by his collar and dragged him in amongst the pirates. "Secure him at all events!" cried Hawkhurst, as they slowly retreated and gained the out-houses. Francisco was overpowered and hauled into one of the boats, all of which in a few minutes afterwards were pulling with all their might to escape from the muskets of the Spaniards, who followed the pirates by the banks of the river, annoying them in their retreat.

XIV
THE MEETING

THE PIRATES RETURNED TO THEIR vessel discomfited. Those on board, who were prepared to hoist in ingots of precious metal, had to receive nought but wounded men, and many of their comrades had remained dead on the shore. Their captain was melancholy and downcast. Hawkhurst was badly wounded, and obliged to be carried below as soon as he came on board. The only capture which they had made was their former associate Francisco, who, by the last words spoken by Hawkhurst as he was supported to his cabin was ordered to be put in irons. The boats were hoisted in without noise, and a general gloom prevailed. All sail was then made upon the schooner, and when day dawned she was seen by the Spaniards far away to the northward.

The report was soon spread through the schooner that Francisco had been the cause of their defeat; and this was only a surmise, still, as they considered that had he not recognised the vessel the Spaniards would not have been prepared, they had good grounds for what had swelled into an assertion. He became, therefore, to many of them, an object of bitter enmity, and they looked forward with pleasure to his destruction, which his present confinement they considered but the precursor of.

"Hist! Massa Francisco!" said a low voice near to where Francisco sat on the chest. Francisco turned round and beheld the Krouman, his old friend.

"Ah! Pompey, are you all still on board?" said Francisco.

"All! no," replied the man, shaking his head; "some die—some get away—only four Kroumen left. Massa Francisco, how you come back again? Everybody tink you dead. I say no, not dead—ab charm with him—ab book."

"If that was my charm, I have it still," replied Francisco, taking the Bible out of his vest; for, strange to say, Francisco himself had a kind of superstition relative to that Bible, and had put it into his bosom previous to the attack made by the pirates.

"Dat very good, Massa Francisco; den you quite safe. Here come Johnson—he very bad man. I go away."

In the meantime Cain had retired to his cabin with feelings scarcely to be analysed. He was in a bewilderment. Notwithstanding the wound he had received by the hand of Francisco, he would never have sanctioned Hawkhurst putting him on shore on a spot which promised nothing but a lingering and miserable death. Irritated as he had been by the young man's open defiance, he loved him—loved him much more than he was aware of himself; and when he had recovered sufficiently from his wound, and had been informed where Francisco had been sent on shore, he quarrelled with Hawkhurst, and reproached him bitterly and sternly, in language which Hawkhurst never forgot or forgave. The vision of the starving lad haunted Cain, and rendered him miserable. His affection for him, now that he was, as he supposed, lost for ever, increased with tenfold force; and since that period Cain had never been seen to smile. He became more gloomy, more ferocious than ever, and the men trembled when he appeared on deck.

The apparition of Francisco after so long an interval, and in such an unexpected quarter of the globe, acted, as we have before described, upon Cain. When he was taken to the boat he was still confused in his ideas, and it was not until they were nearly on board that he perceived that this young man was indeed at his side. He could have fallen on his neck and kissed him: for Francisco had become to him a capture more prized than all the wealth of the Indies. But one pure, good feeling was unextinguished in the bosom of Cain; stained with every crime—with his hands so deeply imbrued in blood—at enmity with all the rest of the world, that one feeling burnt bright and clear, and was not to be quenched. It might have proved a beacon-light to steer him back to repentance and to good works.

But there were other feelings which also crowded upon the mind of the pirate-captain. He knew Francisco's firmness and decision. By some inscrutable means, which Cain considered as supernatural, Francisco had obtained the knowledge, and had accused him, of his mother's death. Would not the affection which he felt for the young man be met with hatred and defiance? He was but too sure that it would. And then his gloomy, cruel disposition would reassume its influence, and he thought of revenging the attack upon his life. His astonishment at the reappearance of Francisco was equally great, and he trembled at the sight of him, as if he were his accusing and condemning spirit. Thus did he wander from one fearful fancy to another, until he at last summoned up resolution to send for him.

A morose, dark man, whom Francisco had not seen when he was before in the schooner, obeyed the commands of the captain. The irons were unlocked, and Francisco was brought down into the cabin. The captain rose and shut the door.

"I little thought to see you here, Francisco," said Cain.

"Probably not," replied Francisco, boldly, "but you have me again, in your power, and may now wreak your vengeance."

"I feel none, Francisco; nor would I have suffered you to have been put on shore as you were, had I known of it. Even now that our expedition has failed through your means, I feel no anger towards you, although I shall have some difficulty in preserving you from the enmity of others. Indeed, Francisco, I am glad to find that you are alive, and I have bitterly mourned your loss:" and Cain extended his hand.

But Francisco folded his arms, and was silent.

"Are you then so unforgiving?" said the captain. "You know that I tell the truth."

"I believe that you state the truth, Captain Cain, for you are too bold to lie; and, as far as I am concerned, you have all the forgiveness you may wish; but I cannot take that hand; nor are our accounts yet settled."

"What would you more? Cannot we be friends again? I do not ask you to remain on board. You are free to go where you please. Come, Francisco, take my hand, and let us forget what is past."

"The hand that is imbrued with my mother's blood, perhaps!" exclaimed Francisco. "Never!"

"Not so, by G—d!" exclaimed Cain. "No, no; not quite so bad as that. In my mood I struck your mother; I grant it. I did not intend to injure her, but I did, and she died. I will not lie—that is the fact. And it is also the fact that I wept over her, Francisco; for I loved her as I do you." ("It was a hasty, bitter blow, that," continued Cain, soliloquising, with his hand to his forehead, and unconscious of Francisco's presence at the moment. "It made me what I am, for it made me reckless.") "Francisco," said Cain, raising his head, "I was bad, but I was no pirate when your mother lived. There is a curse upon me: that which I love most I treat the worst. Of all the world, I loved your mother most: yet did she from me receive much injury, and at last I caused her death. Next to your mother, whose memory I at once revere and love, and tremble when I think of (and each night does she appear to me), I have loved you, Francisco; for you, like her, have an angel's feelings: yet have I treated you as ill. You thwarted me, and you were right. Had you been wrong, I had not cared; but you were right, and it maddened me. Your appeals by day—your mother's in my dreams—"

Francisco's heart was softened; if not repentance, there was at least contrition. "Indeed I pity you," replied Francisco.

"You must do more, Francisco; you must be friends with me," said Cain, again extending his hand.

"I cannot take that hand, it is too deeply dyed in blood," replied Francisco.

"Well, well, so would have said your mother. But hear me, Francisco," said Cain, lowering his voice to a whisper, lest he should be overheard; "I am tired of this life—perhaps sorry for what I have done—I wish to leave it—have wealth in plenty concealed where others know not. Tell me, Francisco, shall we both quit this vessel, and live together happily and without doing wrong? You shall share all, Francisco. Say, now, does that please you?"

"Yes; it pleases me to hear that you will abandon your lawless life, Captain Cain; but share your wealth I cannot, for how has it been gained?"

"It cannot be returned, Francisco; I will do good with it. I will indeed, Francisco. I—will—repent;" and again the hand was extended.

Francisco hesitated.

"I do, so help me God! I do repent, Francisco!" exclaimed the pirate-captain.

"And I, as a Christian, do forgive you all," replied Francisco, taking the still extended hand. "May God forgive you, too!"

"Amen!" replied the pirate, solemnly, covering his face up in his hands.

In this position he remained some minutes, Francisco watching him in silence. At last the face was uncovered, and, to the surprise of Francisco, a tear was on the cheek of Cain and his eyes suffused with moisture. Francisco no longer waited for the hand to be extended; he walked up to the captain, and taking him by the hand, pressed it warmly.

"God bless you, boy! God bless you!" said Cain; "but leave me now."

Francisco returned on deck with a light and grateful heart. His countenance at once told those who were near him that he was not condemned, and many who dared not before take notice of him, now saluted him. The man who had taken him out of irons looked round; he was a creature of Hawkhurst, and he knew not how to act. Francisco observed him, and, with a wave of the hand, ordered him below. That Francisco was again in authority was instantly perceived, and the first proof of it was, that the new second mate reported to him that there was a sail on the weather bow.

Francisco took the glass to examine her. It was a large schooner under all sail. Not wishing that any one should enter the cabin but himself, he went down to the cabin-door, and knocked before he entered, and reported the vessel.

"Thank you, Francisco; you must take Hawkhurst's duty for the present—it shall not be for long; and fear not that I shall make another capture. I swear to you I will not, Francisco. But this schooner—I know very well what she is: she has been looking after us some time: and a week ago, Francisco, I was anxious to meet her, that I might shed more blood. Now I will do all I can to avoid her, and escape. I can do no more, Francisco. I must not be taken."

"There I cannot blame you. To avoid her will be easy, I should think; the *Avenger* outsails everything."

"Except, I believe, the *Enterprise*, which is a sister-vessel. By heaven! it's a fair match," continued Cain, his feelings of combativeness returning for a moment; "and it will look like a craven to refuse the fight: but fear not, Francisco—I have promised you, and I shall keep my word."

Cain went on deck, and surveyed the vessel through the glass.

"Yes, it must be her," said he aloud, so as to be heard by the pirates; "she has been sent out by the admiral on purpose, full of his best men. What a pity we are short-handed!"

"There's enough of us, sir," observed the boatswain.

"Yes," replied Cain, "if there was anything but hard blows to be got; but that is all, and I cannot spare more men. Ready about!" continued he, walking aft.

The *Enterprise*, for she was the vessel in pursuit, was then about five miles distant, steering for the *Avenger*, who was on a wind. As soon as the *Avenger* tacked, the *Enterprise* took in her topmast studding-sail, and hauled her wind. This brought the *Enterprise* well on the weather-quarter of the *Avenger*, who now made all sail. The pirates, who had had quite enough of fighting, and were not stimulated by the presence of Hawkhurst, or the wishes of their captain, now showed as much anxiety to avoid, as they usually did to seek, a combat.

At the first trial of sailing between the two schooners there was no perceptible difference; for half an hour they both continued on a wind, and when Edward Templemore examined his sextant a second time, he could not perceive that he had gained upon the *Avenger* one cable's length.

"We will keep away half a point," said Edward to his second in command. "We can afford that, and still hold the weather-gage."

The *Enterprise* was kept away, and increased her speed: they neared the *Avenger* more than a quarter of a mile.

"They are nearing us," observed Francisco; "we must keep away a point."

Away went the *Avenger*, and would have recovered her distance, but the *Enterprise* was again steered more off the wind.

Thus did they continue altering their course until the studding-sails below and aloft were set by both, and the position of the schooners was changed; the *Enterprise* now being on the starboard instead of the larboard quarter of the *Avenger*. The relative distance between the two schooners was, however, nearly the same, that is, about three miles and a half from each other; and there was every prospect of a long and weary chase on the part of the *Enterprise*, who again kept away a point to near the *Avenger*.

Both vessels were now running to the eastward.

It was about an hour before dark that another sail hove in sight right a-head of the *Avenger*, and was clearly made out to be a frigate. The pirates were alarmed at this unfortunate circumstance, as there was little doubt but that she would prove a British cruiser; and, if not, they had equally reason to expect that she would assist in their capture. She had evidently perceived the two schooners, and had made all sail, tacking every quarter of an hour so as to keep her relative position. The *Enterprise*, who had also made out the frigate, to attract her attention, although not within range of the *Avenger*, commenced firing with her long-gun.

"This is rather awkward," observed Cain.

"It will be dark in less than an hour," observed Francisco; "and that is our only chance."

Cain reflected a minute.

"Get the long-gun ready, my lads! We will return her fire, Francisco, and hoist American colours; that will puzzle the frigate at all events, and the night may do the rest."

The long-gun of the *Avenger* was ready.

"I would not fire the long-gun," observed Francisco, "it will show our force, and will give no reason for our attempt to escape. Now, if we were to fire our broadside-guns, the difference of report between them and the one of large calibre fired by the other schooner would induce them to think that we are an American vessel."

"Very true," replied Cain, "and, as America is at peace with all the world, that our antagonist is a pirate. Hold fast the long-gun, there; and unship the starboard ports. See that the ensign blows out clear."

The *Avenger* commenced firing an occasional gun from her broadside, the reports of which were hardly to be heard by those on board of the frigate; while the long-gun of the *Enterprise* reverberated along the water, and its loud resonance was swept by the wind to the frigate to leeward.

Such was the state of affairs when the sun sank down in the wave, and darkness obscured the vessels from each other's sight, except with the assistance of the night telescopes.

"What do you propose to do, Captain Cain?" said Francisco.

"I have made up my mind to do a bold thing. I will run down to the frigate, as if for shelter; tell him that the other vessel is a pirate, and claim his protection. Leave me to escape afterwards; the moon will not rise till nearly one o'clock."

"That will be a bold ruse, indeed; but suppose you are once under her broadside, and she suspects you?"

"Then I will show her my heels. I should care nothing for her and her broadside if the schooner was not here."

In an hour after dark the *Avenger* was close to the frigate, having steered directly for her. She shortened sail gradually, as if she had few hands on board; and, keeping his men out of sight, Cain ran under the stern of the frigate.

"Schooner ahoy! What schooner is that?"

"*Eliza* of Baltimore, from Carthagena," replied Cain, rounding to under the lee of the man-of-war, and then continuing: "That vessel in chase is a pirate. Shall I send a boat on board?"

"No; keep company with us."

"Ay, ay, sir," replied Cain.

"Hands about ship!" now resounded with the boatswain's whistle on board of the frigate, and in a minute they were on the other tack. The *Avenger* also tacked and kept close under the frigate's counter.

In the meantime, Edward Templemore and those on board of the *Enterprise* who, by the course steered, had gradually neared them, perceiving the motions of the two other vessels, were quite puzzled. At one time they thought they had made a mistake, and that it was not the pirate vessel; at another they surmised that the crew had mutinied and surrendered to the frigate. Edward hauled his wind, and steered directly for them, to ascertain what the real facts were. The captain of the frigate, who had never lost sight of either vessel, was equally astonished at the boldness of the supposed pirate.

"Surely the rascal does not intend to board us?" said he to the first-lieutenant.

"There is no saying, sir; you know what a character he has: and some say there are three hundred men on board, which is equal to our ship's company. Or perhaps, sir, he will pass to windward of us, and give us a broadside, and be off in the wind's eye again."

"At all events we will have a broadside ready for him," replied the captain. "Clear away the starboard guns, and take out the tompions. Pipe starboard watch to quarters."

The *Enterprise* closed with the frigate to windward, intending to run round her stern and bring to on the same tack.

"He does not shorten sail yet, sir," said the first-lieutenant, as the schooner appeared skimming along about a cable's length on their weather bow.

"And she is full of men, sir," said the master, looking at her through the night-glass.

"Fire a gun at her!" said the captain.

Bang! The smoke cleared away, and the schooner's foretopsail, which she was in the act of clewing up, lay over side. The shot had struck the foremast of the *Enterprise*, and cut it in two below the catharpings. The *Enterprise* was, for the time, completely disabled.

"Schooner ahoy! What schooner is that?"

"His Majesty's schooner *Enterprise*."

"Send a boat on board immediately."

"Ay, ay, sir."

"Turn the hands up? Shorten sail!"

The top-gallant and courses of the frigate were taken in, and the mainsail hove to the mast.

"Signalman, whereabouts is that other schooner now?"

"The schooner, sir? On the quarter," replied the signalman, who with everybody else on board, was so anxious about the *Enterprise*, that they had neglected to watch the motions of the supposed American. The man had replied at random, and he now jumped upon the signal-chests abaft to look for her. But she was not to be seen. Cain, who had watched all that passed between the other two vessels, and had been prepared to slip off at a moment's warning, as soon as the gun was fired at the other schooner, had wore round and made all sail on a wind. The night-glass discovered her half a mile astern; and the ruse was immediately perceived. The frigate filled and made sail, leaving Edward to return on board—for there was no time to stop for the boat—tacked, and gave chase. But the *Avenger* was soon in the wind's-eye of her; and at daylight was no longer to be seen.

In the meantime, Edward Templemore had followed the frigate as soon as he could set sail on his vessel, indignant at his treatment, and vowing that he would demand a court-martial. About noon the frigate rejoined him, when matters were fully explained. Annoyed as they all felt at not having captured the pirate, it was unanimously agreed, that by his audacity and coolness he deserved to escape. It was found that the mast of the *Enterprise* could be fished and scarfed, so as to enable her to continue her cruise. The carpenters of the frigate were sent on board; and in two days the injury was repaired, and Edward Templemore once more went in pursuit of the *Avenger*.

XV
THE MISTAKE

THE *AVENGER* STOOD UNDER A press of sail to the northward. She had left her pursuers far behind; and there was not a speck on the horizon, when, on the second morning, Francisco, who had resumed his berth in the captain's cabin, went up on deck. Notwithstanding the request of Cain, Francisco refused to take any part in the command of the schooner, considering himself as a passenger, or prisoner on parole.

He had not been on deck but a few minutes, when he observed the two Spanish fishermen belonging to the establishment of Don Cumanos conversing together forward. Their capture had quite escaped his memory, and he went forward to speak to them. Their surprise at seeing him was great, until Francisco informed them of what had passed. They then recounted what had occurred to them, and showed their thumbs, which had been put into screws to torture from them the truth. Francisco shuddered, but consoled them by promising that they should soon be at liberty, and return to their former master.

As Francisco returned from forward, he found Hawkhurst on the deck. Their eyes met and flashed in enmity. Hawkhurst was pale from loss of blood, and evidently suffering; but he had been informed of the apparent reconciliation between Francisco and the captain, and he could no longer remain in his bed. He knew, also, how the captain had avoided the combat with the *Enterprise*; and something told him that there was a revolution of feeling in more than one point. Suffering as he was, he resolved to be a spectator of what passed, and to watch narrowly. For both Francisco and Cain he had imbibed a deadly hatred, and was watching for an opportunity to wreak his revenge. At present they were too powerful; but he felt that the time was coming when he might be triumphant.

Francisco passed Hawkhurst without speaking.

"You are at liberty again, I see," observed Hawkhurst with a sneer.

"I am not, at all events, indebted to you for it," replied Francisco, haughtily; "nor for my life either."

"No, indeed; but I believe that I am indebted to you for this bullet in my shoulder," replied the mate.

"You are," replied Francisco, coolly.

"And depend upon it the debt shall be repaid with usury."

"I have no doubt of it, if ever it is in your power; but I fear you not."

As Francisco made this reply, the captain came up the ladder. Hawkhurst turned away and walked forward.

"There is mischief in that man, Francisco," said the captain in an under-tone; "I hardly know whom to trust; but he must be watched. He is tampering with the men, and has been for some time; not that it is of much consequence, if he does but remain quiet for a little while. The command of this vessel he is welcome to very soon; but if he attempts too early—"

"I have those I can trust to," replied Francisco. "Let us go below."

Francisco sent for Pompey the Krouman, and gave him his directions in the presence of the captain. That night, to the surprise of all, Hawkhurst kept his watch; and notwithstanding the fatigue, appeared every day to be rapidly recovering from his wound.

Nothing occurred for several days, during which the Avenger still continued her course. What the captain's intentions were did not transpire; they were known only to Francisco.

"We are very short of water, sir," reported Hawkhurst one morning: "shall we have enough to last us to where we are going?"

"How many days of full allowance have we on board?"

"Not above twelve at the most."

"Then we must go on half allowance," replied Cain.

"The ship's company wish to know where we are going, sir."

"Have they deputed you to ask the question?"

"Not exactly, sir; but I wish to know myself," replied Hawkhurst, with an insolent air.

"Turn the hands up," replied Cain: "as one of the ship's company under my orders, you will, with the others, receive the information you require."

The crew of the pirate collected aft.

"My lads," said Cain, "I understand, from the first mate, that you are anxious to know where you are going? In reply, I acquaint you, that having so many wounded men on board, and so much plunder in the hold, I intend to repair to our rendezvous when we were formerly in this part of the world—the *Caicos*. Is there any other question you may wish to ask of me?"

"Yes," replied Hawkhurst; "we wish to know what your intentions are relative to that young man Francisco. We have lost immense wealth; we have now thirty men wounded in the hammocks, and nine we left dead on the shore; and I have a bullet through my body, all of which has been occasioned by him. We demand justice!"

Here Hawkhurst was supported by several of the pirates; and there were many voices which repeated the cry of "Justice!"

"My men! you demand justice, and you shall have it," replied Cain. "This lad you all know well; I have brought him up from a child. He has always disliked our mode of life, and has often requested to leave it, but has been refused. He challenged me by our own laws, 'Blood for blood!' He wounded me; but he was right in his challenge, and, therefore, I bear no malice. Had I been aware that he was to have been sent on shore to die with hunger, I would not have permitted it. What crime had he committed? None; or, if any, it was against me. He was then sentenced to death for no crime, and you yourselves exclaimed against it. Is it not true?"

"Yes—yes," replied the majority of the pirates.

"By a miracle he escapes, and is put in charge of another man's property. He is made a prisoner, and now you demand justice. You shall have it. Allowing that his life is forfeit for this offence,—you have already sentenced him, and left him to death unjustly, and therefore are bound in justice to give his life in this instance. I ask it, my men, not only as his right, but as a favour to your captain."

"Agreed; it's all fair!" exclaimed the majority of the pirate's crew.

"My men, I thank you," replied Cain; "and in return, as soon as we arrive at the Caicos, my share of the plunder on board shall be divided among you."

This last observation completely turned the tables in favour of the captain; and those who had joined Hawkhurst now sided with the captain. Hawkhurst looked like a demon.

"Let those who choose to be bought off, take your money," replied he; "but *I will not*. Blood for blood I will have; and so I give you warning. That lad's life is mine, and have it I will! Prevent me, if you can!" continued the mate, holding up his clenched hand, and shaking it almost in the pirate-captain's face.

The blood mantled even to the forehead of Cain. One moment he raised himself to his utmost height, then seizing a hand spike, which lay near, he felled Hawkhurst to the deck.

"Take that for your mutiny!" exclaimed Cain, putting his foot on Hawkhurst's neck. "My lads, I appeal to you. Is this man worthy to be in command as mate? Is he to live?"

"No! no!" cried the pirates. "Death!"

Francisco stepped forward. "My men, you have granted your captain one favour; grant me another, which is the life of this man. Recollect how often he has led you to conquest, and how brave and faithful he has been until now! Recollect that he is suffering under his wound, which has made him irritable. Command you he cannot any longer, as he will never have the confidence of your captain; but let him live, and quit the vessel."

"Be it so, if you agree," replied Cain, looking at the men; "I do not seek his life."

The pirates consented. Hawkhurst rose slowly from the deck, and was assisted below to his cabin. The second mate was then appointed as the first, and the choice of the man to fill up the vacancy was left to the pirate-crew.

For three days after this scene all was quiet and orderly on board of the pirate. Cain, now that he had more fully made up his mind how to act, imparted to Francisco his plans; and his giving up to the men his share of the booty still on board was, to Francisco, an earnest of his good intentions. A cordiality, even a kind of feeling which never existed before, was created between them; but of Francisco's mother, and the former events of his own life, the pirate never spoke. Francisco more than once put questions on the subject; the answer was,—"You shall know some of these days, Francisco, but not yet; you would hate me too much!"

The *Avenger* was now clear of the English isles, and with light winds running down the shores of Porto Rico. In the evening of the day on which they had made the land, the schooner was becalmed about three miles from the shore, and the new first mate proposed that he should land in the boat and obtain a further supply of water from a fall which they had discovered with the glasses. As this was necessary, Cain gave his consent, and the boat quitted the vessel full of breakers.

Now it happened that the *Avenger* lay becalmed abreast of the country-seat of Don d'Alfarez, the governor of the island. Clara had seen the schooner; and, as usual, had thrown out the white curtain as a signal of recognition; for there was no perceptible difference, even to a sailor, at that distance, between the *Avenger* and the *Enterprise*. She had hastened down to the beach, and hurried into the cave, awaiting the arrival of Edward Templemore. The pirate-boat landed at the very spot of rendezvous, and the mate leaped out of the boat. Clara flew to receive her Edward, and was instantly seized by the mate, before she discovered her mistake.

"Holy Virgin! who and what are you?" cried she, struggling to disengage herself.

"One who is very fond of a pretty girl!" replied the pirate, still detaining her.

"Unhand me, wretch!" cried Clara. "Are you aware whom you are addressing?"

"Not I! nor do I care," replied the pirate.

"You will perhaps, sir, when you learn that I am the daughter of the governor!" exclaimed Clara, pushing him away.

"Yes! by heavens! you are right, pretty lady, I do care; for a governor's daughter will fetch a good ransom at all events. So come, my lads, a little help here; for she is as strong as a young mule. Never mind the water, throw the beakers into the boat again: we have a prize worth taking!"

Clara screamed; but she was gagged with a handkerchief and lifted into the boat, which immediately rowed back to the schooner.

When the mate came on board and reported his capture the pirates were delighted at the prospect of addition to their prize-money. Cain could not, of course, raise any objections; it would have been so different from his general practice, that it would have strengthened suspicions already set afloat by Hawkhurst, which Cain was most anxious just then to remove. He ordered the girl to be taken down into the cabin, hoisted in the boat, and the breeze springing up again, made sail.

In the mean time Francisco was consoling the unfortunate Clara, and assuring her that she need be under no alarm, promising her the protection of himself and the captain.

The poor girl wept bitterly, and it was not until Cain came down into the cabin and corroborated the assurances of Francisco that she could assume any degree of composure; but to find friends when she had expected every insult and degradation—for Francisco had acknowledged that the vessel was a pirate—was some consolation. The kindness and attention of Francisco restored her to comparative tranquillity.

The next day she confided to him the reason of her coming to the beach, and her mistake with regard to the two vessels, and Francisco and Cain promised her that they would themselves pay her ransom, and not wait until she heard from her father. To divert her thoughts Francisco talked much about Edward Templemore, and on that subject Clara could always talk. Every circumstance attending the amour was soon known to Francisco.

But the *Avenger* did not gain her rendezvous as soon as she expected. When to the northward of Porto Rico an English frigate bore down upon her, and the *Avenger* was obliged to run for it. Before the wind is always a schooner's worst point of sailing, and the chase was continued for three days before a fresh wind from the southward, until they had passed the Bahama Isles.

The pirates suffered much from want of water, as it was necessary still further to reduce their allowance. The frigate was still in sight, although the *Avenger* had dropped her astern when the wind became light, and at last it subsided into a calm, which lasted two days more. The boats of the frigate were hoisted out on the eve of the second day to attack the schooner, then distant five miles, when a breeze sprang up from the northward, and the schooner being then to windward, left the enemy hull down.

It was not until the next day that Cain ventured to run again to the southward to procure at one of the keys the water so much required. At last it was obtained, but with difficulty and much loss of time, from the scantiness of the supply, and they again made sail for the Caicos. But they were so much impeded by contrary winds and contrary currents that it was not until three weeks after they had been chased from Porto Rico that they made out the low land of their former rendezvous.

We must now return to Edward Templemore in the *Enterprise*, whom we left off the coast of South America in search of the *Avenger*, which had so strangely slipped through their fingers. Edward had examined the whole coast, ran through the passage and round Trinidad, and then started off to the Leeward Isles in his pursuit. He had spoken every vessel he met with without gaining any information, and had at last arrived off Porto Rico.

This was no time to think of Clara; but, as it was not out of his way, he had run down the island, and as it was just before dark when he arrived off that part of the coast where the governor resided, he had hove to for a little while, and had examined the windows: but the signal of recognition was not made, and after waiting till dark he again made sail, mad with disappointment, and fearing that all had been discovered by the governor; whereas the fact was, that he had only arrived two days after the forcible abduction of Clara. Once more he directed his attention to the discovery of the pirate, and after a fortnight's examination of the inlets and bays of the Island of St. Domingo without success, his provisions and water being nearly expended, he returned, in no very happy mood, to Port Royal.

In the mean time the disappearance of Clara had created the greatest confusion in Porto Rico, and upon the examination of her attendant, who was confronted by the friar and the duenna, the amour of her mistress was confessed. The appearance of the *Avenger* off the coast on that evening confirmed their ideas that the Donna Clara had been carried off by the English lieutenant, and Don Alfarez immediately despatched a vessel to Jamaica, complaining of the outrage, and demanding the restoration of his daughter.

This vessel arrived at Port Royal a few days before the *Enterprise*, and the admiral was very much astonished. He returned a very polite answer to Don Alfarez, promising an investigation immediately upon the arrival of the schooner, and to send a vessel with the result of the said investigation.

"This is a pretty business," said the admiral to his secretary. "Young madcap, I sent him to look after a pirate and he goes after the governor's daughter! By the lord Harry, Mr Templemore, but you and I shall have an account to settle."

"I can hardly believe it, sir," replied the secretary; "and yet it does look suspicious. But on so short an acquaintance—"

"Who knows that, Mr Hadley? Send for his logs, and let us examine them; he may have been keeping up the acquaintance."

The logs of the *Enterprise* were examined, and there were the fatal words—Porto Rico, Porto Rico, bearing in every division of the compass, and in every separate cruise, nay, even when the schooner was charged with despatches.

"Plain enough," said the admiral. "Confounded young scamp, to embroil me in this way! Not that his marrying the girl is any business of mine; but I will punish him for disobedience of orders, at all events. Try him by a court-martial, by heavens!"

The secretary made no reply: he knew very well that the admiral would do no such thing.

"The *Enterprise* anchored at daylight, sir," reported the secretary as the admiral sat down to breakfast.

"And where's Mr Templemore?"

"He is outside in the veranda. They have told him below of what he has been accused, and he swears it is false. I believe him, sir, for he appears half mad at the intelligence."

"Stop a moment. Have you looked over his log?"

"Yes, sir. It appears that he was off Porto Rico on the 19th; but the Spanish governor's letter says that he was there on the 17th, and again made his appearance on the 19th. I mentioned it to him, and he declares upon his honour that he was only there on the 19th, as stated in his log."

"Well, let him come in and speak for himself."

Edward came in, in a state of great agitation.

"Well, Mr Templemore, you have been playing pretty tricks! What is all this, sir? Where is the girl, sir—the governor's daughter?"

"Where she is, sir, I cannot pretend to say; but I feel convinced that she has been carried off by the pirates."

"Pirates! Poor girl, I pity her!—and—I pity you too, Edward. Come, sit down here, and tell me all that has happened."

Edward knew the admiral's character so well, that he immediately disclosed all that had passed between him and Clara. He then stated how the *Avenger* had escaped him by deceiving the frigate, and the agreement made with Clara to meet for the future on the beach, and his conviction that the pirate schooner, so exactly similar in appearance to the *Enterprise*, must have preceded him at Porto Rico, and have carried off the object of his attachment.

Although Edward might have been severely taken to task, yet the admiral pitied him, and, therefore, said nothing about his visits to Porto Rico. When breakfast was over he ordered the signal to be made for a sloop of war to prepare to weigh, and the Enterprise to be revictualled by the boats of the squadron.

"Now, Edward, you and the *Comus* shall sail in company after this rascally pirate, and I trust you will give me a good account of her, and also of the governor's daughter. Cheer up, my boy! depend upon it they will try for ransom before they do her any injury."

That evening the *Enterprise* and *Comus* sailed on their expedition, and having run by Porto Rico and delivered a letter to the governor, they steered to the northward, and early the next morning made the land of the Caicos, just as the *Avenger* had skirted the reefs and bore up for the narrow entrance.

"There she is!" exclaimed Edward; "there she is, by heavens!" making the signal for the enemy, which was immediately answered by the *Comus*.

XVI
THE CAICOS

T HE SMALL PATCH OF ISLANDS called the Caicos, or Cayques, is situated about two degrees to the northward of Saint Domingo, and is nearly the southernmost of a chain which extends up to the Bahamas. Most of the islands of this chain are uninhabited, but were formerly the resort of piratical vessels,—the reefs and shoals with which they are all surrounded afforded them protection from their larger pursuers, and the passages through this dangerous navigation being known only to the pirates who frequented them, proved an additional security. The largest of the Caicos islands forms a curve, like an opened horseshoe, to the southward, with safe and protected anchorage when once in the bay on the southern side; but, previous to arriving at the anchorage, there are coral reefs, extending upwards of forty miles, through which it is necessary to conduct a vessel. This passage is extremely intricate, but was well known to Hawkhurst, who had hitherto been pilot. Cain was not so well acquainted with it and it required the greatest care in taking in the vessel, as, on the present occasion, Hawkhurst could not be called upon for this service. The islands themselves—for there were several of them—were composed of coral rock; a few cocoa-trees raised their lofty heads where there was sufficient earth for vegetation, and stunted brush-wood rose up between the interstices of the rocks. But the chief peculiarity of the islands, and which rendered them suitable to those who frequented them, was the numerous caves with which the rocks were perforated, some above high-water mark, but the majority with the sea-water flowing in and out of them, in some cases merely rushing in, and at high-water filling deep pools, which were detached from each other when the tide receded, in others with a sufficient depth of water at all times to allow you to pull in with a large boat. It is hardly necessary to observe how convenient the higher and dry caves were as receptacles for articles which were intended to be concealed until an opportunity occurred for disposing of them.

In our last chapter we stated that, just as the *Avenger* had entered the passage through the reefs, the *Comus* and *Enterprise* hove in sight and discovered her: but it will be necessary to explain the positions of the vessels. The *Avenger* had entered the southern channel, with the wind from the southward, and had carefully sounded her way for about four miles, under little or no sail.

The *Enterprise* and *Comus* had been examining Turk's Island, to the eastward of the Caicos, and had passed to the northward of it on the larboard tack, standing in for the northern point of the reef, which joined on to the great Caicos Island. They were, therefore, in a situation to intercept the *Avenger* before she arrived at her anchorage, had it not been for the reefs that barred their passage. The only plan which the English vessels could act upon was to beat to the southward, so as to arrive at the entrance of the passage, when the *Enterprise* would, of course, find sufficient water to follow the *Avenger*; for, as the passage was too narrow to beat through, and the wind was from the southward, the *Avenger* could not possibly escape. She was caught in a trap; and all that she had to trust to was the defence which she might be able to make in her stronghold against the force which could be employed in the attack. The breeze was fresh from the southward, and appeared inclined to increase, when the *Comus* and *Enterprise* made all sail, and worked, in short tacks, outside the reef.

On board the *Avenger*, the enemy and their motions were clearly distinguished, and Cain perceived that he was in an awkward dilemma. That they would be attacked he had no doubt; and although, at any other time, he would almost have rejoiced in such an opportunity of discomfiting his assailants, yet now he thought very differently, and would have sacrificed almost everything to have been able to avoid the rencontre, and be permitted quietly to withdraw himself from his associates, without the spilling of more blood. Francisco was equally annoyed at this unfortunate collision; but no words were exchanged between him and the pirate-captain during the time that they were on deck.

It was about nine o'clock, when having safely passed nearly half through the channel, that Cain ordered the kedge-anchor to be dropped, and sent down the people to their breakfast. Francisco went down into the cabin, and was explaining their situation to Clara, when Cain entered. He threw himself on the locker, and appeared lost in deep and sombre meditation.

"What do you intend to do?" said Francisco.

"I do not know; I will not decide myself, Francisco," replied Cain. "If I were to act upon my own judgment, probably I should allow the schooner to remain where she is. They can only attack in the boats, and, in such a case, I do not fear; whereas, if we run right through, we allow the other schooner to follow us, without defending the passage; and we may be attacked by her in the deep water inside, and overpowered by the number of men the two vessels will be able to bring against us. On the other hand, we certainly may defend the schooner from the shore as well as on board; but we are weak-handed. I shall, however, call up the ship's company and let them decide. God knows, if left to me I would not fight at all."

"Is there no way of escape?" resumed Francisco.

"Yes, we might abandon the schooner; and this night, when they would not expect it, run with the boats through the channel between the great island and the north Cayque: but that I daren't propose, and the men would not listen to it: indeed, I very much doubt if the enemy will allow us the time. I knew this morning, long before we saw those vessels, that my fate would be decided before the sun went down."

"What do you mean?"

"I mean this, Francisco," said Cain; "that your mother, who always has visited me in my dreams whenever anything (dreadful now to think of!) was about to take place, appeared to me last night; and there was sorrow and pity in her sweet face as she mournfully waved her hand, as if to summon me to follow her. Yes, thank God! she no longer looked upon me as for many years she has done."

Francisco made no answer; and Cain again seemed to be lost in meditation.

After a little while Cain rose, and taking a small packet from one of the drawers, put it into the hands of Francisco.

"Preserve that," said the pirate-captain; "should any accident happen to me, it will tell you who was your mother; and it also contains directions for finding treasure which I have buried. I leave everything to you, Francisco. It has been unfairly obtained; but you are not the guilty party, and there are none to claim it. Do not answer me now. You may find friends, whom you will make after I am gone, of the same opinion as I am. I tell you again, be careful of that packet."

"I see little chance of it availing me," replied Francisco. "If I live, shall I not be considered as a pirate?"

"No, no; you can prove the contrary."

"I have my doubts. But God's will be done!"

"Yes, God's will be done!" said Cain, mournfully. "I dared not have said that a month ago." And the pirate-captain went on deck, followed by Francisco.

The crew of the *Avenger* were summoned aft, and called upon to decide as to the measures they considered to be most advisable. They preferred weighing the anchor and running into the bay, where they would be able to defend the schooner, in their opinion, much better than by remaining where they were.

The crew of the pirate-schooner weighed the anchor and continued their precarious course: the breeze had freshened, and the water was in strong ripples, so that they could no longer see the danger beneath her bottom. In the meantime, the sloop of war and *Enterprise* continued to turn to windward outside the reef.

By noon the wind had considerably increased, and the breakers now turned and broke in wild foam over the coral reefs, in every direction. The sail was still more reduced on board the *Avenger*, and her difficulties increased from the rapidity of her motion.

A storm-jib was set, and the others hauled down yet even under this small sail she flew before the wind.

Cain stood at the bowsprit, giving his directions to the helmsman. More than once they had grazed the rocks and were clear again. Spars were towed astern, and every means resorted to, to check her way. They had no guide but the breaking of the wild water on each side of them.

"Why should not Hawkhurst, who knows the passage so well, be made to pilot us?" said the boatswain to those who were near him on the forecastle.

"To be sure! let's have him up!" cried several of the crew; and some of them went down below.

In a minute they reappeared with Hawkhurst, whom they led forward. He did not make any resistance, and the crew demanded that he should pilot the vessel.

"And suppose I will not?" said Hawkhurst, coolly.

"Then you lose your passage, that's all," replied the boatswain. "Is it not so, my lads?" continued he, appealing to the crew.

"Yes; either take us safe in, or—overboard," replied several.

"I do not mind that threat, my lads," replied Hawkhurst; "you have all known me as a good man and true, and it's not likely that I shall desert you now. Well, since your captain there cannot save you, I suppose I must; but," exclaimed he, looking about him, "how's this? We are out of the passage already. Yes—and whether we can get into it again I cannot tell."

"We are not out of the passage," said Cain; "you know we are not."

"Well, then, if the captain knows better than I, he had better take you through," rejoined Hawkhurst.

But the crew thought differently, and insisted that Hawkhurst, who well knew the channel, should take charge. Cain retired aft, as Hawkhurst went out on the bowsprit.

"I will do my best, my lads," said Hawkhurst "but recollect, if we strike in trying to get into the right channel, do not blame me. Starboard a little—starboard yet—steady, so—there's the true passage my lads," cried he, pointing to some smoother water between the breakers; "port a little—steady."

But Hawkhurst, who knew that he was to be put on shore as soon as convenient, had resolved to lose the schooner, even if his own life were forfeited, and he was now running her out of the passage on the rocks. A minute after he had conned her, she struck heavily again and again. The third time she struck, she came broadside to the wind and heeled over: a sharp coral rock found its way through her slight timbers and planking, and the water poured in rapidly.

During this there was a dead silence on the part of the marauders.

"My lads," said Hawkhurst, "I have done my best, and now you may throw me overboard if you please. It was not my fault, but his," continued he, pointing to the captain.

"It is of little consequence whose fault it was, Mr Hawkhurst," replied Cain; "we will settle that point by-and-by; at present we have too much on our hands. Out boats, men! as fast as you can, and let every man provide himself with arms and ammunition. Be cool! the schooner is fixed hard enough, and will not go down; we shall save everything by-and-by."

The pirates obeyed the orders of the captain. The three boats were hoisted out and lowered down. In the first were placed all the wounded men and Clara d'Alfarez, who was assisted up by Francisco. As soon as the men had provided themselves with arms, Francisco, to protect Clara, offered to take charge of her, and the boat shoved off.

The men-of-war had seen the *Avenger* strike on the rocks, and the preparations of the crew to take to their boats. They immediately hove to, hoisted out and manned their own boats, with the hopes of cutting them off before they could gain the island and prepare for a vigorous defence; for, although the vessels could not approach the reefs, there was sufficient water in many places for the boats to pass over them. Shortly after Francisco, in the first boat, had shoved off from the *Avenger*, the boats of the men-of-war were darting through the surf to intercept them. The pirates perceived this, and hastened their arrangements; a second boat soon left her, and into that Hawkhurst leaped as it was shoving off. Cain remained on board, going round the lower decks to ascertain if any of the wounded men were left; he then quitted the schooner in the last boat and followed the others, being about a quarter of a mile astern of the second, in which Hawkhurst had secured his place.

At the time that Cain quitted the schooner, it was difficult to say whether the men-of-war's boats would succeed in intercepting any of the pirate's boats. Both parties exerted themselves to their utmost; and when the first boat, with Francisco and Clara, landed, the headmost of the assailants was not much more than half a mile from them; but, shallow water intervening, there was a delay, which was favourable to the pirate. Hawkhurst landed in his boat as the launch of the *Comus* fired her eighteen-pound carronade. The last boat was yet two hundred yards from the beach, when another shot from the *Comus's* launch, which had been unable hitherto to find a passage through the reef, struck her on the counter, and she filled and went down.

"He is gone!" exclaimed Francisco, who had led Clara to a cave, and stood at the mouth of it to protect her: "they have sunk his boat—no, he is swimming to the shore, and will be here soon, long before the English seamen can land."

This was true. Cain was breasting the water manfully, making for a small cove nearer to where the boat was sunk than the one in which Francisco had landed with Clara and the wounded men,

and divided from the other by a ridge of rocks which separated the
sandy beach, and extended some way into the water before they were
submerged. Francisco could easily distinguish the pirate-captain from
the other men, who also were swimming for the beach; for Cain was
far ahead of them, and as he gained nearer to the shore he was shut
from Francisco's sight by the ridge of rocks. Francisco, anxious for
his safety, climbed up the rocks and was watching. Cain was within
a few yards of the beach when there was the report of a musket;
the pirate-captain was seen to raise his body convulsively half out of
the water—he floundered—the clear blue wave was discoloured—he
sank, and was seen no more.

Francisco darted forward from the rocks, and perceived Hawkhurst,
standing beneath them with the musket in his hand, which he was
recharging.

"Villain!" exclaimed Francisco, "you shall account for this."

Hawkhurst had reprimed his musket and shut the pan.

"Not to you," replied Hawkhurst, levelling his piece, and taking
aim at Francisco.

The ball struck Francisco on the breast; he reeled back from his
position, staggered across the sand, gained the cave, and fell at the
feet of Clara.

"Oh, God!" exclaimed the poor girl, "are *you* hurt? who is there
then, to protect me?"

"I hardly know," replied Francisco, faintly; and, at intervals, "I feel
no wound, I feel stronger;" and Francisco put his hand to his heart.

Clara opened his vest, and found that the packet given to Francisco
by Cain, and which he had deposited in his breast, had been struck
by the bullet, which had done him no injury further than the violent
concussion of the blow—notwithstanding he was faint from the
shock, and his head fell upon Clara's bosom.

But we must relate the proceedings of those who were mixed
up in this exciting scene. Edward Templemore had watched from
his vessel, with an eager and painful curiosity, the motions of the

schooner—her running on the rocks, and the subsequent actions of the intrepid marauders. The long telescope enabled him to perceive distinctly all that passed, and his feelings were increased into a paroxysm of agony when his straining eyes beheld the white and fluttering habiliments of a female for a moment at the gunwale of the stranded vessel—her descent, as it appeared to him, nothing loth, into the boat—the arms held out to receive, and the extension of hers to meet those offered. Could it be Clara? Where was the reluctance, the unavailing attempts at resistance, which should have characterised her situation? Excited by feelings which he dared not analyse, he threw down his glass, and seizing his sword, sprang into the boat, which was ready manned alongside, desiring the others to follow him. For once, and the only time in his existence when approaching the enemy, did he feel his heart sink within him—a cold tremor ran through his whole frame, and as he called to mind the loose morals and desperate habits of the pirates, horrible thoughts entered his imagination. As he neared the shore, he stood up in the stern-sheets of the boat, pale, haggard, and with trembling lips; and the intensity of his feelings would have been intolerable but for a more violent thirst for revenge. He clenched his sword, while the quick throbs of his heart seemed, at every pulsation, to repeat to him his thoughts of blood! blood! blood! He approached the small bay and perceived that there was a female at the mouth of the cave—nearer and nearer, and he was certain that it was his Clara—her name was on his lips when he heard the two shots fired one after another by Hawkhurst—he saw the retreat and fall of Francisco—when, madness to behold! he perceived Clara rush forward, and there lay the young man supported by her, and with his head on her bosom. Could he believe what he saw! could she really be his betrothed! Yes, there she was, supporting the handsome figure of a young man, and that man a pirate—she had even put her hand into his vest, and was now watching over his reviving form. Edward could bear no more: he covered his eyes, and now, maddened with jealousy, in a voice of thunder, he called out:

"Give way, my lads! for your lives, give way!"

The gig was within half-a-dozen strokes of the oar from the beach, and Clara, unconscious of wrong, had just taken the packet of papers from Francisco's vest, when Hawkhurst made his appearance from behind the rocks which separated the two little sandy coves. Francisco had recovered his breath, and, perceiving the approach of Hawkhurst, he sprang upon his feet to recover his musket; but, before he could succeed, Hawkhurst had closed in with him, and a short and dreadful struggle ensued. It would soon have terminated fatally to Francisco, for the superior strength of Hawkhurst had enabled him to bear down the body of his opponent with his knee; and he was fast strangling him by twisting his handkerchief round his throat, while Clara shrieked, and attempted in vain to tear the pirate from him. As the prostrate Francisco was fast blackening into a corse, and the maiden screamed for pity, and became frantic in her efforts for his rescue, the boat dashed high up on the sand; and, with the bound of a maddened tiger, Edward sprang upon Hawkhurst, tearing him down on his back, and severing his wrist with his sword-blade until his hold of Francisco was relaxed, and he wrestled in his own defence.

"Seize him, my lads!" said Edward, pointing with his left hand to Hawkhurst; as with his sword directed to the body of Francisco he bitterly continued, "*This victim is mine!*" But whatever were his intentions, they were frustrated by Clara's recognition, who shrieked out, "My Edward!" sprang into his arms, and was immediately in a state of insensibility.

The seamen who had secured Hawkhurst looked upon the scene with curious astonishment, while Edward waited with mingled feelings of impatience and doubt for Clara's recovery: he wished to be assured by her that he was mistaken, and he turned again and again from her face to that of Francisco, who was fast recovering. During this painful suspense, Hawkhurst was bound and made to sit down.

"Edward! dear Edward!" said Clara, at last, in a faint voice, clinging more closely to him; "and am I then rescued by thee, dearest!"

Edward felt the appeal; but his jealousy had not yet subsided.

"Who is that, Clara?" said he sternly.

"It is Francisco. No pirate, Edward, but my preserver."

"Ha, ha!" laughed Hawkhurst, with a bitter sneer, for he perceived how matters stood.

Edward Templemore turned towards him with an inquiring look.

"Ha, ha!" continued Hawkhurst; "why, he is the captain's son! No pirate, eh? Well, what will women not swear to, to save those they dote upon!"

"If the captain's son," said Edward, "why were you contending?"

"Because just now I shot his scoundrel father."

"Edward!" said Clara, solemnly, "this is no time for explanation, but, as I hope for mercy, what I have said is true; believe not the villain."

"Yes," said Francisco, who was now sitting up, "believe him when he says that he shot the captain, for that is true; but, sir, if you value your own peace of mind, believe nothing to the prejudice of that young lady."

"I hardly know what to believe," muttered Edward Templemore; "but, as the lady says, this is no time for explanation. With your permission, madam," said he to Clara, "my coxswain will see you in safety on board of the schooner, or the other vessel, if you prefer it; my duty will not allow me to accompany you."

Clara darted a reproachful yet fond look on Edward, as, with swimming eyes, she was led by the coxswain to the boat, which had been joined by the launch of the *Comus*, the crew of which were, with their officers, wading to the beach. The men of the gig remained until they had given Hawkhurst and Francisco in charge of the other seamen, and then shoved off with Clara for the schooner. Edward Templemore gave one look at the gig as it conveyed Clara on board, and ordering Hawkhurst and Francisco to be taken to the launch, and a guard to be kept over them, went up, with the remainder of the men, in pursuit of the pirates.

During the scene we have described, the other boats of the men-of-war had landed on the island, and the *Avenger's* crew, deprived of their leaders, and scattered in every direction, were many of them slain or captured. In about two hours it was supposed that the majority of the pirates had been accounted for, and the prisoners being now very numerous, it was decided that the boats should return with them to the *Comus*, the captain of which vessel, as commanding officer, would then issue orders as to their future proceedings.

The captured pirates, when mustered on the deck of the *Comus*, amounted to nearly sixty, out of which number one-half were those who had been sent on shore wounded, and had surrendered without resistance. Of killed there were fifteen; and it was conjectured that as many more had been drowned in the boat when she was sunk by the shot from the carronade of the launch. Although, by the account given by the captured pirates, the majority were secured, yet there was reason to suppose that some were still left on the island concealed in the caves.

As the captain of the *Comus* had orders to return as soon as possible, he decided to sail immediately for Port Royal with the prisoners, leaving the *Enterprise* to secure the remainder, if there were any, and recover anything of value which might be left in the wreck of the *Avenger*, and then to destroy her.

With the usual celerity of the service these orders were obeyed. The pirates, among whom Francisco was included, were secured, the boats hoisted up, and in half an hour the *Comus* displayed her ensign, and made all sail on a wind, leaving Edward Templemore with the *Enterprise*, at the back of the reef, to perform the duties entailed upon him; and Clara, who was on board of the schooner, to remove the suspicion and jealousy which had arisen in the bosom of her lover.

XVII
THE TRIAL

IN A WEEK, THE *COMUS* arrived at Port Royal, and the captain went up to the Penn to inform the admiral of the successful result of the expedition.

"Thank God," said the admiral, "we have caught these villains at last! A little hanging will do them no harm. The captain, you say, was drowned?"

"So it is reported, sir," replied Captain Manly; "he was in the last boat which left the schooner, and she was sunk by a shot from the launch."

"I am sorry for that; the death was too good for him. However, we must make an example of the rest; they must be tried by the Admiralty Court, which has the jurisdiction of the high seas. Send them on shore, Manly, and we wash our hands of them."

"Very good, sir: but there are still some left on the island, we have reason to believe; and the *Enterprise* is in search of them."

"By-the-by, did Templemore find his lady?"

"Oh yes, sir; and—all's right, I believe: but I had very little to say to him on the subject."

"Humph!" replied the admiral. "I am glad to hear it. Well, send them on shore, Manly, to the proper authorities. If any more be found, they must be hung afterwards when Templemore brings them in. I am more pleased at having secured these scoundrels than if we had taken a French frigate."

About three weeks after this conversation, the secretary reported to the admiral that the *Enterprise* had made her number outside; but that she was becalmed, and would not probably be in until the evening.

"That's a pity," replied the admiral; "for the pirates are to be tried this morning. He may have more of them on board."

"Very true, sir; but the trial will hardly be over to-day: the judge will not be in court till one o'clock at the soonest."

"It's of little consequence, certainly; as it is, there are so many that they must be hanged by divisions. However, as he is within signal distance, let them telegraph 'Pirates now on trial.' He can pull on shore in his gig, if he pleases."

It was about noon on the same day that the pirates, and among them Francisco, escorted by a strong guard, were conducted to the Court House, and placed at the bar. The Court House was crowded to excess, for the interest excited was intense.

Many of them who had been wounded in the attack upon the property of Don Cumanos, and afterwards captured, had died in their confinement. Still forty-five were placed at the bar; and their picturesque costume, their bearded faces, and the atrocities which they had committed, created in those present a sensation of anxiety mingled with horror and indignation.

Two of the youngest amongst them had been permitted to turn king's evidence. They had been on board of the *Avenger* but a few months; still their testimony as to the murder of the crews of three West India ships, and the attack upon the property of Don Cumanos, was quite sufficient to condemn the remainder.

Much time was necessarily expended in going through the forms of the court; in the pirates answering to their various names; and, lastly, in taking down the detailed evidence of the above men. It was late when the evidence was read over to the pirates, and they were asked if they had anything to offer in their defence. The question was repeated by the judge; when Hawkhurst was the first to speak. To save himself he could scarcely hope; his only object was to prevent Francisco pleading his cause successfully, and escaping the same disgraceful death.

Hawkhurst declared that he had been some time on board the Avenger, but that he had been taken out of a vessel and forced to serve against his will, as could be proved by the captain's son, who stood there (pointing to Francisco), who had been in the schooner since her first fitting out:—that he had always opposed the captain, who would not part with him, because he was the only one on board who was competent to navigate the schooner: that he had intended to rise against him, and take the vessel, having often stimulated the crew so to do; and that, as the other men, as well as the captain's son, could prove, if they chose, he actually was in confinement for that attempt when the schooner was entering the passage to the Caicos; and that he was only released because he was acquainted with the passage, and threatened to be thrown overboard if he did not take her in; that, at every risk, he had run her on the rocks; and aware that the captain would murder him, he had shot Cain as he was swimming to the shore, as the captain's son could prove; for he had taxed him with it, and he was actually struggling with him for life, when the officers and boat's crew separated them, and made them both prisoners: that he hardly expected that Francisco, the captain's son, would tell the truth to save him, as he was his bitter enemy, and in the business at the Magdalen river, which had been long planned (for Francisco had been sent on shore under the pretence of being wrecked, but, in fact, to ascertain where the booty was, and to assist the pirates in their attack), Francisco had taken the opportunity of putting a bullet through his shoulder, which was well known to the other pirates, and Francisco could not venture to deny. He trusted that the court would order the torture to Francisco, and then he would probably speak the truth; at all events, let him speak now.

When Hawkhurst had ceased to address the court, there was an anxious pause for some minutes. The day was fast declining, and most parts of the spacious Court House were already deeply immersed in gloom; while the light, sober, solemn, and almost sad, gleamed upon the savage and reckless countenances of the prisoners at the bar. The sun had sunk down behind a mass of heavy yet gorgeous clouds, fringing their edges with molten gold. Hawkhurst had spoken fluently and energetically, and there was an appearance of almost honesty in his coarse and deep-toned voice. Even the occasional oaths with which his speech was garnished, but which we have omitted, seemed to be pronounced more in sincerity than in blasphemy, and gave a more forcible impression to his narrative.

We have said, that when he concluded there was a profound silence; and amid the fast-falling shadows of the evening, those who were present began to feel, for the first time, the awful importance of the drama before them, the number of lives which were trembling upon the verge of existence, depending upon the single word of "Guilty." This painful silence, this harrowing suspense, was at last broken by a restrained sob from a female; but owing to the obscurity involving the body of the court, her person could not be distinguished. The wail of a woman so unexpected—for who could there be of that sex interested in the fate of these desperate men?—touched the heart of its auditors, and appeared to sow the first seeds of compassionate and humane feeling among those who had hitherto expressed and felt nothing but indignation towards the prisoners.

The judge upon the bench, the counsel at the bar, and the jury impannelled in their box, felt the force of the appeal; and it softened down the evil impression created by the address of Hawkhurst against the youthful Francisco. The eyes of all were now directed towards the one doubly accused—accused not only by the public prosecutor, but even by his associate in crime,—and the survey was favourable. They acknowledged that he was one whose personal qualities might indeed challenge the love of woman in his pride, and her lament in his disgrace; and as their regard was directed towards him, the sun, which had been obscured, now pierced through a break in the mass of clouds, and threw a portion of his glorious beams from a window opposite upon him, and him alone, while all the other prisoners who surrounded him were buried more or less in deep shadow. It was at once evident that his associates were bold yet commonplace villains—men who owed their courage, their only virtue perhaps, to their habits, to their physical organisation, or the influence of those around them. They were mere human butchers, with the only adjunct that, now that the trade was to be exercised upon themselves, they could bear it with sullen apathy—a feeling how far removed from true fortitude! Even Hawkhurst, though more commanding than the rest, with all his daring mien and scowl of defiance, looked nothing more than a distinguished ruffian. With the exception of Francisco, the prisoners had wholly neglected their personal appearance; and in them the squalid and sordid look of the mendicant seemed allied with the ferocity of the murderer.

Francisco was not only an exception, but formed a beautiful contrast to the others; and as the evening beams lighted up his figure, he stood at the bar, if not with all the splendour of a hero of romance, certainly a most picturesque and interesting personage, elegantly if not richly attired.

The low sobs at intervals repeated, as if impossible to be checked, seemed to rouse and call him to a sense of the important part which he was called upon to act in the tragedy there and then performing. His face was pale, yet composed; his mien at once proud and sorrowful: his eye was bright, yet his glance was not upon those in court, but far away, fixed, like an eagle's, upon the gorgeous beams of the setting sun, which glowed upon him through the window that was in front of him.

At last the voice of Francisco was heard, and all in that wide court started at the sound—deep, full, and melodious as the evening chimes. The ears of those present had, in the profound silence, but just recovered from the harsh, deep-toned, and barbarous idiom of Hawkhurst's address, when the clear, silvery, yet manly voice of Francisco, riveted their attention. The jury stretched forth their heads, the counsel and all in court turned anxiously round towards the prisoner, even the judge held up his forefinger to intimate his wish for perfect silence.

"My lord and gentlemen," commenced Francisco, "when I first found myself in this degrading situation, I had not thought to have spoken or to have uttered one word in my defence. He that has just now accused me has recommended the torture to be applied; he has already had his wish, for what torture can be more agonising than to find myself where I now am? So tortured, indeed, have I been through a short yet wretched life, that I have often felt that anything short of self-destruction which would release me would be a blessing; but within these few minutes I have been made to acknowledge that I have still feelings in unison with my fellow-creatures; that I am not yet fit for death, and all too young, too unprepared to die: for who would not reluctantly leave this world while there is such a beauteous sky to love and look upon, or while there is one female breast who holds him innocent, and has evinced her pity for his misfortunes? Yes, my lord! mercy, and pity, and compassion, have not yet fled from earth; and therefore do I feel I am too young to die. God forgive me! but I thought they had—for never have they been shown in those with whom by fate I have been connected; and it has been from this conviction that I have so often longed for death. And now may that righteous God who judges us not here, but hereafter, enable me to prove that I do not deserve an ignominious punishment from my fellow-sinners—men!

"My lord, I know not the subtleties of the laws, nor the intricacy of pleadings. First, let me assert that I have never robbed; but I have restored unto the plundered: I have never murdered; but I have stood between the assassin's knife and his victim. For this have I been hated and reviled by my associates, and for this, is my life now threatened by those laws against which I never had offended. The man who last addressed you has told you that I am the pirate-captain's son; it is the assertion of the only irreclaimable and utterly remorseless villain among those who now stand before you to be judged—the assertion of one whose glory, whose joy, whose solace has been blood-shedding.

"My lord, I had it from the mouth of the captain himself, previous to his murder by that man, that I was not his son. His son! thank God, not so. Connected with him and in his power I was, most certainly and most incomprehensibly. Before he died, he delivered me a packet that would have told me who I am; but I have lost it, and deeply have I felt the loss. One only fact I gained from him whom they would call my father, which is, that with his own hand he slew—yes, basely slew—my mother."

The address of Francisco was here interrupted by a low deep groan of anguish, which startled the whole audience. It was now quite dark, and the judge ordered the court to be lighted previous to the defence being continued. The impatience and anxiety of those present were shown in low murmurs of communication until the lights were brought in. The word "Silence!" from the judge produced an immediate obedience, and the prisoner was ordered to proceed.

Francisco then continued his address, commencing with the remembrances of his earliest childhood. As he warmed with his subject, he became more eloquent; his action became energetical without violence; and the pallid and modest youth gradually grew into the impassioned and inspired orator. He recapitulated rapidly, yet distinctly and with terrible force, all the startling events in his fearful life. There was truth in the tones of his voice, there was conviction in his animated countenance, there was innocence in his open and expressive brow.

All who heard believed; and scarcely had he concluded his address, when the jury appeared impatient to rise and give their verdict in his favour. But the judge stood up, and, addressing the jury, told them that it was his most painful duty to remind them that as yet they had heard but assertion, beautiful and almost convincing assertion truly; but still it was not proof.

"Alas!" observed Francisco, "what evidence can I bring forward, except the evidence of those around me at the bar, which will not be admitted? Can I recall the dead from the grave? Can I expect those who have been murdered to rise again to assert my innocence? Can I expect that Don Cumanos will appear from distant leagues to give evidence on my behalf? Alas he knows not how I am situated, or he would have flown to my succour. No, no; not even can I expect that the sweet Spanish maiden, the last to whom I offered my protection, will appear in such a place as this to meet the bold gaze of hundreds!"

"She is here!" replied a manly voice; and a passage was made through the crowd; and Clara, supported by Edward Templemore, dressed in his uniform, was ushered into the box for the witnesses. The appearance of the fair girl, who looked round her with alarm, created a great sensation. As soon as she was sufficiently composed, she was sworn, and gave her evidence as to Francisco's behaviour during the time that she was a prisoner on board of the *Avenger*. She produced the packet which had saved the life of Francisco, and substantiated a great part of his defence. She extolled his kindness and his generosity; and when she had concluded, every one asked of himself, "Can this young man be a pirate and a murderer?" The reply was, "It is impossible."

"My lord," said Edward Templemore, "I request permission to ask the prisoner a question. When I was on board of the wreck of the *Avenger*, I found this book floating in the cabin. I wish to ask the prisoner, whether, as that young lady has informed me, it is his?" And Edward Templemore produced the Bible.

"It is mine," replied Francisco.

"May I ask you by what means it came into your possession?"

"It is the only relic left of one who is now no more. It was the consolation of my murdered mother; it has since been mine. Give it to me, sir; I may probably need its support now more than ever."

"Was your mother murdered, say you?" cried Edward Templemore, with much agitation.

"I have already said so; and I now repeat it."

The judge again rose, and recapitulated the evidence to the jury. Evidently friendly to Francisco he was obliged to point out to them, that although the evidence of the young lady had produced much which might be offered in extenuation, and induce him to submit it to His Majesty, in hopes of his gracious pardon after condemnation, yet, that many acts in which the prisoner had been involved had endangered his life and no testimony had been brought forward to prove that he had not, at one time, acted with the pirates, although he might since have repented. They would of course, remember that the evidence of the mate, Hawkhurst, was not of any value, and must dismiss any impression which it might have made against Francisco. At the same time he had the unpleasant duty to point out, that the evidence of the Spanish lady was so far prejudicial, that it pointed out the good terms subsisting between the young man and the pirate-captain. Much as he was interested in his fate, he must reluctantly remind the jury, that the evidence on the whole was not sufficient to clear the prisoner; and he considered it their duty to return a verdict of *guilty against all the prisoners at the bar.*

"My lord," said Edward Templemore, a few seconds after the judge had resumed his seat; "may not the contents of this packet, the seal of which I have not ventured to break, afford some evidence in favour of the prisoner? Have you any objection that it should be opened previous to the jury delivering their verdict?"

"None," replied the judge: "but what are its supposed contents?"

"The contents, my lord," replied Francisco, "are in the writing of the pirate-captain. He delivered that packet into my hands previous to our quitting the schooner, stating that it would inform me who were my parents. My lord, in my present situation I claim that packet, and refuse that its contents should be read in court. If I am to die an ignominious death, at least those who are connected with me shall not have to blush at my disgrace, for the secret of my parentage shall die with me."

"Nay—nay; be ruled by me," replied Edward Templemore, with much emotion. "In the narrative, the handwriting of which can be proved by the king's evidence, there may be acknowledgment of all you have stated, and it will be received as evidence; will it not, my lord?"

"If the handwriting is proved, I should think it may," replied the judge, "particularly as the lady was present when the packet was delivered, and heard the captain's assertion. Will you allow it to be offered as evidence, young man?"

"No, my lord," replied Francisco; "unless I have permission first to peruse it myself. I will not have its contents divulged, unless I am sure of an honourable acquittal. The jury must deliver their verdict."

The jury turned round to consult, during which Edward Templemore walked to Francisco, accompanied by Clara, to entreat him to allow the packet to be opened; but Francisco was firm against both their entreaties. At last the foreman of the jury rose to deliver the verdict. A solemn and awful silence prevailed throughout the court; the suspense was painful to a degree.

"My lord," said the foreman of the jury, "our verdict is—"

"Stop, sir!" said Edward Templemore as he clasped one arm round the astonished Francisco, and extended the other towards the foreman. "Stop, sir! harm him not! for he is my brother!"

"And my preserver!" cried Clara, kneeling on the other side of Francisco, and holding up her hands in supplication.

The announcement was electrical; the foreman dropped into his seat; the judge and whole court were in mute astonishment. The dead silence was followed by confusion, to which, after a time, the judge in vain attempted to put a stop.

Edward Templemore, Clara, and Francisco, continued to form the same group; and never was there one more beautiful. And now that they were together, every one in court perceived the strong resemblance between the two young men.

Francisco's complexion was darker than Edward's from his constant exposure, from infancy, to a tropical sun; but the features of the two were the same.

It was some time before the judge could obtain silence in the court; and when it had been obtained, he was himself puzzled how to proceed.

Edward and Francisco, who had exchanged a few words, were now standing side by side.

"My lord," said Edward Templemore, "the prisoner consents that the packet shall be opened."

"I do," said Francisco, mournfully; "although I have but little hope from its contents. Alas! now that I have everything to live for—not that I cling to life, I feel as if every chance was gone! The days of miracles have passed; and nothing but the miracle of the reappearance of the pirate-captain from the grave can prove my innocence."

"He reappears from the grave to prove thine innocence, Francisco!" said a deep, hollow voice, which startled the whole court, and most of all Hawkhurst and the prisoners at the bar. Still more did fear and horror distort their countenances when into the witness-box stalked the giant form of Cain.

But it was no longer the figure which we have described in the commencement of this narrative; his beard had been removed, and he was pale, wan, and emaciated. His sunken eyes, his hollow cheek, and a short cough, which interrupted his speech, proved that his days were nearly at a close.

"My lord," said Cain, addressing the judge, "I am the pirate Cain, and was the captain of the Avenger! Still am I free! I come here voluntarily, that I may attest the innocence of that young man! As yet, my hand has not known the manacle, nor my feet the gyves! I am not a prisoner, nor included in the indictment, and at present my evidence is good. None know me in this court, except those whose testimony, as prisoners, is unavailing; and therefore, to save that boy, and only to save him, I demand that I may be sworn."

The oath was administered, with more than usual solemnity.

"My lord, and gentlemen of the jury, I have been in court since the commencement of the trial, and I declare that every word which Francisco has uttered in his own defence is true. He is totally innocent of any act of piracy or murder; the packet would, indeed, have proved as much: but in that packet there are secrets which I wished to remain unknown to all but Francisco; and, rather than it should be opened, I have come forward myself. How that young officer discovered that Francisco is his brother I know not; but if he also is the son of Cecilia Templemore, it is true. But the packet will explain all.

"And now, my lords, that my evidence is received, I am content: I have done one good deed before I die, and I surrender myself, as a pirate and a foul murderer, to justice. True, my life is nearly closed— thanks to that villain there; but I prefer that I should meet that death I merit, as an expiation of my many deeds of guilt."

Cain then turned to Hawkhurst, who was close to him, but the mate appeared to be in a state of stupor; he had not recovered from his first terror, and still imagined the appearance of Cain to be supernatural.

"Villain!" exclaimed Cain, putting his mouth close to Hawkhurst's ear; "doubly d—d villain! thou'lt die like a dog, and unrevenged! The boy is safe, and I'm alive!"

"Art thou really living?" said Hawkhurst, recovering from his fear.

"Yes, living—yes, flesh and blood; feel, wretch! feel this arm, and be convinced: thou hast felt the power of it before now," continued Cain, sarcastically. "And now, my lord, I have done. Francisco, fare thee well! I loved thee, and have proved my love. Hate not, then, my memory, and forgive me—yes, forgive me when I'm no more," said Cain, who then turned his eyes to the ceiling of the court-house.—"Yes, there she is, Francisco!—there she is! and see," cried he, extending both arms above his head, "she smiles upon—yes, Francisco, your sainted mother smiles and pardons—"

The sentence was not finished; for Hawkhurst, when Cain's arms were upheld, perceived his knife in his girdle, and, with the rapidity of thought, he drew it out, and passed it through the body of the pirate-captain.

Cain fell heavily on the floor while the court was again in confusion. Hawkhurst was secured, and Cain raised from the ground.

"I thank thee, Hawkhurst!" said Cain, in an expiring voice; "another murder thou hast to answer for: and you have saved me from the disgrace, not of the gallows, but of the gallows in thy company. Francisco, boy, farewell!" and Cain groaned deeply, and expired.

Thus perished the renowned pirate-captain, who in his life had shed so much blood, and whose death produced another murder. "Blood for blood!"

The body was removed; and it now remained but for the jury to give their verdict. All the prisoners were found guilty, with the exception of Francisco, who left the dock accompanied by his newly-found brother, and the congratulations of every individual who could gain access to him.

XVIII
CONCLUSION

O<small>UR FIRST OBJECT WILL BE</small> to explain to the reader by what means Edward Templemore was induced to surmise that in Francisco, whom he considered as a rival, he had found a brother; and also to account for the reappearance of the pirate Cain.

In pursuance of his orders, Edward Templemore had proceeded on board of the wreck of the *Avenger*, and while his men were employed in collecting articles of great value which were on board of her, he had descended into the cabin, which was partly under water. He had picked up a book floating near the lockers, and on examination found it to be a Bible.

Surprised at seeing such a book on board of a pirate, he had taken it with him when he returned to the *Enterprise*, and had shown it to Clara, who immediately recognised it as the property of Francisco. The book was saturated with the salt water, and as Edward mechanically turned over the pages, he referred to the title-page to see if there was any name upon it. There was not: but he observed that the blank or fly-leaf next to the binding had been pasted down, and that there was writing on the other side. In its present state it was easily detached from the cover; and then, to his astonishment, he read the name of

Cecilia Templemore—his own mother. He knew well the history; how he had been saved, and his mother and brother supposed to be lost; and it may readily be imagined how great was his anxiety to ascertain by what means her Bible had come into the possession of Francisco. He dared not think Francisco was his brother—that he was so closely connected with one he still supposed to be a pirate: but the circumstance was possible; and although he had intended to have remained a few days longer, he now listened to the entreaties of Clara, whose peculiar position on board was only to be justified by the peculiar position from which she had been rescued, and returning that evening to the wreck he set fire to her, and then made all sail for Port Royal.

Fortunately he arrived, as we have stated, on the day of the trial; and as soon as the signal was made by the admiral he immediately manned his gig, and, taking Clara with him, in case her evidence might be of use, arrived at the Court House when the trial was about half over.

In our last chapter but one, we stated that Cain had been wounded by Hawkhurst, when he was swimming on shore, and had sunk; the ball had entered his chest, and passed through his lungs. The contest between Hawkhurst and Francisco, and their capture by Edward, had taken place on the other side of the ridge of rocks in the adjacent cove, and although Francisco had seen Cain disappear, and concluded that he was dead, it was not so; he had again risen above the water, and dropping his feet and finding bottom, he contrived to crawl out, and wade into a cave adjacent, where he lay down to die.

But in this cave there was one of the *Avenger's* boats, two of the pirates mortally wounded, and the four Kroumen, who had concealed themselves there with the intention of taking no part in the conflict, and, as soon as it became dark, of making their escape in the boat, which they had hauled up dry into the cave.

Cain staggered in, recovered the dry land; and fell. Pompey, the Krouman, perceiving his condition, went to his assistance and bound up his wound, and the stanching of the blood soon revived the pirate-captain. The other pirates died unaided.

Although the island was searched in every direction, this cave, from the water flowing into it, escaped the vigilance of the British seamen; and when they re-embarked, with the majority of the pirates captured, Cain and the Kroumen were undiscovered.

As soon as it was dark, Cain informed them of his intentions; and although the Kroumen would probably have left him to his fate, yet, as they required his services to know how to steer to some other island, he was assisted into the stern-sheets, and the boat was backed out of the cave.

By the direction of Cain they passed through the passage between the great island and the northern Caique, and before daylight were far away from any chance of capture.

Cain had now to a certain degree recovered, and knowing that they were in the channel of the small traders, he pointed out to the Kroumen that, if supposed to be pirates, they would inevitably be punished, although not guilty, and that they must pass off as the crew of a small coasting-vessel which had been wrecked. He then, with the assistance of Pompey, cut off his beard as close as he could, and arranged his dress in a more European style. They had neither water nor provisions, and were exposed to a vertical sun. Fortunately for them, and still more fortunately for Francisco, on the second day they were picked up by an American brig bound to Antigua.

Cain narrated his fictitious disasters, but said nothing about his wound, the neglect of which would certainly have occasioned his death a very few days after he appeared at the trial, had he not fallen by the malignity of Hawkhurst.

Anxious to find his way to Port Royal, for he was indifferent as to his own life, and only wished to save Francisco, he was overjoyed to meet a small schooner trading between the islands, bound to Port Royal. In that vessel he obtained a passage for himself and the Kroumen, and had arrived three days previous to the trial, and during

that time had remained concealed until the day that the Admiralty Court assembled.

It may be as well here to remark, that Cain's reason for not wishing the packet to be opened was, that among the other papers relative to Francisco were directions for the recovery of the treasure which he had concealed, and which, of course, he wished to be communicated to Francisco alone.

We will leave the reader to imagine what passed between Francisco and Edward after the discovery of their kindred, and proceed to state the contents of the packet, which the twin-brothers now opened in the presence of Clara alone.

We must, however, condense the matter, which was very voluminous. It stated that Cain, whose real name was Charles Osborne, had sailed in a fine schooner from Bilboa, for the coast of Africa, to procure a cargo of slaves; and had been out about twenty-four hours when the crew perceived a boat apparently with no one in her, about a mile ahead of them. The water was then smooth, and the vessel had but little way. As soon as they came up with the boat, they lowered down their skiff to examine her.

The men sent in the skiff soon returned, towing the boat alongside. Lying at the bottom of the boat were found several men almost dead, and reduced to skeletons; and in the stern-sheets a negro woman, with a child at her breast, and a white female in the last state of exhaustion.

Osborne was then a gay and unprincipled man, but not a hardened villain and murderer, as he afterwards became; he had compassion and feeling—they were all taken on board the schooner: some recovered, others were too much exhausted. Among those restored was Cecilia Templemore and the infant, who at first had been considered quite dead; but the negro woman, exhausted by the demands of her nursling and her privations, expired as she was being removed from the boat. A goat, that fortunately was on board, proved a substitute for the negress; and before Osborne had arrived off the coast, the child had recovered its health and vigour, and the mother her extreme beauty.

We must now pass over a considerable portion of the narrative. Osborne was impetuous in his passions, and Cecilia Templemore became his victim. He had, indeed, afterwards quieted her qualms of conscience by a pretended marriage, when he arrived at the Brazils with his cargo of human flesh. But that was little alleviation of her sufferings; she who had been indulged in every luxury, who had been educated with the greatest care, was now lost for ever, an outcast from the society to which she could never hope to return, and associating with those she both dreaded and despised. She passed her days and her nights in tears; and had soon more cause for sorrow from the brutal treatment she received from Osborne, who had been her destroyer. Her child was her only solace; but for him, and the fear of leaving him to the demoralising influence of those about him, she would have laid down and died: but she lived for him—for him attempted to recall Osborne from his career of increasing guilt—bore meekly with reproaches and with blows. At last Osborne changed his nefarious life for one of deeper guilt: he became a pirate, and still carried with him Cecilia and her child.

This was the climax of her misery: she now wasted from day to day, and grief would soon have terminated her existence, had it not been hastened by the cruelty of Cain, who, upon an expostulation on her part, followed up with a denunciation of the consequences of his guilty career, struck her with such violence that she sank under the blow. She expired with a prayer that her child might be rescued from a life of guilt; and when the then repentant Cain promised what he never did perform, she blessed him, too, before she died.

Such was the substance of the narrative, as far as it related to the unfortunate mother of these two young men, who, when they had concluded, sat hand-in-hand in mournful silence. This, however, was soon broken by the innumerable questions asked by Edward of his brother, as to what he could remember of their ill-fated parent, which were followed up by the history of Francisco's eventful life.

"And the treasure, Edward," said Francisco; "I cannot take possession of it."

"No, nor shall you either," replied Edward; "it belongs to the captors, and must be shared as prize-money. You will never touch one penny of it, but I shall, I trust, pocket a very fair proportion of it! However, keep this paper, as it is addressed to you."

The admiral had been made acquainted with all the particulars of the eventful trial, and had sent a message to Edward, requesting that, as soon as he and his brother could make it convenient, he would be happy to see them at the Penn, as well as the daughter of the Spanish governor, whom he must consider as being under his protection during the time that she remained at Port Royal. This offer was gladly accepted by Clara; and on the second day after the trial they proceeded up to the Penn. Clara and Francisco were introduced, and apartments and suitable attendance provided for the former.

"Templemore," said the admiral, "I'm afraid I must send you away to Porto Rico, to assure the governor of his daughter's safety."

"I would rather you would send some one else, sir, and I'll assure her happiness in the meantime."

"What! by marrying her? Humph! you've a good opinion of yourself! Wait till you're a captain, sir."

"I hope I shall not have to wait long, sir," replied Edward, demurely.

"By-the-bye," said the admiral, "did you not say you have notice of treasure concealed in those islands?"

"My brother has: I have not."

"We must send for it. I think we must send you, Edward. Mr Francisco, you must go with him."

"With pleasure, sir," replied Francisco, laughing; "but I think I'd rather wait till Edward is a captain. His wife and his fortune ought to come together. I think I shall not deliver up my papers until the day of his marriage!"

"Upon my word," said Captain Manly, "I wish, Templemore, you had your commission, for there seems so much depending on it—

the young lady's happiness, my share of the prize-money, and the admiral's eighth. Really, admiral, it becomes a common cause; and I'm sure he deserves it!"

"So do I, Manly," replied the admiral; "and to prove that I have thought so here comes Mr Hadley with it in his hand; it only wants one little thing to complete it—"

"Which is your signature, admiral, I presume," replied Captain Manly, taking a pen full of ink, and presenting it to his senior officer.

"Exactly," replied the admiral, scribbling at the bottom of the paper; "and now—it does not want that. Captain Templemore, I wish you joy!"

Edward made a very low obeisance, as his flushed countenance indicated his satisfaction.

"I cannot give commissions, admiral," said Francisco, presenting a paper in return; "but I can give information—and you will find it not unimportant—for the treasure appears of great value."

"God bless my soul! Manly, you must start at daylight!" exclaimed the admiral; "why, there is enough to load your sloop! There!—read it!—and then I will write your orders, and enclose a copy of it, for fear of accident."

"That was to have been my fortune," said Francisco, with a grave smile; "but I would not touch it."

"Very right, boy!—a fine principle! But we are not quite so particular," said the admiral. "Now, where's the young lady? Let her know that dinner's on the table."

A fortnight after this conversation, Captain Manly returned with the treasure; and the *Enterprise*, commanded by another officer, returned from Porto Rico, with a letter from the governor in reply to one from the admiral, in which the rescue of his daughter by Edward had been communicated. The letter was full of thanks to the admiral, and compliments to Edward; and, what was of more importance, it sanctioned the union of the young officer with his daughter, with a dozen boxes of gold doubloons.

About six weeks after the above-mentioned important conversation, Mr Witherington, who had been reading a voluminous packet of letters in his breakfast-room in Finsbury Square, pulled his bell so violently that old Jonathan thought his master must be out of his senses. This, however, did not induce him to accelerate his solemn and measured pace; and he made his appearance at the door, as usual, without speaking.

"Why don't that fellow answer the bell?" cried Mr Witherington.

"I am here, sir," said Jonathan, solemnly.

"Well, so you are! but, confound you! you come like the ghost of a butler!—But who do you think is coming here, Jonathan?"

"I cannot tell, sir."

"But I can!—you solemn old—! Edward's coming here!—coming home directly?"

"Is he to sleep in his old room, sir?" replied the imperturbable butler.

"No! the best bedroom! Why, Jonathan, he is married—he is made a captain—Captain Templemore!"

"Yes—sir."

"And he has found his brother, Jonathan; his twin-brother!"

"Yes—sir."

"His brother Francis—that was supposed to be lost! But it's a long story, Jonathan—and a very wonderful one—! his poor mother has long been dead!"

"*In caelo quies!*" said Jonathan, casting up his eyes.

"But his brother has turned up again."

"*Resurgam!*" said the butler.

"They will be here in ten days—so let everything be in readiness, Jonathan. God bless my soul!" continued the old gentleman, "I hardly know what I'm about. It's a Spanish girl, Jonathan!"

"What is, sir?"

"What is, sir!—who, Captain Templemore's wife; and he was tried as a pirate!"

"Who, sir?"

"Who sir! why, Francis, his brother! Jonathan, you're a stupid old fellow!"

"Have you any further commands, sir?"

"No—no!—there—that'll do—go away."

And in three weeks after this conversation, Captain and Mrs Templemore, and his brother Frank, were established in the house, to the great delight of Mr Witherington; for he had long been tired of solitude and old Jonathan.

The twin-brothers were a comfort to him in his old age: they closed his eyes in peace—they divided his blessing and his large fortune and thus ends our history of THE PIRATE!

THE THREE CUTTERS

I
CUTTER THE FIRST

READER, HAVE YOU EVER BEEN at Plymouth? If you have, your eye must have dwelt with ecstasy upon the beautiful property of the Earl of Mount Edgcumbe: if you have not been at Plymouth, the sooner that you go there, the better. At Mount Edgcumbe you will behold the finest timber in existence, towering up to the summits of the hills, and feathering down to the shingle on the beach. And from this lovely spot you will witness one of the most splendid panoramas in the world. You will see—I hardly know what you will not see—you will see Ram Head, and Cawsand Bay; and then you will see the Breakwater, and Drake's Island, and the Devil's Bridge below you; and the town of Plymouth and its fortifications, and the Hoe; and then you will come to the Devil's Point, round which the tide runs devilish strong; and then you will see the New Victualling Office,—about which Sir James Gordon used to stump all day, and take a pinch of snuff from every man who carried a box, which all were delighted to give, and he was delighted to receive, proving how much pleasure may be communicated merely by a pinch of snuff—and then you will see Mount Wise and Mutton Cove; the town of Devonport, with its magnificent dockyard and arsenals, North Corner, and the way which leads to Saltash. And you will see ships building and ships in ordinary; and ships repairing and ships fitting; and hulks and convict ships, and the guardship; ships ready to sail and ships under sail; besides lighters, men-of-war's boats, dockyard-boats, bumboats, and shore-boats. In short, there is a great deal to see at Plymouth besides the sea itself: but what I particularly wish now, is, that you will stand at the battery of Mount Edgecumbe and look into Barn Pool below you, and there you will see, lying at single anchor, a cutter; and you may also see, by her pendant and ensign, that she is a yacht.

Of all the amusements entered into by the nobility and gentry of our island there is not one so manly, so exciting, so patriotic, or so national, as yacht-sailing. It is peculiar to England, not only from our insular position and our fine harbours, but because it requires a certain degree of energy and a certain amount of income rarely to be found elsewhere. It has been wisely fostered by our sovereigns, who have felt that the security of the kingdom is increased by every man being more or less a sailor, or connected with the nautical profession. It is an amusement of the greatest importance to the country; as it has much improved our ship-building and our ship-fitting, while it affords employment to our seamen and shipwrights. But if I were to say all that I could say in praise of yachts, I should never advance with my narrative. I shall therefore drink a bumper to the health of Admiral Lord Yarborough and the Yacht Club, and proceed.

You observe that this yacht is cutter-rigged, and that she sits gracefully on the smooth water. She is just heaving up her anchor; her foresail is loose, all ready to cast her—in a few minutes she will be under weigh. You see that there are some ladies sitting at the taffrail; and there are five haunches of venison hanging over the stern. Of all amusements, give me yachting. But we must go on board. The deck, you observe, is of narrow deal planks as white as snow; the guns are of polished brass; the bitts and binnacles of mahogany; she is painted with taste; and all the mouldings are gilded. There is nothing wanting; and yet how clear and unencumbered are her decks! Let us go below. This is the ladies' cabin: can anything be more tasteful or elegant? is it not luxurious? and, although so small, does not its very confined space astonish you, when you view so many comforts so beautifully arranged? This is the dining-room, and where the gentlemen repair. What can be more complete or *recherché*? and just peep into their state-rooms and bed-places. Here is the steward's room and the beaufet: the steward is squeezing lemons for the punch, and there is the champagne in ice; and by the side of the pail the long-corks are ranged up, all ready. Now, let us go forwards: here are the men's berths, not confined as in a man-of-war. No! luxury starts from abaft, and is not wholly lost, even at the fore-peak. This is the kitchen: is it not admirably arranged? What a *multum in parvo*! And how delightful are the fumes of the turtle-soup! At sea we do meet with rough weather at times; but, for roughing it out, give me a *yacht*. Now that I have shown you round the vessel, I must introduce the parties on board.

You observe that florid, handsome man in white trousers and blue jacket, who has a telescope in one hand, and is sipping a glass of brandy and water which he has just taken off the skylight. That is the owner of the vessel, and a member of the Yacht Club. It is Lord B—: he looks like a sailor, and he does not much belie his looks; yet I have seen him in his robes of state at the opening of the House of Lords. The one near to him is Mr Stewart, a lieutenant in the navy. He holds on by the rigging with one hand, because, having been actively employed all his life, he does not know what to do with hands which have nothing in them. He is *protégé* of Lord B., and is now on board as sailing-master of the yacht.

That handsome, well-built man who is standing by the binnacle, is a Mr Hautaine. He served six years as midshipman in the navy, and

did not like it. He then served six years in a cavalry regiment, and
did not like it. He then married, and in a much shorter probation,
found that he did not like that. But he is very fond of yachts and
other men's wives, if he does not like his own; and wherever he goes,
he is welcome.

That young man with an embroidered silk waistcoat and white
gloves, bending to talk to one of the ladies, is a Mr Vaughan. He is to
be seen at Almack's, at Crockford's, and everywhere else. Everybody
knows him, and he knows everybody. He is a little in debt, and
yachting is convenient.

The one who sits by the lady is a relation of Lord B.; you see
at once what he is. He apes the sailor; he has not shaved, because
sailors have no time to shave every day; he has not changed his linen,
because sailors cannot change every day. He has a cigar in his mouth,
which makes him half sick and annoys his company. He talks of the
pleasure of a rough sea, which will drive all the ladies below—and
then they will not perceive that he is more sick than themselves. He
has the misfortune to be born to a large estate, and to be a *fool*. His
name is Ossulton.

The last of the gentlemen on board whom I have to introduce,
is Mr Seagrove. He is slightly made, with marked features full of
intelligence. He has been brought up to the bar; and has every
qualification but application. He has never had a brief, nor has he a
chance of one. He is the fiddler of the company, and he has locked
up his chambers, and come, by invitation of his lordship, to play on
board of his yacht.

I have yet to describe the ladies—perhaps I should have commenced
with them—I must excuse myself upon the principle of reserving the
best to the last. All puppet-showmen do so: and what is this but the
first scene in my puppet-show?

We will describe them according to seniority. That tall, thin, cross-
looking lady of forty-five is a spinster, and sister to Lord B. She has
been persuaded very much against her will to come on board; but her

notions of propriety would not permit her niece to embark under the protection of *only* her father. She is frightened at everything: if a rope is thrown down on the deck, up she starts, and cries, "Oh!" if on the deck, she thinks the water is rushing in below; if down below, and there is a noise, she is convinced there is danger; and, if it be perfectly still, she is sure there is something wrong. She fidgets herself and everybody, and is quite a nuisance with her pride and ill-humour; but she has strict notions of propriety, and sacrifices herself as a martyr. She is the Hon. Miss Ossulton.

The lady who, when she smiles, shows so many dimples in her pretty oval face, is a young widow of the name of Lascelles. She married an old man to please her father and mother, which was very dutiful on her part. She was rewarded by finding herself a widow with a large fortune. Having married the first time to please her parents, she intends now to marry to please herself; but she is very young, and is in no hurry.

The young lady with such a sweet expression of countenance is the Hon. Miss Cecilia Ossulton. She is lively, witty, and has no fear in her composition; but she is very young yet, not more than seventeen—and nobody knows what she really is—she does not know herself. These are the parties who meet in the cabin of the yacht. The crew consists of ten fine seamen, the steward, and the cook. There is also Lord B.'s valet, Mr Ossulton's gentleman, and the lady's maid of Miss Ossulton. There not being accommodation for them, the other servants have been left on shore.

The yacht is now under weigh, and her sails are all set. She is running between Drake's Island and the main. Dinner has been announced. As the reader has learnt something about the preparations, I leave him to judge whether it be not very pleasant to sit down to dinner in a yacht. The air has given everybody an appetite; and it was not until the cloth was removed that the conversation became general.

"Mr Seagrove," said his lordship, "you very nearly lost your passage; I expected you last Thursday."

"I am sorry, my lord, that business prevented my sooner attending to your lordship's kind summons."

"Come, Seagrove, don't be nonsensical," said Hautaine; "you told me yourself, the other evening, when you were talkative, that you had never had a brief in your life."

"And a very fortunate circumstance," replied Seagrove; "for if I had had a brief I should not have known what to have done with it. It is not my fault; I am fit for nothing but a commissioner. But still I had business, and very important business, too; I was summoned by Ponsonby to go with him to Tattersall's, to give my opinion about a horse he wishes to purchase, and then to attend him to Forest Wild to plead his cause with his uncle."

"It appears, then, that you were retained," replied Lord B.; "may I ask you whether your friend gained his cause?"

"No, my lord, he lost his cause, but he gained a suit."

"Expound your riddle, sir," said Cecilia Ossulton.

"The fact is, that old Ponsonby is very anxious that William should marry Miss Percival, whose estates join on to Forest Wild. Now, my friend William is about as fond of marriage as I am of law, and thereby issue was joined."

"But why were you to be called in?" inquired Mrs Lascelles.

"Because, madam, as Ponsonby never buys a horse without consulting me—"

"I cannot see the analogy, sir," observed Miss Ossulton, senior, bridling up.

"Pardon me, madam: the fact is," continued Seagrove, "that, as I always have to back Ponsonby's horses, he thought it right that, in this instance, I should back him: he required special pleading, but his uncle tried him for the capital offence, and he was not allowed counsel. As soon as we arrived, and I had bowed myself into the room, Mr Ponsonby bowed me out again—which would have been infinitely more jarring to my feelings, had not the door been left a-jar."

"Do anything but pun, Seagrove," interrupted Hautaine.

"Well, then, I will take a glass of wine."

"Do so," said his lordship; "but, recollect, the whole company are impatient for your story."

"I can assure you, my lord, that it was equal to any scene in a comedy."

Now be it observed that Mr Seagrove had a great deal of comic talent; he was an excellent mimic, and could alter his voice almost as he pleased. It was a custom of his to act a scene as between other people, and he performed it remarkably well. Whenever he said that anything he was going to narrate was "as good as a comedy," it was generally understood by those who were acquainted with him, that he was to be asked so to do. Cecilia Ossulton therefore immediately said, "Pray act it, Mr Seagrove."

Upon which, Mr Seagrove—premising that he had not only heard, but also seen all that passed—changing his voice, and suiting the action to the word, commenced.

"It may," said he, "be called

'FIVE THOUSAND ACRES IN A RING-FENCE.'"

We shall not describe Mr Seagrove's motions; they must be inferred from his words.

"'It will, then, William,' observed Mr Ponsonby, stopping, and turning to his nephew, after a rapid walk up and down the room with his hands behind him under his coat, so as to allow the tails to drop their perpendicular about three inches clear of his body, 'I may say, without contradiction, be the finest property in the county—five thousand acres in a ring-fence.'

"'I dare say it will, uncle,' replied William, tapping his foot as he lounged in a green morocco easy-chair; 'and so, because you have set your fancy upon having these two estates enclosed together in a ring-fence, you wish that I should also be enclosed in a *ring*-fence.'

"'And a beautiful property it will be,' replied Mr Ponsonby.

"'Which, uncle?—the estate, or the wife?'

"'Both, nephew, both; and I expect your consent.'

"'Uncle, I am not avaricious. Your present property is sufficient for me. With your permission, instead of doubling the property, and doubling myself, I will remain your sole heir, and single.'

"'Observe, William, such an opportunity may not occur again for centuries. We shall restore Forest Wild to its ancient boundaries. You know it has been divided nearly two hundred years. We now have a glorious, golden opportunity of re-uniting the two properties; and when joined, the estate will be exactly what it was when granted to our ancestors by Henry the Eighth, at the period of the Reformation. This house must be pulled down, and the monastery left standing. Then we shall have our own again, and the property without encumbrance.'

"'Without encumbrance, uncle! You forget that there will be a wife.'

"'And you forget that there will be five thousand acres in a ring-fence.'

"'Indeed, uncle, you ring it too often in my ears that I should forget it; but much as I should like to be the happy possessor of such a property, I do not feel inclined to be the happy possessor of Miss Percival; and the more so, as I have never seen the property.'

"'We will ride over it to-morrow, William."

"'Ride over Miss Percival, uncle! That will not be very gallant. I will, however, one of these days, ride over the property with you, which, as well as Miss Percival, I have not as yet seen.'

"'Then I can tell you, she is a very pretty property.'

"'If she were not in a ring-fence.'

"'In good heart, William. That is, I mean an excellent disposition.'

"'Valuable in matrimony.'

"'And well tilled—I should say well-educated, by her thee maiden aunts, who are the patterns of propriety.'

"'Does any one follow the fashion?'

"'In a high state of cultivation; that is, her mind highly cultivated, and according to the last new system—what is it?'

"'A four-course shift, I presume,' replied William, laughing; 'that is, dancing, singing, music, and drawing.'

"'And only seventeen! Capital soil, promising good crops. What would you have more?'

"'A very pretty estate, uncle, if it were not the estate of matrimony. I am sorry, very sorry, to disappoint you; but I must decline taking a lease of it for life.'

"'Then, sir, allow me to hint to you that in my testament you are only tenant-at-will. I consider it a duty that I owe to the family, that the estate should be re-united. That can only be done by one of our family marrying Miss Percival; and, as you will not, I shall now write to your cousin James, and if he accept my proposal, shall make *him* my heir. Probably he will more fully appreciate the advantages of five thousand acres in a ring-fence.'

"And Mr Ponsonby directed his steps towards the door.

"'Stop, my dear uncle,' cried William, rising up from his easy-chair; 'we do not quite understand one another. It is very true that I would prefer half the property and remaining single to the two estates and the estate of marriage; but, at the same time I did not tell you that I would prefer beggary to a wife and five thousand acres in a ring-fence. I know you to be a man of your word;—I accept your proposal, and you need not put my cousin James to the expense of postage.'

"'Very good, William; I require no more: and as I know you to be a man of your word, I shall consider this match as settled. It was on this account only that I sent for you, and now you may go back again as soon as you please. I will let you know when all is ready.'

"'I must be at Tattersall's on Monday, uncle; there is a horse I must have for next season. Pray, uncle, may I ask when you are likely to want me?'

"'Let me see—this is May—about July, I should think.'

"'July, uncle! Spare me—I cannot marry in the dog-days. No, hang it, not July.'

"'Well, William, perhaps, as you must come down once or twice to see the property—Miss Percival, I should say—it may be too soon—suppose we put it off till October.'

"'October—I shall be down at Melton.'

"'Pray, sir, may I then inquire what portion of the year is not, with you, *dog*-days?'

"'Why, uncle, next April, now—I think that would do.'

"'Next April. Eleven months, and a winter between. Suppose Miss Percival was to take a cold, and die.'

"'I should be excessively obliged to her,' thought William.

"'No! no!' continued Mr Ponsonby: 'there is nothing certain in this world, William.'

"'Well, then, uncle, suppose we arrange it for the first *hard frost*.'

"'We have had no hard frosts lately, William.—We may wait for years.—The sooner it is over the better.—Go back to town, buy your horse, and then come down here—my dear William—to oblige your uncle—never mind the dog-days.'

"'Well, sir, if I am to make a sacrifice, it shall not be done by halves; out of respect for you I will even marry in July, without any regard to the thermometer.'

"'You are a good boy, William.—Do you want a cheque?'

"'I have had one to-day,' thought William, and was almost at fault. 'I shall be most thankful, sir—they sell horse-flesh by the ounce now-a-days.'

"'And you pay in pounds.—There, William.'

"'Thank you, sir, I'm all obedience; and I'll keep my word, even if there should be a comet. I'll go and buy the horse, and then I shall be ready to take the ring-fence as soon as you please.'

"'Yes, and you'll get over it cleverly, I've no doubt.—Five thousand acres, William, and—a pretty wife!'

"'Have you any further commands, uncle?' said William, depositing the cheque in his pocket-book.

"'Now, my dear boy, are you going?'

"'Yes, sir; I dine at the Clarendon.'

"'Well, then, good-bye. Make my compliments and excuses to your friend Seagrove.—You will come on Tuesday or Wednesday.'

"Thus was concluded the marriage between William Ponsonby and Emily Percival, and the junction of the two estates, which formed together the great desideratum,—*five thousand acres in a ring-fence*."

Mr Scagrove finished, and he looked round for approbation.

"Very good, indeed, Seagrove," said his lordship, "you must take a glass of wine after that."

"I would not give much for Miss Percival's chance of happiness," observed the elder Miss Ossulton.

"Of two evils choose the least, they say," observed Mr Hautaine. "Poor Ponsonby could not help himself."

"That's a very polite observation of yours, Mr Hautaine—I thank you in the name of the sex," replied Cecilia Ossulton.

"Nay, Miss Ossulton; would you like to marry a person whom you never saw?"

"Most certainly not; but when you mentioned the two evils, Mr Hautaine, I appeal to your honour, did you not refer to marriage or beggary?"

"I must confess it, Miss Ossulton; but it is hardly fair to call on my honour to get me into a scrape."

"I only wish that the offer had been made to me," observed Vaughan; "I should not have hesitated as Ponsonby did."

"Then I beg you will not think of proposing for me," said Mrs Lascelles, laughing;—for Mr Vaughan had been excessively attentive.

"It appears to me, Vaughan," observed Seagrove, "that you have slightly committed yourself by that remark."

Vaughan, who thought so too, replied: "Mrs Lascelles must be aware that I was only joking."

"Fie! Mr Vaughan," cried Cecilia Ossulton; "you know it came from your heart."

"My dear Cecilia," said the elder Miss Ossulton, "you forget yourself—what can you possibly know about gentlemen's hearts?"

"The Bible says, 'that they are deceitful and desperately wicked,' aunt."

"And cannot we also quote the Bible against your sex, Miss Ossulton?" replied Seagrove.

"Yes, you could, perhaps, if any of you had ever read it," replied Miss Ossulton, carelessly.

"Upon my word, Cissy, you are throwing the gauntlet down to the gentlemen," observed Lord B.; "but I shall throw my warder down, and not permit this combat à l'outrance.—I perceive you drink no more wine, gentlemen, we will take our coffee on deck."

"We were just about to retire, my lord," observed the elder Miss Ossulton, with great asperity: "I have been trying to catch the eye of Mrs Lascelles for some time, but—"

"I was looking another way, I presume," interrupted Mrs Lascelles, smiling.

"I am afraid that I am the unfortunate culprit," said Mr Seagrove. "I was telling a little anecdote to Mrs Lascelles—"

"Which, of course, from its being communicated in an undertone, was not proper for all the company to hear," replied the elder Miss Ossulton; "but if Mrs Lascelles is now ready—" continued she, bridling up, as she rose from her chair. "At all events, I can hear the remainder of it on deck," replied Mrs Lascelles. The ladies rose, and went into the cabin, Cecilia and Mrs Lascelles exchanging very significant smiles, as they followed the precise spinster, who did not choose that Mrs Lascelles should take the lead, merely because she had once happened to have been married.—The gentlemen also broke up, and went on deck.

"We have a nice breeze now, my lord," observed Mr Stewart, who had remained on deck, "and we lie right up Channel."

"So much the better," replied his lordship; "we ought to have been anchored at Cowes a week ago. They will all be there before us."

"Tell Mr Simpson to bring me a light for my cigar," said Mr Ossulton to one of the men.

Mr Stewart went down to his dinner; the ladies and the coffee came on deck; the breeze was fine, the weather (it was April) almost warm; and the yacht, whose name was the *Arrow*, assisted by the tide, soon left the Mewstone far astern.

II
CUTTER THE SECOND

R EADER, HAVE YOU EVER BEEN at Portsmouth? If you have, you
must have been delighted with the view from the saluting
battery; and, if you have not, you had better go there as soon as
you can. From the saluting battery you may look up the harbour,
and see much of what I have described at Plymouth; the scenery is
different; but similar arsenals and dockyards, and an equal portion
of our stupendous navy, are to be found there.—And you will see
Gosport on the other side of the harbour, and Sally Port close to you;
besides a great many other places, which, from the saluting battery,
you cannot see. And then there is Southsea Beach to your left. Before
you, Spithead, with the men-of-war, and the Motherbank, crowded
with merchant vessels;—and there is the buoy where the *Royal George*
was wrecked, and where she still lies, the fish swimming in and out
of her cabin windows; but that is not all; you can also see the Isle of
Wight,—Ryde, with its long wooden pier, and Cowes, where the
yachts lie. In fact, there is a great deal to be seen at Portsmouth as well
as at Plymouth; but what I wish you particularly to see, just now, is
a vessel holding fast to the buoy, just off the saluting battery. She is a
cutter; and you may know that she belongs to the Preventive Service

by the number of gigs and galleys which she has hoisted up all round her. She looks like a vessel that was about to sail with a cargo of boats. Two on deck, one astern, one on each side of her. You observe that she is painted black, and all her boats are white. She is not such an elegant vessel as the yacht, and she is much more lumbered up. She has no haunches of venison over the stern; but I think there is a leg of mutton, and some cabbages hanging by their stalks. But revenue-cutters are not yachts.—You will find no turtle or champagne; but, nevertheless, you will, perhaps, find a joint to carve at, a good glass of grog, and a hearty welcome.

Let us go on board.—You observe the guns are iron, and painted black, and her bulwarks are painted red; it is not a very becoming colour; but then it lasts a long while, and the dock-yard is not very generous on the score of paint—or lieutenants of the navy troubled with much spare cash. She has plenty of men, and fine men they are; all dressed in red flannel shirts, and blue trousers; some of them have not taken off their canvas or tarpaulin petticoats, which are very useful to them, as they are in the boats night and day, and in all weathers. But we will at once go down into the cabin, where we shall find the lieutenant who commands her, a master's mate, and a midshipman. They have each their tumbler before them, and are drinking gin-toddy, hot, with sugar—capital gin, too, 'bove proof; it is from that small anker, standing under the table. It was one that they forgot to return to the custom-house when they made their last seizure. We must introduce them.

The elderly personage, with grizzly hair and whiskers, a round pale face, and a somewhat red nose (being too much in the wind will make the nose red, and this old officer is very often "in the wind," of course, from the very nature of his profession), is a Lieutenant Appleboy. He has served in every class of vessel in the service, and done the duty of first lieutenant for twenty years; he is now on promotion—that is to say, after he has taken a certain number of tubs of gin, he will be rewarded with his rank as commander. It is a pity that what he takes inside of him does not count, for he takes it morning, noon, and night.—He is just filling his fourteenth glass: he always keeps a regular account, as he never exceeds his limited number, which is seventeen; then he is exactly down to his bearings.

The master's mate's name is Tomkins; he has served his six years three times over, and has now outgrown his ambition; which is fortunate for him, as his chances of promotion are small. He prefers a small vessel to a large one, because he is not obliged to be so particular in his dress—and looks for his lieutenancy whenever there shall be another charity promotion. He is fond of soft bread, for his teeth are all absent without leave; he prefers porter to any other liquor, but he can drink his glass of grog, whether it be based upon rum, brandy, or the liquor now before him.

Mr Smith is the name of that young gentleman, whose jacket is so out at the elbows; he has been intending to mend it these last two months, but is too lazy to go to his chest for another. He has been turned out of half the ships in the service for laziness; but he was born so—and therefore it is not his fault.—A revenue-cutter suits him, she is half her time hove to; and he has no objection to boat-service, as he sits down always in the stern-sheets, which is not fatiguing. Creeping for tubs is his delight, as he gets over so little ground. He is fond of grog, but there is some trouble in carrying the tumbler so often to his mouth; so he looks at it, and lets it stand. He says little, because he is too lazy to speak. He has served more than *eight years*; but as for passing—it has never come into his head. Such are the three persons who are now sitting in the cabin of the revenue-cutter, drinking hot gin-toddy.

"Let me see, it was, I think, in ninety-three or ninety-four. Before you were in the service, Tomkins.—"

"Maybe, sir; it's so long ago since I entered, that I can't recollect dates,—but this I know, that my aunt died three days before."

"Then the question is, when did your aunt die?"

"Oh! she died about a year after my uncle."

"And when did your uncle die?"

"I'll be hanged if I know!"

"Then, d'ye see, you've no departure to work from. However, I think you cannot have been in the service at that time. We were not quite so particular about uniform as we are now."

"Then I think the service was all the better for it. Now-a-days, in your crack ships, a mate has to go down in the hold or spirit-room, and after whipping up fifty empty casks, and breaking out twenty full ones, he is expected to come on quarter-deck as clean as if he was just come out of a band-box."

"Well, there's plenty of water alongside, as far as the outward man goes, and iron dust is soon brushed off. However, as you say, perhaps a little too much is expected; at least, in five of the ships in which I was first-lieutenant, the captain was always hauling me over the coals about the midshipmen not dressing properly, as if I was their dry-nurse. I wonder what Captain Prigg would have said, if he had seen such a turn-out as you, Mr Smith, on his quarter-deck."

"I should have had one turn-out more," drawled Smith.

"With your out-at-elbows jacket, there, heh!" continued Mr Appleboy.

Smith turned up his elbows, looked at one and then at the other: after so fatiguing an operation, he was silent.

"Well, where was I? Oh! it was about ninety-three or ninety-four, as I said, that it happened—Tomkins, fill your glass, and hand me the sugar—how do I get on? This is No. 15," said Appleboy, counting some white lines on the table by him; and taking up a piece of chalk, he marked one more line on his tally. "I don't think this is so good a tub as the last, Tomkins, there's a twang about it—a want of juniper—however, I hope we shall have better luck this time. Of course, you know we sail to-morrow?"

"I presume so, by the leg of mutton coming on board."

"True—true—I'm regular—as clock-work.—After being twenty years a first-lieutenant, one gets a little method—I like regularity.

Now the admiral has never omitted asking me to dinner once, every time I have come into harbour, except this time—I was so certain of it, that I never expected to sail; and I have but two shirts clean in consequence."

"That's odd, isn't it? and the more so, because he has had such great people down here, and has been giving large parties every day."

"And yet I made three seizures, besides sweeping up those thirty-seven tubs."

"I swept them up," observed Smith.

"That's all the same thing, *younker*.—When you've been a little longer in the service, you'll find out that the commanding officer has the merit of all that is done—but you're *green* yet. Let me see, where was I? Oh!—It was about ninety-three or ninety-four, as I said. At that time I was in the Channel fleet—Tomkins, I'll trouble you for the hot water; this water's cold.—Mr Smith, do me the favour to ring the bell.—Jem, some more hot water."

"Please, sir," said Jem, who was barefooted as well as bare-headed, touching the lock of hair on his forehead, "the cook has capsized the kettle—but he has put more on."

"Capsized the kettle! Ha!—very well—we'll talk about that to-morrow. Mr Tomkins, do me the favour to put him in the report, I may forget it. And pray, sir, how long is it since he has put more on?"

"Just this moment, sir, as I came aft."

"Very well, we'll see to that to-morrow:—You bring the kettle aft as soon as it is ready. I say, Mr Jem, is that fellow sober?"

"Yees, sir, he be sober as you be."

"It's quite astonishing what a propensity the common sailors have to liquor. Forty odd years have I been in the service, and I've never found any difference: I only wish I had a guinea for every time that I have given a fellow seven-water grog during my servitude as first-lieutenant, I wouldn't call the king my cousin. Well, if there's no hot water, we must take lukewarm—it won't do to heave to. By the Lord Harry! who would have thought it?—I'm at number sixteen! Let me count—yes!—surely I must have made a mistake. A fact, by Heaven!" continued Mr Appleboy, throwing the chalk down on the table. "Only one more glass, after this—that is, if I have counted right—I may have seen double."

"Yes," drawled Smith.

"Well, never mind—let's go on with my story.—It was either in the year ninety-three or ninety-four, that I was in the Channel fleet—we were then abreast of Torbay—"

"Here be the hot water, sir," cried Jem, putting the kettle down on the deck.

"Very well, boy—by-the-bye, has the jar of butter come on board?"

"Yes, but it broke all down the middle; I tied him up with a ropeyarn."

"Who broke it, sir?"

"Coxswain says as how he didn't."

"But who did, sir?"

"Coxswain handed it up to Bill Jones, and he says as how he didn't."

"But who did, sir?"

"Bill Jones gave it to me, and I'm sure as how I didn't."

"Then who did, sir, I ask you?"

"I think it be Bill Jones, sir, 'cause he's fond of butter, I know, and there be very little left in the jar."

"Very *well*, we'll see to that to-morrow morning. Mr Tomkins, you'll oblige me by putting the butter-jar down in the report, in case it should slip my memory. Bill Jones, indeed, looks as if butter wouldn't melt in his mouth—never mind. Well, it was, as I said before—it was in the year ninety-three or ninety-four, when I was in the Channel fleet; we were then off Torbay, and had just taken two reefs in the top-sails. Stop, before I go on with my story, I'll take my last glass—I think it's the last: let me count—yes, by heavens I make out sixteen, well told. Never mind, it shall be a stiff one. Boy, bring the kettle, and mind you don't pour the hot water into my shoes, as you did the other night. There, that will do. Now, Tomkins, fill up yours; and you, Mr Smith: let us all start fair, and then you shall have my story—and a very curious one it is, I can tell you; I wouldn't have believed it myself if I hadn't seen it. Hilloa! what's this? confound it! what's the matter with the toddy? Heh, Mr Tomkins?"

Mr Tomkins tasted, but, like the lieutenant, he had made it very stiff; and, as he had also taken largely before, he was, like him, not quite so clear in his discrimination: "It has a queer *twang*, sir: Smith, what is it?"

Smith took up his glass, tasted the contents.

"*Salt water*" drawled the midshipman.

"Salt water! so it is, by heavens!" cried Mr Appleboy.

"Salt as Lot's wife!—by all that's infamous!" cried the master's mate.

"Salt water, sir!" cried Jem in a fright, expecting a *salt* eel for supper.

"Yes, sir," replied Mr Appleboy, tossing the contents of the tumbler in the boy's face, "salt water. Very well, sir,—very well!"

"It warn't me, sir," replied the boy, making up a piteous look.

"No, sir, but you said the cook was sober."

"He was not so *very* much disguised, sir," replied Jem.

"Oh! very well—never mind. Mr Tomkins, in case I should forget it, do me the favour to put the kettle of salt water down in the report. The scoundrel! I'm very sorry, gentlemen, but there's no means of having any more gin-toddy,—but never mind, we'll see to this to-morrow. Two can play at this; and if I don't salt-water their grog, and make them drink it, too, I have been twenty years a first-lieutenant for nothing—that's all. Good night, gentlemen; and," continued the lieutenant, in a severe tone, "you'll keep a sharp look-out, Mr Smith—do you hear, sir?"

"Yes," drawled Smith, "but it's not my watch; it was my first watch, and, just now, it struck one bell."

"You'll keep the middle watch, then, Mr Smith," said Mr Appleboy, who was not a little put out; "and, Mr Tomkins, let me know as soon as it's daylight. Boy, get my bed made. Salt water, by all that's blue! However, we'll see to that to-morrow morning."

Mr Appleboy then turned in; so did Mr Tomkins; and so did Mr Smith, who had no idea of keeping the middle watch because the cook was drunk and had filled up the kettle with salt water. As for what happened in ninety-three or ninety-four, I really would inform the reader if I knew, but I am afraid that that most curious story is never to be handed down to posterity.

The next morning, Mr Tomkins, as usual, forgot to report the cook, the jar of butter, and the kettle of salt water; and Mr Appleboy's wrath had long been appeased before he remembered them. At daylight the lieutenant came on deck, having only slept away half of the sixteen, and a taste of the seventeenth salt-water glass of gin-toddy. He rubbed his grey eyes, that he might peer through the grey of the morning; the fresh breeze blew about his grizzly locks, and cooled his rubicund nose. The revenue-cutter, whose name was the *Active*, cast off from the buoy; and, with a fresh breeze, steered her course for the Needles' passage.

III
CUTTER THE THIRD

R EADER! HAVE YOU BEEN TO St Maloes? If you have, you were glad enough to leave the hole; and, if you have not, take my advice, and do not give yourself the trouble to go and see that, or any other French port in the Channel. There is not one worth looking at. They have made one or two artificial ports, and they are no great things; there is no getting out, or getting in. In fact, they have no harbours in the Channel, while we have the finest in the world; a peculiar dispensation of Providence, because it knew that we should want them, and France would not. In France, what are called ports are all alike, nasty narrow holes, only to be entered at certain times of tide and certain winds; made up of basins and back-waters, custom-houses, and cabarets; just fit for smugglers to run into, and nothing more; and, therefore, they are used for very little else.

Now, in the dog-hole called St Maloes there is some pretty land, although a great deficiency of marine scenery. But never mind that: stay at home, and don't go abroad to drink sour wine, because they call it Bordeaux, and eat villanous trash, so disguised by cooking that you cannot possibly tell which of the birds of the air, or beasts of the field, or fishes of the sea, you are cramming down your throat. "If all is right, there is no occasion for disguise," is an old saying; so depend upon it, that there is something wrong, and that you are eating offal, under a grand French name. They eat everything in France, and would serve you up the head of a monkey who has died of the smallpox, as *singe au petite vérole*—that is, if you did not understand French; if you did, they would call it, *Tête d'amour a l'Ethiopique*, and then you would be even more puzzled. As for their wine, there is no disguise in that—it's half vinegar. No, no! stay at home; you can live just as cheaply, if you choose; and then you will have good meat, good vegetables, good ale, good beer, and a good glass of grog—and what is of more importance, you will be in good company. Live with your friends, and don't make a fool of yourself.

I would not have condescended to have noticed this place, had it not been that I wish you to observe a vessel which is lying along the pier-wharf, with a plank from the shore to her gunnel. It is low water, and she is aground, and the plank dips down at such an angle that it is a work of danger to go either in or out of her. You observe that there is nothing very remarkable in her. She is a cutter, and a good sea-boat, and sails well before the wind. She is short for her breadth of beam, and is not armed. Smugglers do not arm now—the service is too dangerous; they effect their purpose by cunning, not by force. Nevertheless, it requires that smugglers should be good seamen, smart, active fellows, and keen-witted, or they can do nothing. This vessel has not a large cargo in her, but it is valuable. She has some thousand yards of lace, a few hundred pounds of tea, a few bales of silk, and about forty ankers of brandy—just as much as they can land in one boat. All they ask is a heavy gale or a thick fog, and they trust to themselves for success.

There is nobody on board except a boy; the crew are all up at the cabaret, settling their little accounts of every description—for they smuggle both ways, and every man has his own private venture. There they are all, fifteen of them, and fine-looking fellows, too, sitting at that long table. They are very merry, but quite sober, as they are to sail to-night.

The captain of the vessel (whose name, by-the-bye is the "*Happy-go-lucky*,"—the captain christened her himself) is that fine-looking young man, with dark whiskers, meeting under his throat. His name is Jack Pickersgill. You perceive, at once, that he is much above a common sailor in appearance. His manners are good, he is remarkably handsome, very clean, and rather a dandy in his dress. Observe, how very politely he takes off his hat to that Frenchman, with whom he has just settled accounts; he beats Johnny Crapeau at his own weapons. And then there is an air of command, a feeling of conscious superiority about Jack; see how he treats the landlord, *de haut en bas*, at the same time that he is very civil. The fact is, that Jack is of a very good, old family, and received a very excellent education; but he was an orphan, his friends were poor, and could do but little for him: he went out to India as a cadet, ran away, and served in a schooner which smuggled opium into China, and then came home. He took a liking to the employment, and is now laying up a very pretty little sum: not that he intends to stop: no, as soon as he has enough to fit out a vessel for himself, he intends to start again for India, and with two cargoes of opium, he will return, he trusts, with a handsome fortune, and re-assume his family name. Such are Jack's intentions; and, as he eventually means to reappear as a gentleman, he preserves his gentlemanly habits: he neither drinks, nor chews, nor smokes. He keeps his hands clean, wears rings, and sports a gold snuff-box; notwithstanding which, Jack is one of the boldest and best of sailors, and the men know it. He is full of fun, and as keen as a razor. Jack has a very heavy venture this time—all the lace is his own speculation, and if he gets it in safe, he will clear some thousands of pounds. A certain fashionable shop in London has already agreed to take the whole off his hands.

That short, neatly-made young man is the second in command, and the companion of the captain. He is clever, and always has a remedy to propose when there is a difficulty, which is a great quality in a second in command. His name is Corbett. He is always merry—

half-sailor, half-tradesman; knows the markets, runs up to London, and does business as well as a chapman—lives for the day, and laughs at to-morrow.

That little punchy old man, with long gray hair and fat face, with a nose like a note of interrogation, is the next personage of importance. He ought to be called the sailing-master, for, although he goes on shore in France, off the English coast he never quits the vessel. When they leave her with the goods, he remains on board; he is always to be found off any part of the coast where he may be ordered; holding his position in defiance of gales, and tides, and fogs: as for the revenue vessels, they all know him well enough, but they cannot touch a vessel in ballast, if she has no more men on board than allowed by her tonnage. He knows every creek, and hole, and corner, of the coast; how the tide runs in—tide, half-tide, eddy, or current. That is his value. His name is Morrison.

You observe that Jack Pickersgill has two excellent supporters in Corbett and Morrison; his other men are good seamen, active, and obedient, which is all that he requires. I shall not particularly introduce them.

"Now you may call for another *litre*, my lads, and that must be the last; the tide is flowing fast, and we shall be afloat in half an hour, and we have just the breeze we want. What d'ye think, Morrison, shall we have dirt?"

"I've been looking just now, and if it were any other month in the year I should say, yes; but there's no trusting April, captain. Howsomever, if it does blow off, I'll promise you a fog in three hours afterwards."

"That will do as well. Corbett, have you settled with Duval?"

"Yes, after more noise and *charivari* than a panic in the Stock Exchange would make in England. He fought and squabbled for an hour, and I found that, without some abatement, I never should have settled the affair."

"What did you let him off?"

"Seventeen sous," replied Corbett, laughing.

"And that satisfied him?" inquired Pickersgill.

"Yes—it was all he could prove to be a *surfaire*: two of the knives were a little rusty. But he will always have something off; he could not be happy without it. I really think he would commit suicide, if he had to pay a bill without a deduction."

"Let him live," replied Pickersgill. "Jeannette, a bottle of Volnay, of 1811, and three glasses."

Jeannette, who was the *fille de cabaret*, soon appeared with a bottle of wine, seldom called for, except by the captain of the *Happy-go-lucky*.

"You sail to-night?" said she, as she placed the bottle before him.

Pickersgill nodded his head.

"I had a strange dream," said Jeannette; "I thought you were all taken by a revenue cutter, and put in a *cachot*. I went to see you, and I did not know one of you again—you were all changed."

"Very likely, Jeannette—you would not be the first who did not know their friends again when in misfortune. There was nothing strange in your dream."

"*Mais, mon Dieu! je ne suis pas comme ça moi.*"

"No, that you are not, Jeannette; you are a good girl, and some of these fine days I'll marry you," said Corbett.

"*Doit être bien beau ce jour là, par exemple,*" replied Jeannette, laughing; "you have promised to marry me every time you have come in, these last three years."

"Well, that proves I keep to my promise, any how."

"Yes; but you never go any further."

"I can't spare him, Jeannette, that is the real truth," said the captain: "but wait a little—in the meantime, here is a five-franc piece to add to your *petite* fortune."

"*Merci bien, monsieur le capitaine; bon voyage!*" Jeannette held her finger up to Corbett, saying, with a smile, "*méchant!*" and then quitted the room.

"Come, Morrison, help us to empty this bottle, and then we will all go on board."

"I wish that girl wouldn't come here with her nonsensical dreams," said Morrison, taking his seat; "I don't like it. When she said that we should be taken by a revenue cutter, I was looking at a blue and a white pigeon sitting on the wall opposite; and I said to myself, now, if that be a warning, I will see: if the *blue* pigeon flies away first, I shall be in jail in a week; if the *white*, I shall be back here."

"Well?" said Pickersgill, laughing.

"It wasn't well," answered Morrison, tossing off his wine, and putting the glass down with a deep sigh; "for the cursed *blue* pigeon flew away immediately."

"Why, Morrison, you must have a chicken-heart to be frightened at a blue pigeon," said Corbett, laughing, and looking out of the window; "at all events, he has come back again, and there he is sitting by the white one."

"It's the first time that ever I was called chicken-hearted," replied Morrison, in wrath.

"Nor do you deserve it, Morrison," replied Pickersgill; "but Corbett is only joking."

"Well, at all events, I'll try my luck in the same way, and see whether I am to be in jail: I shall take the blue pigeon as my bad omen, as you did."

The sailors and Captain Pickersgill all rose and went to the window, to ascertain Corbett's fortune by this new species of augury. The blue pigeon flapped his wings, and then he sidled up to the white one; at last, the white pigeon flew off the wall and settled on the roof of the adjacent house. "Bravo, white pigeon!" said Corbett; "I shall be here again in a week." The whole party, laughing, then resumed their seats; and Morrison's countenance brightened up. As he took the glass of wine poured out by Pickersgill, he said, "Here's your health, Corbett; it was all nonsense, after all—for, d'ye see, I can't be put in jail without you are. We all sail in the same boat, and when you leave me, you take with you everything that can condemn the vessel—so here's success to our trip."

"We will all drink that toast, my lads, and then on board," said the captain; "here's success to our trip."

The captain rose, as did the mates and men, drank the toast, turned down the drinking-vessels on the table, hastened to the wharf, and, in half an hour, the *Happy-go-lucky* was clear of the port of St Maloes.

IV
PORTLAND BILL

THE *HAPPY-GO-LUCKY* SAILED WITH A fresh breeze and a flowing sheet from St Maloes, the evening before the *Arrow* sailed from Barn Pool. The *Active* sailed from Portsmouth the morning after.

The yacht, as we before observed, was bound to Cowes, in the Isle of Wight. The *Active* had orders to cruise wherever she pleased within the limits of the admiral's station; and she ran for West Bay, on the other side of the Bill of Portland. The *Happy-go-lucky* was also bound for that bay to land her cargo.

The wind was light, and there was every appearance of fine weather, when the *Happy-go-lucky*, at ten o'clock on the Tuesday night, made the Portland lights; as it was impossible to run her cargo that night, she hove to.

At eleven o'clock, the Portland lights were made by the revenue cutter *Active*. Mr Appleboy went up to have a look at them, ordered the cutter to be hove to, and then went down to finish his allowance of gin-toddy. At twelve o'clock, the yacht *Arrow* made the Portland lights, and continued her course, hardly stemming the ebb tide.

Day broke, and the horizon was clear. The first on the look-out were, of course, the smugglers; they, and those on board the revenue cutter, were the only two interested parties—the yacht was neuter.

"There are two cutters in sight, sir," said Corbett, who had the watch; for Pickersgill, having been up the whole night, had thrown himself down on the bed with his clothes on.

"What do they look like?" said Pickersgill, who was up in a moment.

"One is a yacht, and the other may be; but I rather think, as far as I can judge in the gray, that it is our old friend off here."

"What! old Appleboy?"

"Yes, it looks like him; but the day has scarcely broke yet."

"Well, he can do nothing in a light wind like this; and before the wind we can show him our heels; but are you sure the other is a yacht?" said Pickersgill, coming on deck.

"Yes; the king is more careful of his canvas."

"You're right," said Pickersgill, "that is a yacht; and you're right there again in your guess—that is the stupid old *Active*, which creeps about creeping for tubs. Well, I see nothing to alarm us at present, provided it don't fall a dead calm, and then we must take to our boat as soon as he takes to his; we are four miles from him at least. Watch his motions, Corbett, and see if he lowers a boat. What does she go now? Four knots?—that will soon tire their men."

The positions of the three cutters were as follows:—

The *Happy-go-lucky* was about four miles off Portland Head, and well into West Bay. The revenue cutter was close to the Head. The yacht was outside of the smuggler, about two miles to the westward, and about five or six miles from the revenue cutter.

"Two vessels in sight, sir," said Mr Smith, coming down into the cabin to Mr Appleboy.

"Very well," replied the lieutenant, who was *lying* down in his *standing* bed-place.

"The people say one is the *Happy-go-lucky*, sir," drawled Smith.

"Heh? what! *Happy-go-lucky*? Yes, I recollect; I've boarded her twenty times—always empty. How's she standing?"

"She stands to the westward now, sir; but she was hove to, they say, when they first saw her."

"Then she has a cargo in her;" and Mr Appleboy shaved himself, dressed, and went on deck.

"Yes," said the lieutenant, rubbing his eyes again and again, and then looking through the glass, "it is her sure enough. Let draw the fore sheet—hands make sail. What vessel's the other?"

"Don't know, sir,—she's a cutter."

"A cutter? yes; may be a yacht, or may be the new cutter ordered on the station. Make all sail, Mr Tomkins; hoist our pendant, and fire a gun—they will understand what we mean then; they don't know the *Happy-go-lucky* as well as we do."

In a few minutes the *Active* was under a press of sail; she hoisted her pendant, and fired a gun. The smuggler perceived that the *Active* had recognised her, and she also threw out more canvas, and ran off more to the westward.

"There's a gun, sir," reported one of the men to Mr Stewart, on board of the yacht.

"Yes; give me the glass—a revenue cutter; then this vessel in shore, running towards us, must be a smuggler."

"She has just now made all sail, sir."

"Yes, there's no doubt of it; I will go down to his lordship—keep her as she goes."

Mr Stewart then went down to inform Lord B. of the circumstance. Not only Lord B., but most of the gentlemen came on deck; as did soon afterwards the ladies, who had received the intelligence from Lord B., who spoke to them through the door of the cabin.

But the smuggler had more wind than the revenue cutter, and increased her distance.

"If we were to wear round now, my lord," observed Mr Stewart, "she is just abreast of us and in shore, we could prevent her escape."

"Round with her, Mr Stewart," said Lord B.; "we must do our duty, and protect the laws."

"That will not be fair, papa," said Cecilia Ossulton; "we have no quarrel with the smugglers: I'm sure the ladies have not, for they bring us beautiful things."

"Miss Ossulton," observed her aunt, "it is not proper for you to offer an opinion."

The yacht wore round, and, sailing so fast, the smuggler had little chance of escaping her; but to chase is one thing—to capture, another.

"Let us give her a gun," said Lord B., "that will frighten her; and he dare not cross our hawse."

The gun was loaded, and not being more than a mile from the smuggler, actually threw the ball almost a quarter of the way.

The gentlemen, as well as Lord B., were equally excited by the ardour of pursuit; but the wind died away, and at last it was nearly calm. The revenue cutter's boats were out, and coming up fast.

"Let us get our boat out, Stewart," said his lordship; "and help them; it is quite calm now."

The boat was soon out: it was a very large one, usually stowed on, and occupied a large portion of, the deck. It pulled six oars; and when it was manned, Mr Stewart jumped in, and Lord B. followed him.

"But you have no arms," said Mr Hautaine.

"The smugglers never resist now," observed Stewart.

"Then you are going on a very gallant expedition, indeed," observed Cecilia Ossulton; "I wish you joy."

But Lord B. was too much excited to pay attention. They shoved off, and pulled towards the smuggler.

At this time, the revenue boats were about five miles astern of the *Happy-go-lucky*, and the yacht about three-quarters of a mile from her in the offing. Pickersgill had, of course, observed the motions of the yacht; had seen her wear on chase, hoist her ensign and pendant, and fire her gun.

"Well," said he, "this is the blackest ingratitude; to be attacked by the very people whom we smuggle for. I only wish she may come up with us; and, let her attempt to interfere, she shall rue the day: I don't much like this, though."

As we before observed, it fell nearly calm, and the revenue boats were in chase. Pickersgill watched them as they came up.

"What shall we do," said Corbett,—"get the boat out?"

"Yes," replied Pickersgill, "we will get the boat out, and have the goods in her all ready; but we can pull faster than they do, in the first place; and, in the next, they will be pretty well tired before they come up to us. We are fresh, and shall soon walk away from them; so I shall not leave the vessel till they are within half a mile. We must sink the ankers, that they may not seize the vessel, for it is not worth while taking them with us. Pass them along ready to run them over the bows, that they may not see us and swear to it. But we have a good half hour, and more."

"Ay, and you may hold all fast if you choose," said Morrison, "although it's better to be on the right side and get ready; otherwise, before half an hour, I'll swear that we are out of their sight. Look there," said he, pointing to the eastward at a heavy bank, "it's coming right down upon us, as I said it would."

"True enough; but still there is no saying which will come first, Morrison; the boats or the fog, so we must be prepared."

"Hilloa! what's this? why, there's a boat coming from the yacht!"

Pickersgill took out his glass.

"Yes, and the yacht's own boat, with the name painted on her bows. Well, let them come—we will have no ceremony in resisting them; they are not in the Act of Parliament, and must take the consequences. We have nought to fear. Get stretchers, my lads, and hand-spikes; they row six oars, and are three in the stern sheets—they must be good men if they take us."

In a few minutes Lord B. was close to the smuggler.

"Boat, ahoy! what do you want?"

"Surrender in the king's name."

"To what, and to whom, and what are we to surrender? We are an English vessel coasting along shore."

"Pull on board, my lads," cried Stewart; "I am a king's officer—we know her."

The boat darted alongside, and Stewart and Lord B., followed by the men, jumped on the deck.

"Well, gentlemen, what do you want?" said Pickersgill.

"We seize you—you are a smuggler; there's no denying it: look at the casks of spirits stretched along the deck."

"We never said that we were not smugglers," replied Pickersgill; "but what is that to you? You are not a king's ship, or employed by the revenue."

"No, but we carry a pendant, and it is our duty to protect the laws."

"And who are you?" said Pickersgill.

"I am Lord B."

"Then, my lord, allow me to say that you would do much better to attend to the framing of laws, and leave people of less consequence, like those astern of me, to execute them. 'Mind your own business,' is an old adage. We shall not hurt you, my lord, as you have only employed words, but we shall put it out of your power to hurt us. Come aft, my lads. Now, my lord, resistance is useless; we are double your numbers, and you have caught a Tartar."

Lord B. and Mr Stewart perceived that they were in an awkward predicament.

"You may do what you please," observed Mr Stewart, "but the revenue boats are coming up, recollect."

"Look you, sir, do you see the revenue cutter?" said Pickersgill.

Stewart looked in that direction, and saw that she was hidden in the fog.

"In five minutes, sir, the boats will be out of sight also, and so will your vessel; we have nothing to fear from them."

"Indeed, my lord, we had better return," said Mr Stewart, who perceived that Pickersgill was right.

"I beg your pardon, you will not go on board your yacht so soon as you expect. Take the oars out of the boat, my lads, two or three of you, and throw in a couple of our paddles for them to reach the shore with. The rest of you knock down the first man who offers to resist. You are not aware, perhaps, my lord, that you have attempted *piracy* on the high seas?"

Stewart looked at Lord B. It was true enough. The men of the yacht could offer no resistance; the oars were taken out of the boat, and the men put in again.

"My lord," said Pickersgill, "your boat is manned—do me the favour to step into it; and you, sir, do the same. I should be sorry to lay my hands upon a peer of the realm, or a king's officer even on half pay."

Remonstrance was vain; his lordship was led to the boat by two of the smugglers, and Stewart followed.

"I will leave your oars, my lord, at the Weymouth Custom-house; and I trust this will be a lesson to you in future to 'mind your own business.'"

The boat was shoved off from the sloop by the smugglers, and was soon lost sight of in the fog, which had now covered the revenue boats as well as the yacht; at the same time, it brought down a breeze from the eastward.

"Haul to the wind, Morrison," said Pickersgill, "we will stand out to get rid of the boats; if they pull on, they will take it for granted that we shall run into the bay, as will the revenue cutter."

Pickersgill and Corbett were in conversation abaft for a short time, when the former desired the course to be altered two points.

"Keep silence all of you, my lads, and let me know if you hear a gun or a bell from the yacht," said Pickersgill.

"There is a gun, sir, close to us," said one of the men; "the sound was right ahead."

"That will do, keep her as she goes. Aft here, my lads; we cannot run our cargo in the bay, for the cutter has been seen to chase us, and they will all be on the look-out at the preventive stations for us on shore. Now, my lads, I have made up my mind that, as these yacht gentlemen have thought proper to interfere, I will take possession of the yacht for a few days. We shall then out-sail everything, go where we like unsuspected, and land our cargo with ease. I shall run alongside of her—she can have but few hands on board; and mind, do not hurt anybody, but be civil and obey my orders. Morrison, you and your four men and the boy will remain on board as before, and take the vessel to Cherbourg, where we will join you."

In a short time another gun was fired from the yacht.

Those on board, particularly the ladies, were alarmed; the fog was very thick, and they could not distinguish the length of the vessel. They had seen the boat board, but had not seen her turned adrift without oars, as the fog came on just at that time. The yacht was left with only three seamen on board, and, should it come on bad weather, they were in an awkward predicament. Mr Hautaine had taken the command, and ordered the guns to be fired that the boat might be enabled to find them. The fourth gun was loading, when they perceived the smuggler's cutter close to them looming through the fog.

"Here they are," cried the seamen; "and they have brought the prize along with them! Three cheers for the *Arrow!*"

"Hilloa! you'll be on board of us?" cried Hautaine.

"That's exactly what I intended to be, sir," replied Pickersgill, jumping on the quarter-deck, followed by his men.

"Who the devil are you?"

"That's exactly the same question that I asked Lord B. when he boarded us," replied Pickersgill, taking off his hat to the ladies.

"Well, but what business have you here?"

"Exactly the same question which I put to Lord B.," replied Pickersgill.

"Where is Lord B., sir?" said Cecilia Ossulton, going up to the smuggler; "is he safe?"

"Yes, madam, he is safe; at least he is in his boat with all his men, and unhurt: but you must excuse me if I request you and the other ladies to go down below while I speak to these gentlemen. Be under no alarm, miss; you will receive neither insult nor ill-treatment—I have only taken possession of this vessel for the present."

"Take possession," cried Hautaine, "of a yacht."

"Yes, sir, since the owner of the yacht thought proper to attempt to take possession of me. I always thought that yachts were pleasure-vessels, sailing about for amusement, respected themselves, and not interfering with others; but it appears that such is not the case. The owner of this yacht has thought proper to break through the neutrality, and commence aggression, and under such circumstances I have now, in retaliation, taken possession of her."

"And, pray, what do you mean to do, sir?"

"Simply for a few days to make an exchange. I shall send you on board of my vessel as smugglers, while I remain here with the ladies and amuse myself with yachting."

"Why, sir, you cannot mean—"

"I have said, gentlemen, and that is enough; I should be sorry to resort to violence, but I must be obeyed. You have, I perceive, three seamen only left: they are not sufficient to take charge of the vessel, and Lord B. and the others you will not meet for several days. My regard for the ladies, even common humanity, points out to me that I cannot leave the vessel in this crippled condition. At the same time, as I must have hands on board of my own, you will oblige me by going on board and taking her safely into port. It is the least return you can make for my kindness. In those dresses, gentlemen, you will not be able to do your duty; oblige me by shifting, and putting on these." Corbett handed a flannel shirt, a rough jacket and trousers, to Messrs Hautaine, Ossulton, Vaughan, and Seagrove. After some useless resistance they were stripped, and having put on the smugglers' attire, they were handed on board of the *Happy-go-lucky*.

The three English seamen were also sent on board and confined below, as well as Ossulton's servant, who was also equipped like his master, and confined below with the seamen. Corbett and the men then handed up all the smuggled goods into the yacht, dropped the boat, and made it fast astern; and, Morrison having received his directions, the vessels separated—Morrison running for Cherbourg, and Pickersgill steering the yacht along shore to the westward. About an hour after this exchange had been effected, the fog cleared up, and showed the revenue cutter hove to for her boats, which had pulled back and were close on board of her; and the *Happy-go-lucky*, about three miles in the offing. Lord B. and his boat's crew were about four miles in shore, paddling and drifting with the tide towards Portland. As soon as the boats were on board, the revenue cutter made all sail after the smuggler, paying no attention to the yacht, and either not seeing or not caring about the boat which was drifting about in West Bay.

V
THE TRAVESTIE

"HERE WE ARE, CORBETT, AND now I only wish my venture had been double," observed Pickersgill; "but I shall not allow business to absorb me wholly—we must add a little amusement. It appears to me, Corbett, that the gentleman's clothes which lie there will fit you, and those of the good-looking fellow who was spokesman will, I am sure, suit me well. Now, let us dress ourselves, and then for breakfast."

Pickersgill then exchanged his clothes for those of Mr Hautaine, and Corbett fitted on those of Mr Ossulton. The steward was summoned up, and he dared not disobey; he appeared on deck, trembling.

"Steward—you will take these clothes below," said Pickersgill, "and, observe, I now command this yacht; and, during the time that I am on board, you will pay me the same respect as you did Lord B.: nay, more, you will always address me as Lord B. You will prepare dinner and breakfast, and do your duty just as if his lordship was on board, and take care that you feed us well, for I will not allow the ladies to be entertained in a less sumptuous manner than before.—You will tell the cook what I say,—and now that you have heard me, take care that you obey; if not, recollect that I have my own men here, and if I but point with my finger, *overboard you go.*—Do you perfectly comprehend me?"

"Yes,—sir," stammered the steward.

"Yes, *sir*!—What did I tell you, sirrah?—Yes, my lord.—Do you understand me?"

"Yes—my lord."

"Pray, steward, whose clothes has this gentleman put on?"

"Mr—Mr Ossulton's, I think—sir—my lord, I mean."

"Very well, steward; then recollect, in future you always address that gentleman as *Mr Ossulton*"

"Yes, my lord," and the steward went down below, and was obliged to take a couple of glasses of brandy, to keep himself from fainting.

"Who are they, and what are they! Mr Maddox?" cried the lady's-maid, who had been weeping.

"Pirates!—*bloody, murderous, stick-at-nothing* pirates!" replied the steward.

"Oh!" screamed the lady's-maid, "what will become of us, poor unprotected females?" And she hastened into the cabin, to impart this dreadful intelligence.

The ladies in the cabin were not in a very enviable situation. As for the elder Miss Ossulton (but, perhaps, it will be better in future to distinguish the two ladies, by calling the elder simply Miss Ossulton, and her niece, Cecilia), she was sitting with her salts to her nose, agonised with a mixture of trepidation and wounded pride. Mrs Lascelles was weeping, but weeping gently. Cecilia was sad, and her heart was beating with anxiety and suspense—when the maid rushed in.

"O madam! O miss! O Mrs Lascelles! I have found it all out!—they are murderous, bloody, do-everything pirates!!!"

"Mercy on us!" exclaimed Miss Ossulton; "surely they will never dare—?"

"Oh, ma'am, they dare anything!—they just now were throwing the steward overboard—and they have rummaged all the portmanteaus, and dressed themselves in the gentlemen's best clothes—the captain of them told the steward that he was Lord B.—and that if he dared to call him anything else, he would cut his throat from ear to ear—and if the cook don't give them a good dinner, they swear that they'll chop his right hand off, and make him eat it, without pepper or salt!"

Miss Ossulton screamed, and went off into hysterics. Mrs Lascelles and Cecilia went to her assistance; but the latter had not forgotten the very different behaviour of Jack Pickersgill, and his polite manners, when he boarded the vessel. She did not, therefore, believe what the maid had reported, but still her anxiety and suspense were great, especially about her father. After having restored her aunt, she put on her bonnet, which was lying on the sofa.

"Where are you going, dear?" said Mrs Lascelles.

"On deck," replied Cecilia. "I must and will speak to these men."

"Gracious heaven, Miss Ossulton going on deck! have you heard what Phoebe says?"

"Yes, aunt, I have; but I can wait here no longer."

"Stop her! stop her!—she will be murdered!—she will be—she is mad!" screamed Miss Ossulton; but no one attempted to stop Cecilia, and on deck she went. On her arrival, she found Jack Pickersgill and Corbett walking the deck; one of the smugglers at the helm, and the rest forward, and as quiet as the crew of the yacht. As soon as she made her appearance, Jack took off his hat, and made her a bow.

"I do not know whom I have the honour of addressing, young lady! but I am flattered with this mark of confidence. You feel, and I assure you, you feel correctly, that you are not exactly in lawless hands."

Cecilia looked with more surprise than fear at Pickersgill; Mr Hautaine's dress became him, he was a handsome, fine-looking man, and had nothing of the ruffian in his appearance; unless, like Byron's Corsair, he was *half savage, half soft*. She could not help thinking that she had met many with less pretensions, as far as appearance went, to the claims of a gentleman, at Almack's, and other fashionable circles.

"I have ventured on deck, sir," said Cecilia, with a little tremulousness in her voice, "to request, as a favour, that you will inform me what your intentions may be, with regard to the vessel, and with regard to the ladies!"

"And I feel much obliged to you, for so doing, and I assure you, I will, as far as I have made up my own mind, answer you candidly: but you tremble—allow me to conduct you to a seat. In few words, then, to remove your present alarm, I intend that the vessel shall be returned to its owner, with every article in it, as religiously respected as if they were church property. With respect to you, and the other ladies on board, I pledge you my honour, that you have nothing to fear; that you shall be treated with every respect; your privacy never invaded; and that, in a few days, you will be restored to your friends. Young lady, I pledge my hopes of future salvation to the truth of this; but, at the same time, I must make a few conditions, which, however, will not be very severe."

"But, sir," replied Cecilia, much relieved, for Pickersgill had stood by her in the most respectful manner, "you are, I presume, the captain of the smuggler? Pray, answer me one question more—What became of the boat, with Lord B.,—he is my father?"

"I left him in his boat, without a hair of his head touched, young lady; but I took away the oars."

"Then he will perish!" cried Cecilia, putting her handkerchief to her eyes.

"No, young lady, he is on shore probably by this time; although I took away his means of assisting to capture us, I left him the means of gaining the land. It is not every one who would have done that, after his conduct to us."

"I begged him not to go," said Cecilia; "I told him that it was not fair, and that he had no quarrel with the smugglers."

"I thank you even for that," replied Pickersgill. "And now, Miss—I have not the pleasure of recollecting his lordship's family name—"

"Ossulton, sir," said Cecilia, looking at Pickersgill with surprise.

"Then, with your permission, Miss Ossulton, I will now make you my confidant: excuse my using so free a term, but it is because I wish to relieve your fears; at the same time, I cannot permit you to divulge all my intentions to the whole party on board; I feel that I may trust you, for you have courage, and where there is courage, there generally is truth; but you must first tell me whether you will condescend to accept these terms?"

Cecilia demurred a moment—the idea of being the confidant of a smuggler rather startled her; but still, her knowledge of what his intentions were, if she might not reveal them, might be important; as, perhaps, she might dissuade him. She could be in no worse position than she was now, and she might be in a much better. The conduct of Pickersgill had been such, up to the present, as to inspire confidence; and, although he defied the laws, he appeared to regard the courtesies of life. Cecilia was a courageous girl, and at length she replied:—

"Provided what you desire me to keep secret will not be injurious to any one, or compromise me, in my peculiar situation, I consent."

"I would not hurt a fly, Miss Ossulton, but in self-defence, and I have too much respect for you, from your conduct during our short meeting, to compromise you. Allow me now to be very candid; and then, perhaps, you will acknowledge that, in my situation, others would do the same; and, perhaps, not show half so much forbearance. Your father, without any right whatever, interferes with me, and my calling: he attempts to make me a prisoner, to have me thrown in jail; heavily fined, and, perhaps, sent out of the country. I will not enter into any defence of smuggling, it is sufficient to say, that there are pains and penalties attached to the infraction of certain laws, and that I choose to risk them—but Lord B. was not empowered by Government to attack me; it was a gratuitous act—and had I thrown him, and all his crew into the sea, I should have been justified, for it was in short, an act of piracy on their part. Now, as your father has thought to turn a yacht into a revenue cutter, you cannot be surprised at my retaliating, in turning her into a smuggler; and as he has mixed up looking after the revenue with yachting, he cannot be surprised if I retaliate, by mixing up a little yachting with smuggling. I have dressed your male companions as smugglers, and have sent them in the smuggling vessel to Cherbourg, where they will be safely landed; and I have dressed myself, and the only person whom I could join with me in this frolic, as gentlemen, in their places. My object is twofold: one is, to land my cargo, which I have now on board, and which is very valuable; the other is, to retaliate upon your father and his companions, for their attempt upon me, by stepping into their shoes, and enjoying, for a day or two, their luxuries. It is my intention to make free with nothing, but his lordship's wine and eatables,—that you may be assured of; but I shall have no pleasure, if the ladies do not sit down to the dinner-table with us, as they did before with your father and his friends."

"You can hardly expect that, sir," said Cecilia.

"Yes, I do; and that will be not only the price of the early release of the yacht and themselves, but it will also be the only means by which they will obtain anything to eat. You observe, Miss Ossulton, the sins of the fathers are visited on the children. I have now told you what I mean to do, and what I wish. I leave you to think of it, and decide whether it will not be the best for all parties to consent. You have my permission to tell the other ladies, that whatever may be their conduct, they are as secure from ill-treatment or rudeness, as if they were in Grosvenor Square; but I cannot answer that they will not be hungry, if, after such forbearance in every point, they show so little gratitude, as not to honour me with their company."

"Then I am to understand that we are to be starved into submission?"

"No, not starved, Miss Ossulton; but recollect that you will be on bread and water, and detained until you do consent, and your detention will increase the anxiety of your father."

"You know how to persuade, sir," said Cecilia. "As far as I am concerned, I trust I shall ever be ready to sacrifice any feelings of pride, to spare my father so much uneasiness. With your permission, I will now go down into the cabin, and relieve my companions from the worst of their fears. As for obtaining what you wish, I can only say, that, as a young person, I am not likely to have much influence with those older than myself, and must inevitably be overruled, as I have not permission to point out to them reasons which might avail. Would you so far allow me to be relieved from my promise, as to communicate all you have said to me, to the only married woman on board? I think I then might obtain your wishes, which, I must candidly tell you, I shall attempt to effect, *only* because I am most anxious to rejoin my friends."

"And be relieved of my company," replied Pickersgill, smiling, ironically,—"of course you are; but I must and will have my petty revenge: and although you may, and probably will detest me, at all events you shall not have any very formidable charge to make against me Before you go below, Miss Ossulton, I give you my permission to add the married lady to the number of my confidants; and you must permit me to introduce my friend, Mr Ossulton;" and Pickersgill waved his hand in the direction of Corbett, who took off his hat, and made a low obeisance.

It was impossible for Cecilia Ossulton to help smiling.

"And," continued Pickersgill, "having taking the command of this yacht, instead of his lordship, it is absolutely necessary that I also take his lordship's name. While on board I am Lord B.; and allow me to introduce myself under that name—I cannot be addressed otherwise. Depend upon it, Miss Ossulton, that I shall have a most paternal solicitude to make you happy and comfortable."

Had Cecilia Ossulton dared to have given vent to her real feelings at that time, she would have burst into a fit of laughter, it was too ludicrous. At the same time, the very burlesque reassured her still more. She went into the cabin with a heavy weight removed from her heart.

In the meantime, Miss Ossulton and Mrs Lascelles remained below, in the greatest anxiety at Cecilia's prolonged stay; they knew not what to think, and dared not go on deck. Mrs Lascelles had once determined at all risks to go up; but Miss Ossulton and Phoebe had screamed, and implored her so fervently not to leave them, that she unwillingly consented to remain. Cecilia's countenance, when she entered the cabin, reassured Mrs Lascelles, but not her aunt, who ran to her, crying and sobbing, and clinging to her, saying, "What have they done to you, my poor, poor Cecilia?"

"Nothing at all, aunt," replied Cecilia, "the captain speaks very fairly, and says he shall respect us in every possible way, provided that we obey his orders, but if not— "

"If not—what, Cecilia?" said Miss Ossulton, grasping her niece's arm.

"He will starve us, and not let us go!"

"God have mercy on us!"—cried Miss Ossulton, renewing her sobs.

Cecilia then went to Mrs Lascelles, and communicated to her, apart, all that had passed. Mrs Lascelles agreed with Cecilia, that they were in no danger of insult; and as they talked over the matter, they at last began to laugh; there was a novelty in it, and there was something so ridiculous in all the gentlemen being turned into smugglers. Cecilia was glad that she could not tell her aunt, as she wished her to be so frightened, as never to have her company on board of the yacht again; and Mrs Lascelles was too glad to annoy her for many and various insults received. The matter was, therefore, canvassed over very satisfactorily, and Mrs Lascelles felt a natural curiosity to see this new Lord B. and the second Mr Ossulton. But they had had no breakfast and were feeling very hungry, now that their alarm was over. They desired Phoebe to ask the steward for some tea or coffee. The reply was, that, "Breakfast was laid in the cabin, and Lord B. trusted that the ladies would come to partake of it."

"No, no," replied Mrs Lascelles, "I never can, without being introduced to them first."

"Nor will I go," replied Cecilia, "but I will write a note, and we will have our breakfast here." Cecilia wrote a note in pencil as follows:—

> "Miss Ossulton's compliments to Lord B., and, as the ladies feel rather indisposed after the alarm of this morning, they trust that his lordship will excuse their coming to breakfast; but hope to meet his lordship at dinner, if not before that time, on deck."

The answer was propitious, and the steward soon appeared with the breakfast in the ladies' cabin.

"Well Maddox," said Cecilia, "how do you get on with your new master?"

The steward looked at the door to see if it was closed, shook his head, and then said with a look of despair, "He has ordered a haunch of venison for dinner, miss, and he has twice threatened to toss me overboard."

"You must obey him, Maddox, or he certainly will. These pirates are dreadful fellows; be attentive, and serve him just as if he was my father."

"Yes, yes, ma'am, I will, but our time may come; it's *burglary* on the high seas, and I'll go fifty miles to see him hanged."

"Steward!" cried Pickersgill, from the cabin.

"O lord! he can't have heard me—d'ye-think he did, miss?"

"The partitions are very thin, and you spoke very loud," said Mrs Lascelles; "at all events, go to him quickly."

"Good-bye, miss; good-bye, ma'am; if I shouldn't see you any more," said Maddox, trembling with fear, as he obeyed the awful summons—which was to demand a tooth-pick.

Miss Ossulton would not touch the breakfast; not so Mrs Lascelles and Cecilia, who ate very heartily.

"It's very dull to be shut up in this cabin," said Mrs Lascelles; "come, Cecilia, let's go on deck."

"And leave me," cried Miss Ossulton.

"There is Phoebe here, aunt; we are going up to persuade the pirates to put us all on shore."

Mrs Lascelles and Cecilia put on their bonnets and went up. Lord B. took off his hat, and begged the honour of being introduced to the pretty widow. He handed the ladies to a seat, and then commenced conversing upon various subjects, which, at the same time, possessed great novelty. His lordship talked about France, and described its ports; told now and then a good anecdote; pointed out the different headlands, bays, towns, and villages, which they were passing rapidly, and always had some little story connected with each. Before the ladies had been two hours on deck, they found themselves, to their infinite surprise, not only interested, but in conversation with the captain of the smuggler, and more than once they laughed outright. But the *soi-disant* Lord B. had inspired them with confidence; they fully believed that what he had told them was true, and that he had taken possession of the yacht to smuggle his goods, to be revenged, and to have a laugh. Now none of these three offences are capital in the eyes of the fair sex; and Jack was a handsome, fine-looking fellow, of excellent manners, and very agreeable conversation, at the same time, neither he nor his friend were in their general deportment and behaviour otherwise than most respectful.

"Ladies, as you are not afraid of me, which is a greater happiness than I had reason to expect, I think you may be amused to witness the fear of those who accuse your sex of cowardice. With your permission, I will send for the cook and steward, and inquire about the dinner."

"I should like to know what there is for dinner," observed Mrs Lascelles demurely; "wouldn't you, Cecilia?"

Cecilia put her handkerchief to her mouth.

"Tell the steward and the cook both to come aft immediately," cried Pickersgill.

In a few seconds they both made their appearance.

"Steward!" cried Pickersgill, with a loud voice.

"Yes, my lord," replied Maddox, with his hat in his hand.

"What wines have you put out for dinner?"

"Champagne, my lord; and claret, my lord; and Madeira and sherry, my lord."

"No Burgundy, sir?"

"No, my lord; there is no Burgundy on board."

"No Burgundy, sir! do you dare to tell me that?"

"Upon my soul, my lord," cried Maddox, dropping on his knees, "there is no Burgundy on board—ask the ladies."

"Very well, sir; you may go."

"Cook, what have you got for dinner?"

"Sir, a haunch of mutt—of venison, my lord," replied the cook, with his white night-cap in his hand.

"What else, sirrah?"

"A boiled calf's head, my lord."

"A boiled calf's head! Let it be roasted, or I'll roast you, sir!" cried Pickersgill in an angry tone.

"Yes, my lord; I'll roast it."

"And what else, sir?"

"Maintenon cutlets, my lord."

"Maintenon cutlets! I hate them—I won't have them, sir. Let them be dressed à l'ombre Chinoise."

"I don't know what that is, my lord."

"I don't care for that, sirrah; if you don't find out by dinner-time, you're food for fishes—that's all; you may go."

The cook walked off wringing his hands and his night-cap as well—for he still held it in his right hand—and disappeared down the fore-hatchway.

"I have done this to pay you a deserved compliment, ladies; you have more courage than the other sex."

"Recollect that we have had confidence given to us in consequence of your pledging your word, my lord."

"You do me, then, the honour of believing me?"

"I did not until I saw you," replied Mrs Lascelles; "but now I am convinced that you will perform your promise."

"You do, indeed, encourage me, madam, to pursue what is right," said Pickersgill, bowing; "for your approbation I should be most sorry to lose, still more sorry to prove myself unworthy of it."

As the reader will observe, everything was going on remarkably well.

VI
THE SMUGGLING YACHT

CECILIA RETURNED TO THE CABIN, to ascertain whether her aunt was more composed; but Mrs Lascelles remained on deck. She was much pleased with Pickersgill; and they continued their conversation. Pickersgill entered into a defence of his conduct to Lord B.; and Mrs Lascelles could not but admit the provocation. After a long conversation, she hinted at his profession, and how superior he appeared to be to such a lawless life.

"You may be incredulous, madam," replied Pickersgill, "if I tell you that I have as good a right to quarter my arms as Lord B. himself; and that I am not under my real name. Smuggling is, at all events, no crime; and I infinitely prefer the wild life I lead at the head of my men, to being spurned by society because I am poor. The greatest crime in this country is poverty. I may, if I am fortunate, some day resume my name. You may, perhaps, meet me, and, if you please, you may expose me."

"That I should not be likely to do," replied the widow; "but still I regret to see a person, evidently intended for better things, employed in so disreputable a profession."

"I hardly know, madam, what is and what is not disreputable in this conventional world. It is not considered disreputable to cringe to the vices of a court, or to accept a pension wrung from the industry of the nation, in return for base servility. It is not considered disreputable to take tithes, intended for the service of God, and lavish them away at watering-places or elsewhere, seeking pleasure instead of doing God service. It is not considered disreputable to take fee after fee to uphold injustice, to plead against innocence, to pervert truth, and to aid the devil. It is not considered disreputable to gamble on the Stock Exchange, or to corrupt the honesty of electors by bribes, to doing which the penalty attached is equal to that decreed to the offence of which I am guilty. All these, and much more, are not considered disreputable; yet, by all these are the moral bonds of society loosened, while in mine we cause no guilt in others—"

"But still it is a crime."

"A violation of the revenue laws, and no more. Observe, madam, the English Government encourage the smuggling of our manufactures to the Continent, at the same time that they take every step to prevent articles being smuggled into this country. Now, madam, can that be a *crime*, when the head of the vessel is turned north, which becomes *no crime* when she steers the opposite way?"

"There is a stigma attached to it, you must allow."

"That I grant you, madam; and as soon as I can quit the profession I shall. No captive ever sighed more to be released from his chains; but I will not leave it, till I find that I am in a situation not to be spurned and neglected by those with whom I have a right to associate."

At this moment, the steward was seen forward making signs to Mrs Lascelles, who excused herself, and went to him.

"For the love of God, madam," said Maddox, "as he appears to be friendly with you, do pray find out how these cutlets are to be dressed; the cook is tearing his hair, and we shall never have any dinner; and then it will all fall upon me, and I—shall be tossed overboard."

Mrs Lascelles desired poor Maddox to wait there while she obtained the desired information. In a few minutes she returned to him.

"I have found it out. They are first to be boiled in vinegar; then fried in batter, and served up with a sauce of anchovy and Malaga raisins!"

"First fried in vinegar; then boiled in batter, and served up with almonds and raisins!"

"No—no!" Mrs Lascelles repeated the injunction to the frightened steward; and then returned aft, and re-entered into a conversation with Pickersgill, in which for the first time, Corbett now joined. Corbett had sense enough to feel, that the less he came forward until his superior had established himself in the good graces of the ladies, the more favourable would be the result.

In the mean time Cecilia had gone down to her aunt, who still continued to wail and lament. The young lady tried all she could to console her, and to persuade her that if they were civil and obedient they had nothing to fear.

"Civil and obedient, indeed!" cried Miss Ossulton, "to a fellow who is a smuggler and a pirate! I, the sister of Lord B.! Never! The presumption of the wretch!"

"That is all very well, aunt; but recollect, we must submit to circumstances. These men insist upon our dining with them; and we must go, or we shall have no dinner."

"I sit down with a pirate! Never! I'll have no dinner—I'll starve—I'll die!"

"But, my dear aunt, it's the only chance we have of obtaining our release; and if you do not do it Mrs Lascelles will think that you wish to remain with them."

"Mrs Lascelles judges of other people by herself."

"The captain is certainly a very well-behaved, handsome man. He looks like a nobleman in disguise. What an odd thing it would be, aunt, if this should be all a hoax!"

"A hoax, child?" replied Miss Ossulton, sitting up on the sofa.

Cecilia found that she had hit the right nail, as the saying is; and she brought forward so many arguments to prove that she thought it was a hoax to frighten them, and that the gentleman above was a man of consequence, that her aunt began to listen to reason, and at last consented to join the dinner-party. Mrs Lascelles now came down below; and when dinner was announced they repaired to the large cabin, where they found Pickersgill and Corbett waiting for them.

Miss Ossulton did not venture to look up, until she heard Pickersgill say to Mrs Lascelles, "Perhaps, madam, you will do me the favour to introduce me to that lady, whom I have not had the honour of seeing before?"

"Certainly, my lord," replied Mrs Lascelles. "Miss Ossulton, the aunt of this young lady."

Mrs Lascelles purposely did not introduce *his lordship* in return, that she might mystify the old spinster.

"I feel highly honoured in finding myself in the company of Miss Ossulton," said Pickersgill. "Ladies, we wait but for you to sit down. Ossulton, take the head of the table and serve the soup."

Miss Ossulton was astonished; she looked at the smugglers, and perceived two well-dressed gentlemanly men, one of whom was apparently a lord, and the other having the same family name.

"It must be all a hoax," thought she; and she very quietly took to her soup.

The dinner passed off very pleasantly; Pickersgill was agreeable, Corbett funny, and Miss Ossulton so far recovered herself as to drink wine with his lordship, and to ask Corbett what branch of their family he belonged to.

"I presume it's the Irish branch," said Mrs Lascelles, prompting him.

"Exactly, madam," replied Corbett.

"Have you ever been to Torquay, ladies?" inquired Pickersgill.

"No, my lord," answered Mrs Lascelles.

"We shall anchor there in the course of an hour, and probably remain there till to-morrow. Steward, bring coffee. Tell the cook these cutlets were remarkably well dressed."

The ladies retired to the cabin. Miss Ossulton was now convinced that it was all a hoax; but said she, "I shall tell Lord B. my opinion of their practical jokes when he returns. What is his lordship's name who is on board?"

"He won't tell us," replied Mrs Lascelles; "but I think I know; it is Lord Blarney."

"Lord Blaney you mean, I presume," said Miss Ossulton; "however, the thing is carried too far. Cecilia, we will go on shore at Torquay, and wait till the yacht returns with Lord B. I don't like these jokes; they may do very well for widows, and people of no rank."

Now, Mrs Lascelles was sorry to find Miss Ossulton so much at her ease. She owed her no little spite, and wished for revenge. Ladies will go very far to obtain this. How far Mrs Lascelles would have gone, I will not pretend to say; but this is certain, that the last innuendo of Miss Ossulton very much added to her determination. She took her bonnet and went on deck, at once told Pickersgill that he could not please her or Cecilia more than by frightening Miss Ossulton, who, under the idea that it was all a hoax, had quite recovered her spirits; talked of her pride and ill-nature, and wished her to receive a useful lesson. Thus, to follow up her revenge, did Mrs Lascelles commit herself so far, as to be confidential with the smuggler in return.

"Mrs Lascelles, I shall be able to obey you, and, at the same time, to combine business with pleasure."

After a short conversation, the yacht dropped her anchor at Torquay. It was then about two hours before sunset. As soon as the sails were furled, one or two gentlemen, who resided there, came on board to pay their respects to Lord B.; and, as Pickersgill had found out from Cecilia that her father was acquainted with no one there, he received them in person; asked them down in the cabin; called for wine; and desired them to send their boat away, as his own was going on shore. The smugglers took great care, that the steward, cook, and lady's maid, should have no communication with the guests; one of them, by Corbett's direction, being a sentinel over each individual. The gentlemen remained about half-an-hour on board, during which Corbett and the smugglers had filled the portmanteaus found in the cabin with the lace, and they were put in the boat. Corbett then landed the gentlemen in the same boat, and went up to the hotel, the smugglers following him with the portmanteaus, without any suspicion or interruption. As soon as he was there, he ordered post-horses, and set off for a town close by, where he had correspondents; and thus the major part of the cargo was secured. Corbett then returned in the night, bringing with him people to receive the goods, and the smugglers landed the silks, teas, &c., with the same good fortune. Everything was out of the yacht except a portion of the lace, which the portmanteaus would not hold. Pickersgill might easily have sent this on shore; but, to please Mrs Lascelles, he arranged otherwise.

The next morning, about an hour after breakfast was finished, Mrs Lascelles entered the cabin pretending to be in the greatest consternation, and fell on the sofa as if she were going to faint.

"Good heavens! what is the matter?" exclaimed Cecilia, who knew very well what was coming.

"Oh, the wretch! he has made such proposals!"

"Proposals! what proposals? what! Lord Blaney?" cried Miss Ossulton.

"Oh, he's no lord! he's a villain and a smuggler! and he insists that we shall both fill our pockets full of lace, and go on shore with him."

"Mercy on me! Then it is no hoax after all; and I've been sitting down to dinner with a smuggler!"

"Sitting down, madam!—if it were to be no more than that—but we are to take his arm up to the hotel. Oh, dear! Cecilia, I am ordered on deck, pray come with me!"

Miss Ossulton rolled on the sofa, and rang for Phoebe; she was in a state of great alarm.

A knock at the door.

"Come in," said Miss Ossulton, thinking it was Phoebe; when Pickersgill made his appearance.

"What do you want, sir? Go out, sir! go out directly, or I'll scream!"

"It is no use screaming, madam; recollect that all on board are at my service. You will oblige me by listening to me, Miss Ossulton. I am, as you know, a smuggler, and I must send this lace on shore. You will oblige me by putting it into your pockets, or about your person, and prepare to go on shore with me. As soon as we arrive at the hotel, you will deliver it to me, and I then shall reconduct you on board of the yacht. You are not the first lady who has gone on shore with contraband articles about her person."

"Me, sir! go on shore in that way? No, sir, never! What will the world say? the Hon. Miss Ossulton walking with a smuggler! No, sir, never!"

"Yes, madam, walking arm-in-arm with a smuggler: I shall have you on one arm, and Mrs Lascelles on the other; and I would advise you to take it very quietly; for, in the first place, it will be you who smuggle, as the goods will be found on your person, and you will certainly be put in prison, for, at the least appearance of insubordination, we run and inform against you; and, further, your niece will remain on board as a hostage for your good behaviour, and if you have any regard for her liberty, you will consent immediately."

Pickersgill left the cabin, and shortly afterwards Cecilia and Mrs Lascelles entered, apparently much distressed. They had been informed of all, and Mrs Lascelles declared, that, for her part, sooner than leave her poor Cecilia to the mercy of such people, she had made up her mind to submit to the smuggler's demands. Cecilia also begged so earnestly, that Miss Ossulton, who had no idea that it was a trick, with much sobbing and blubbering, consented.

When all was ready, Cecilia left the cabin; Pickersgill came down, handed up the two ladies, who had not exchanged a word with each other during Cecilia's absence; the boat was ready alongside—they went in, and pulled on shore. Everything succeeded to the smuggler's satisfaction. Miss Ossulton, frightened out of her wits, took his arm; and, with Mrs Lascelles on the other, they went up to the hotel, followed by four of his boat's crew. As soon as they were shown into a room, Corbett, who was already on shore, asked for Lord B., and joined them. The ladies retired to another apartment, divested themselves of their contraband goods, and, after calling for some sandwiches and wine, Pickersgill waited an hour, and then returned on board. Mrs Lascelles was triumphant; and she rewarded her new ally, the smuggler, with one of her sweetest smiles. Community of interest will sometimes make strange friendships.

VII
CONCLUSION

WE MUST NOW RETURN TO the other parties who have assisted in the acts of this little drama. Lord B., after paddling and paddling, the men relieving each other in order to make head against the wind which was off shore, arrived about midnight at a small town in West Bay, from whence he took a chaise on to Portsmouth, taking it for granted that his yacht would arrive as soon as, if not before himself, little imagining that it was in possession of the smugglers. There he remained three or four days, when, becoming impatient, he applied to one of his friends who had a yacht at Cowes, and sailed with him to look after his own.

We left the *Happy-go-lucky* chased by the revenue cutter. At first the smuggler had the advantage before the wind; but, by degrees, the wind went round with the sun, and brought the revenue cutter to leeward: it was then a chase on a wind, and the revenue cutter came fast up with her.

Morrison, perceiving that he had no chance of escape, let run the ankers of brandy that he might not be condemned; but still he was in an awkward situation, as he had more men on board than allowed by Act of Parliament. He therefore stood on, notwithstanding the shot of the cutter went over and over him, hoping that a fog or night might enable him to escape; but he had no such good fortune,—one of the shot carried away the head of his mast, and the *Happy-go-lucky*'s luck was all over. He was boarded and taken possession of; he asserted that the extra men were only passengers; but, in the first place, they were dressed in seamen's clothes; and, in the second, as soon as the boat was aboard of her, Appleboy had gone down to his gin-toddy, and was not to be disturbed. The gentlemen smugglers therefore passed an uncomfortable night; and the cutter going to Portland by daylight before Appleboy was out of bed, they were taken on shore to the magistrate. Hautaine explained the whole affair, and they were immediately released and treated with respect; but they were not permitted to depart until they were bound over to appear against the smugglers, and prove the brandy having been on board. They then set off for Portsmouth in the seamen's clothes, having had quite enough of yachting for that season, Mr Ossulton declaring that he only wanted to get his luggage, and then he would take care how he put himself again in the way of the shot of a revenue cruiser, or of sleeping a night on her decks.

In the mean time Morrison and his men were locked up in the jail, the old man, as the key was turned on him, exclaiming, as he raised his foot in vexation, "That cursed blue pigeon!"

We will now return to the yacht.

About an hour after Pickersgill had come on board, Corbett had made all his arrangements and followed him. It was not advisable to remain at Torquay any longer, through fear of discovery; he, therefore, weighed the anchor before dinner, and made sail.

"What do you intend to do now, my lord?" said Mrs Lascelles.

"I intend to run down to Cowes, anchor the yacht in the night; and an hour before daylight have you in my boat with all my men. I will take care that you are in perfect safety, depend upon it, even if I run a risk. I should, indeed, be miserable, if, through my wild freaks, any accident should happen to Mrs Lascelles or Miss Ossulton."

"I am very anxious about my father," observed Cecilia. "I trust that you will keep your promise."

"I always have hitherto, Miss Ossulton; have I not?"

"Ours is but a short and strange acquaintance."

"I grant it; but it will serve for you to talk about long after. I shall disappear as suddenly as I have come—you will neither of you, in all probability, ever see me again."

The dinner was announced, and they sat down to table as before; but the elderly spinster refused to make her appearance; and Mrs Lascelles and Cecilia, who thought she had been frightened enough, did not attempt to force her. Pickersgill immediately yielded to these remonstrances, and, from that time she remained undisturbed in the ladies' cabin, meditating over the indignity of having sat down to table, having drank wine, and been obliged to walk on shore, taking the arm of a smuggler, and appear in such a humiliating situation.

The wind was light, and they made but little progress, and were not abreast of Portland till the second day, when another yacht appeared in sight, and the two vessels slowly neared until in the afternoon they were within four miles of each other. It then fell a dead calm—signals were thrown out by the other yacht, but could not be distinguished, and, for the last time, they sat down to dinner. Three days' companionship on board of a vessel, cooped up together, and having no one else to converse with, will produce intimacy; and Pickersgill was a young man of so much originality and information, that he was listened to with pleasure. He never attempted to advance beyond the line of strict decorum and politeness; and his companion was equally unpresuming. Situated as they were, and feeling what must have been the case had they fallen into other hands, both Cecilia and Mrs Lascelles felt some degree of gratitude towards him; and, although anxious to be relieved from so strange a position, they had gradually acquired a perfect confidence in him, and this had produced a degree of familiarity, on their parts, although never ventured upon by the smuggler. As Corbett was at the table, one of the men came down and made a sign. Corbett shortly after quitted the table and went on deck. "I wish, my lord, you would come up a moment, and see if you can make this flag out," said Corbett, giving a significant nod to Pickersgill. "Excuse me, ladies, one moment," said Pickersgill, who went on deck.

"It is the boat of the yacht coming on board," said Corbett; "and Lord B. is in the stern-sheets with the gentleman who was with him."

"And how many men in the boat?—let me see—only four. Well, let his lordship and his friend come: when they are on the deck, have the men ready in case of accident; but if you can manage to tell the boat's crew that they are to go on board again, and get rid of them that way, so much the better. Arrange this with Adams, and then come down again—his lordship must see us all at dinner."

Pickersgill then descended, and Corbett had hardly time to give his directions and to resume his seat, before his lordship and Mr Stewart pulled up alongside and jumped on deck. There was no one to receive them but the seamen, and those whom they did not know. They looked round in amazement; at last his lordship said to Adams, who stood forward,

"What men are you?"

"Belong to the yacht, ye'r honour."

Lord B. heard laughing in the cabin; he would not wait to interrogate the men; he walked aft, followed by Mr Stewart, looked down the skylight, and perceived his daughter and Mrs Lascelles with, as he supposed, Hautaine and Ossulton.

Pickersgill had heard the boat rub the side, and the sound of the feet on deck, and he talked the more loudly, that the ladies might be caught by Lord B. as they were. He heard their feet at the skylight, and knew that they could hear what passed; and at that moment he proposed to the ladies that as this was their last meeting at table they should all take a glass of champagne to drink to "their happy meeting with Lord B." This was a toast which they did not refuse. Maddox poured out the wine, and they were all bowing to each other, when his lordship, who had come down the ladder, walked into the cabin, followed by Mr Stewart. Cecilia perceived her father; the champagne-glass dropped from her hand—she flew into his arms, and burst into tears.

"Who would not be a father, Mrs Lascelles?" said Pickersgill, quietly seating himself, after having first risen to receive Lord B.

"And pray, whom may I have the honour of finding established here?" said Lord B., in an angry tone, speaking over his daughter's head, who still lay in his arms. "By heavens, yes?—Stewart, it is the smuggling captain dressed out."

"Even so, my lord," replied Pickersgill. "You abandoned your yacht to capture me; you left these ladies in a vessel crippled for want of men; they might have been lost. I have returned good for evil by coming on board with my own people, and taking charge of them. This night, I expected to have anchored your vessel in Cowes, and have left them in safety."

"By the—" cried Stewart.

"Stop, sir, if you please!" cried Pickersgill; "recollect you have once already attacked one who never offended. Oblige me by refraining from intemperate language; for I tell you I will not put up with it. Recollect, sir, that I have refrained from that, and also from taking advantage of you when you were in my power. Recollect, sir, also, that the yacht is still in possession of the smugglers, and that you are in no condition to insult with impunity. My lord, allow me to observe, that we men are too hot of temperament to argue, or listen coolly. With your permission, your friend, and my friend, and I, will repair on deck, leaving you to hear from your daughter and that lady all that has passed. After that, my lord, I shall be most happy to hear anything which your lordship may please to say."

"Upon my word—" commenced Mr Stewart.

"Mr Stewart," interrupted Cecilia Ossulton, "I request your silence; nay, more, if ever we are again to sail in the same vessel together, I *insist* upon it."

"Your lordship will oblige me by enforcing Miss Ossulton's request," said Mrs Lascelles.

Mr Stewart was dumbfounded, no wonder, to find the ladies siding with the smuggler.

"I am obliged to you ladies for your interference," said Pickersgill; "for, although I have the means of enforcing conditions, I should be sorry to avail myself of them. I wait for his lordship's reply."

Lord B. was very much surprised. He wished for an explanation; he bowed with *hauteur*. Everybody appeared to be in a false position; even he, Lord B., somehow or another had bowed to a smuggler.

Pickersgill and Stewart went on deck, walking up and down, crossing each other without speaking, but reminding you of two dogs who both are anxious to fight, but have been restrained by the voice of their masters. Corbett followed, and talked in a low tone to Pickersgill; Stewart went over to leeward to see if the boat was still alongside, but it had long before returned to the yacht. Miss Ossulton had heard her brother's voice, but did not come out of the after-cabin; she wished to be magnificent and, at the same time, she was not sure whether all was right, Phoebe having informed her that there was nobody with her brother and Mr Stewart, and that the smugglers still had the command of the vessel. After a while, Pickersgill and Corbett went down forward, and returned dressed in the smuggler's clothes, when they resumed their walk on the deck.

In the mean time, it was dark; the cutter flew along the coast; and the Needles' lights were on the larboard bow. The conversation between Cecilia, Mrs Lascelles, and her father, was long. When all had been detailed, and the conduct of Pickersgill duly represented, Lord B. acknowledged that, by attacking the smuggler, he had laid himself open to retaliation; that Pickersgill had shown a great deal of forbearance in every instance; and, after all, had he not gone on board the yacht she might have been lost, with only three seamen on board. He was amused with the smuggling and the fright of his sister; still more with the gentlemen being sent to Cherbourg, and much consoled that he was not the only one to be laughed at. He was also much pleased with Pickersgill's intention of leaving the yacht safe in Cowes harbour, his respect to the property on board, and his conduct to the ladies. On the whole, he felt grateful to Pickersgill; and where there is gratitude there is always good will.

"But who can he be?" said Mrs Lascelles; "his name he acknowledges not to be Pickersgill; and he told me confidentially that he was of good family."

"Confidentially, my dear Mrs Lascelles!" said Lord B.

"Oh, yes! we are both his confidants. Are we not, Cecilia?"

"Upon my honour, Mrs Lascelles, this smuggler appears to have made an impression which many have attempted in vain."

Mrs Lascelles did not reply to that remark, but said, "Now, my lord, you must decide—and I trust you will to oblige us—treat him as he has treated us, with the greatest respect and kindness."

"Why should you suppose otherwise?" replied Lord B.; "it is not only my wish but my interest so to do. He may take us over to France to-night, or anywhere else. Has he not possession of the vessel?"

"Yes," replied Cecilia; "but we flatter ourselves that we have *the command*. Shall we call him down, papa?"

"Ring for Maddox. Maddox, tell Mr Pickersgill, who is on deck, that I wish to speak with him, and shall be obliged by his stepping down into the cabin."

"Who, my lord? What? *Him?*"

"Yes, *him*," replied Cecilia, laughing.

"Must I call him, my lord, now, miss?"

"You may do as you please, Maddox; but recollect, he is still in possession of the vessel," replied Cecilia.

"Then, with your lordship's permission, I will; it's the safest way."

The smuggler entered the cabin; the ladies started as he appeared in his rough costume, with his throat open, and his loose black handkerchief. He was the *beau idéal* of a handsome sailor.

"Your lordship wishes to communicate with me?"

"Mr Pickersgill, I feel that you have had cause of enmity against me, and that you have behaved with forbearance. I thank you for your considerate treatment of the ladies; and I assure you, that I feel no resentment for what has passed."

"My lord, I am quite satisfied with what you have said; and I only hope that, in future, you will not interfere with a poor smuggler, who may be striving, by a life of danger and privation, to procure subsistence for himself and, perhaps, his family. I stated to these ladies my intention of anchoring the yacht this night at Cowes, and leaving her as soon as she was in safety. Your unexpected presence will only make this difference, which is, that I must previously obtain your lordship's assurance that those with you will allow me and my men to quit her without molestation, after we have performed this service."

"I pledge you my word, Mr Pickersgill, and I thank you into the bargain. I trust you will allow me to offer some remuneration."

"Most certainly not, my lord."

"At all events, Mr Pickersgill, if, at any other time, I can be of service, you may command me."

Pickersgill made no reply.

"Surely, Mr Pickersgill,—"

"Pickersgill! how I hate that name!" said the smuggler, musing. "I beg your lordship's pardon—if I may require your assistance for any of my unfortunate companions—"

"Not for yourself, Mr Pickersgill?" said Mrs Lascelles.

"Madam, I smuggle no more."

"For the pleasure I feel in hearing that resolution, Mr Pickersgill," said Cecilia, "take my hand and thanks."

"And mine," said Mrs Lascelles, half crying.

"And mine, too," said Lord B., rising up.

Pickersgill passed the back of his hand across his eyes, turned round, and left the cabin.

"I'm so happy!" said Mrs Lascelles, bursting into tears.

"He's a magnificent fellow," observed Lord B. "Come, let us all go on deck."

"You have not seen my aunt, papa."

"True; I'll go in to her, and then follow you."

The ladies went upon deck. Cecilia entered into conversation with Mr Stewart, giving him a narrative of what had happened. Mrs Lascelles sat abaft at the taffrail, with her pretty hand supporting her cheek, looking very much *à la Juliette*.

"Mrs Lascelles," said Pickersgill, "before we part, allow me to observe, that it is *you* who have induced me to give up my profession—"

"Why me, Mr Pickersgill?"

"You said that you did not like it."

Mrs Lascelles felt the force of the compliment. "You said, just now, that you hated the name of Pickersgill: why do you call yourself so?"

"It was my smuggling name, Mrs Lascelles."

"And now, that you have left off smuggling, pray what may be the name we are to call you by?"

"I cannot resume it till I have not only left this vessel, but shaken hands with, and bid farewell to, my companions; and by that time, Mrs Lascelles, I shall be away from you."

"But I've a great curiosity to know it, and a lady's curiosity must be gratified. You must call upon me some day, and tell it me. Here is my address."

Pickersgill received the card with a low bow: and Lord B. coming on deck, Mrs Lascelles hastened to meet him.

The vessel was now passing the Bridge at the Needles, and the smuggler piloted her on. As soon as they were clear and well inside, the whole party went down into the cabin, Lord B. requesting Pickersgill and Corbett to join him in a parting glass. Mr Stewart, who had received the account of what had passed from Cecilia, was very attentive to Pickersgill, and took an opportunity of saying, that he was sorry that he had said or done anything to annoy him. Every one recovered his spirits; and all was good humour and mirth, because Miss Ossulton adhered to her resolution of not quitting the cabin till she could quit the yacht. At ten o'clock the yacht was anchored. Pickersgill took his leave of the honourable company, and went in his boat with his men; and Lord B. was again in possession of his vessel, although he had not a ship's company. Maddox recovered his usual tone; and the cook flourished his knife, swearing that he should like to see the smuggler who would again order him to dress cutlets à l'ombre Chinoise.

The yacht had remained three days at Cowes, when Lord B. received a letter from Pickersgill, stating that the men of his vessel had been captured, and would be condemned, in consequence of their having the gentlemen on board, who were bound to appear against them, to prove that they had sunk the brandy. Lord B. paid all the recognisances, and the men were liberated for want of evidence.

It was about two years after this that Cecilia Ossulton, who was sitting at her work-table in deep mourning for her aunt, was presented with a letter by the butler. It was from her friend Mrs Lascelles, informing her that she was married again to a Mr Davenant, and intended to pay her a short visit on her way to the Continent. Mr and Mrs Davenant arrived the next day; and when the latter introduced her husband, she said to Miss Ossulton, "Look, Cecilia, dear, and tell me if you have ever seen Davenant before."

Cecilia looked earnestly: "I have, indeed," cried she at last, extending her hand with warmth; "and happy am I to meet with him again."

For in Mr Davenant she recognised her old acquaintance, the captain of the *Happy-go-lucky*, Jack Pickersgill, the smuggler.

THE END

ALSO AVAILABLE IN THE NONSUCH CLASSICS SERIES

For forthcoming titles and sales information see
www.nonsuch-publishing.com